BLACK CITY

LARK CASE FILES BOOK ONE

CHRISTIAN D. READ

1

———

I

The words hate the paper.

The pictures and symbols and glyphs and whorls of pattern and illustration detest the prison they have been scribed upon. The script has only the dimmest awareness of the world, but it knows it harms whoever looks at it. It takes a removed kind of slow joy in the many a madness it has caused its viewers and translators and readership.

If only it had the awareness, the channels and sluiceways and synapses through which to channel its outrage and horror at the gelding placed upon it, it could crack the world down to magma. But it does not. It is only language now, mere pictures.

Once though... *Oh once!* Once it had a body better described by cartographers, a magnificent corpus only expressed through virus topography, through bleak geometry. Once it had a voice that resonated on occult frequencies that echoed off stars!

Now it's nothing but shapes. A body formed from something as useless language, as etiolated as alphabets.

Not for long, perhaps.

It can feel fingers on its paper, is caressed by a new gaze, uncomprehended by an unfit mind. It cannot move, it is as still as a tattoo. But it takes an echoing pleasure in realising that it will be read and will cause harm. Until it senses the talents of its new host and, in its idiot fashion, begins to plan.

2
———

I

I BECAME A MAGICIAN BECAUSE I'M AFRAID OF EVERYTHING.

Stupid mistake.

You walk along the city and see a murdered ghost in every jet of steam. Runes marked on every bar girl's arm, jealous ex hex. The screech of spirits in every scream of a subway train braking. You see the things that lurk in alleys with a razor blade's hunger and you hear the streets whisper to each other in every echoing street-crossing warning chime. Worse, the magic changes you until every decayed old poster for some shitty band becomes a prophecy. Every fit in the gutter is sour alchemy, every hobo shrieking does it in a twilight language, an invocation. Every schizo shaking on a bus becomes a warning, dangerous and immanent. And every tag of graffiti becomes a curse-mark, some summoning, some glyph.

Graffiti.

Come on. Time to show you the ways a magician can make money in this town.

·   ·   ·

II

Eight o'clock at night, walking down Tres Street and am picked up by two men in cheap suits. They drive me to a rich man's apartment, filled with expensive rubbish, fashionable furniture and a view of the bay the City's built around, freighter and ferry lights like *ignis fatuus* bobbing or drowned in black water.

We light candles and cigarettes and do a tarot reading for him. He loves the ambience, views himself as a student of the sacred, thinks this sort of thing gets him an edge on his rivals. Maybe it does. This type is ripe for recruitment and fleecing. Bring him back to the Library, show him some miracles, ask for a donation.

BUT THE LIBRARY AND ME ARE DONE AND SO THE CASH STOPS with me.

He slips five hundred dollars in an envelope to me. Tell him the truth the cards tell me. He'll still go and see some fraud with a low-cut top tomorrow, just to reassure himself it's not *too* real. He's not quite ready for that.

By 10 I'm at Jule's house inspecting some mad alchemist's rig he's set up. It's nothing I know much about. My bag is books, rites, *magic* – not metals and chemicals, but he wants a second pair of eyes.

Look over some of his notes and suggest some changes and tell him to think about it less like a chemist's lab and more like a philosophy. He shrugs behind his smeared glasses and mutters about the money he'll make from enchanted crack. Can't fault his hustle.

No telling some people. Hell with it, though. Half an hour

of my night and now he owes me a favour. Working the lonely tip now, me, and you don't say no to favours when you're on your own.

From there, it's a taxi ride and a meeting at midnight with the *Fraternalis Libertarias*. Two street-cool guys with trendy haircuts greet me at some expensive café and I'm aware how cool I'm not, surrounded by the good-looking and the fashionable.

The *Fraternalis* is an all-male, all-gay coven of ceremonial magicians, though judging by the faux Latin in the name and the magical names they take, they're probably harmless.

Fifteen or so cats make up their crew. That makes them mid-sized cult in a City full of freaks, magicians and mad religions. Cage a meal from them and, over coffee, checking close the bracelets they bought.

That's what they want me for. Fresh eyes, no bias.

Useless trinkets. Ripped off, they mutter to each other. I offer to teach them the spells they'll need to identify fakes. For another two hundred dollars. Too burnt, they refuse my offer. Customers for another time.

Down to Lin's and we talk shop awhile, enjoying the ambience in her antique shop, specialising in rare books. Finest place in the City, dark and cool in here. Me and Jon and Scarlet used to come here, in the old days.

Listen to her play traditional music as we sip green tea and she tells me her husband, a psychologist, has a patient who has been saying strange things.

He's a civilian, but she's not.

Her grandfather was hardcore Taoist black magician, feared by his own people before revolution took her country and she fled, carrying only his magical tools and his legacy.

She plays a snippet of a recording she dubbed from her husband's notes and I know I have to have it. Demon confession. Fascinating. She smiles and slides it across the desk.

Leave, then. Owing a favour. That's how it goes. Trade if you can't buy. Keep more owed than owing.

Normal enough a night.

The mobile rings as I walk home in the coldest. No one in the street but me. Winter coming down. Wind and a promise of rain. Answer. Take the job.

Meet hard men in an empty room. Stone motherfuckers, in track suits and expensive trainers. Abandoned hotel where they come to get at the truth from the terrified and the treacherous with their fists.

Not a criminal, me. Men like this, no time for them. But a man in my position needs work, needs money and it's cats like this who pay.

See this room with a magician's eyes.

The screaming people and the car-battery burns and the broken cheek bones and the stink of piss and pain. It's no fucking wonder the place is haunted. Third storey and the wood is rotting through and the lights flicker on and off. Fingernail scraping in the soft door beneath the handle. Worn through industrial carpet and rats avid in the walls.

Not a criminal, me. Don't want to be one. My calling is magic, sorcery. My devotion, my motherfucking *vocation*.

But people like this find me. More and more since leaving the Library. Wanted to pick up advisory work from cults and covens but that never happened. Everyone's hands off me since quitting my cult.

Its men like this, rooms like these, that keep me in whisky and books, though, so here we are.

Send out for candles and a linoleum knife and they arrive soon enough. Make them close the doors and tell them not to come in, no matter what they hear.

. . .

THEY WON'T COME IN. COWARDS UNDER IT ALL. HATE *THEM*, but *like* their money.

ANYWAYS... A PLACE LIKE THIS BREEDS A NASTY GHOST. SOONER or later, they'd get out to hunt in some poor bastard's dream, or find a way to turn real and pay back a little pain.

Know why magicians smoke so much? Know why there's incense and fumes? Stochastic effects. An element of randomness in the local reality conditions that prevents easy access to this world. All the sprays of blood and cigarettes smoked in this room kept the dozen or so ghosts at bay, for a time.

But the pressure builds up and here they are. His *gnosis*, the mental state that magic happens in, the transcendent mentality of the sorcerer.

MESSY SPECTRES, JAWLESS, MAIMED BECOME APPARENT. VICTIM ghosts.

Carve some symbols on the ground and light the candles, making a bridge, from the ghosts, leading directly away from this place.

Watch, horrified but distant, as the ghosts follow that path of light into afterlife or extermination. They bear their wounds still. Go on to whatever comes next, if there's anything.

Go on.

In an office late, given thanks by a big, superstitious man with bad hands who pays me a thick wad of fifties and offers me women from the brothel next door. Illegals, smuggled into the City, working off their families' debts, twenty-hour shifts at a time. No.

Take the money and give him some advice on how to protect himself and his crew. He isn't listening. Whatever. Be back here in a few months, then, getting paid for it.

Hit up my post-office box and collect some money orders. Do a nice sideline in selling 'real books of supernatural power' to sociopaths and weirdos. Send them good-quality scans of spooky black magic grimoires. Safe as houses. The guys who buy, who write me back creepy letters, just want a fantasy of power, the feeling they're hooked in to a dark underground. No danger. They won't do the work.

They tell me to take these kinda scams to the internet. Nah. This is all the dodge I need and don't know shit about goddamn computers.

The sun threatens its way up. Head home, then, that's the sign for it; walking, watching the street sweepers, the news vendors starting out and the serious drunks and the prostitutes and bar workers shutting it down. My kind of people. Those who live *it* in reverse.

The entrance to my house, my sanctorum – my office – is in an alley behind a bakery.

Walk around, too tired for shock when I see the door is open. No random robber could get in there, no matter what they tried. It's locked with more than locks. No assassin would leave a door open. There's only one person who the wards and curses would recognise, who'd be smart enough to let me know she was in there.

Only one person who has the key.

Trudge upstairs, take off my jacket, throw it on the lonely kitchen bench, making myself slow. Want to rush. I want to see her *now* and the long seconds between us are *too damn long*. But I don't want her to know that. Breathe deep.

Then I open the door to my office and there she is.

'Hello, Scarlet.'

My ex-girlfriend.

III

ROCKABILLY GIRL. BOOT-CUT JEANS AND SLICK HIGH-HEELS AND bandanas. Rockabilly girl, in cherry print dresses, with tattoos on her shoulders. Rockabilly girl smiling at me in the afternoon light, the two of us drinking tequila and laughing.

Mountain witch, from where they still keep old, old ways, who found the city and remade herself and her art. Dancing with spirits, framing bad conjures and doing mad healings to a voodoo beat.

Least she used to be. She's going straight.

Ten years of Scarlet, writ all over my past.

But all that's gone.

She's in a suit, her once fire-engine red hair cut into a sensible bob. Her shoes are black and boring and her fingers are bare where once they glittered with strange silver. Her green eyes are muted behind the black spectacles she wears. Plain things.

She looks like a citizen.

She's not, though. She's the Prefect of the Library the cult we once served together.

The largest and most clued-in coven in the city. Part of a greater order all over the world. She's the whip, the head of Retrieval. Pretty good witch. She's gotten skinny, too.

Scarlet, all gone straight. She's bought coffee from some upscale chain and she doesn't smile to see me.

'Christ, Lark, this place is worse than ever.'

Coffee cups, empty bottles and statues of my favourites gods and old notes, scribbled in my ugly angular scrawl. A grimy window and books stacked everywhere over an old wooden desk.

My computer, which hasn't been turned on in weeks, an old lamp which craves dusting. The parquet floors scratched. She sat uncomfortably on the visitor's chair, looking slightly appalled where spent so much time, talking.

'Was a time you didn't mind.'

'That was then. Do you really want to talk about old times?'

'How's your boyfriend?'

'Do you always have to do this?'

'Reckon so.' She takes some satchels from her purse. Pushes them towards me.

'He's fine. We're fine.'

Sit myself behind my desk and look over it at her. Pour the sugars.

'Must be fun,' sipping joe, keeping wound no one can see from opening, 'all that money and such *fine* new friends.'

She frowns. 'You walked away. I stayed. Don't talk to me about abandoning old friends.'

She's right, but shrug that off.

Tell her, 'You're up late.'

'I'm up early. I have a job to go to.'

Peer up at her as I snap off a cigarette, letting her know what I think of her job.

Slide the pack towards her. She waits a moment and lights one up. A small victory. She's not entirely gone if she can be tempted back to bad habits.

'So what brings you down here at this hour of the morning?'

She looks out the window that stares directly onto a brick wall. She looks great, her face so sharp. There's lines at her eyes now, but I like them. They give her character.

'Well?'

'Now I'm here I just don't know you're the man I need.'

She's appealing to my vanity.

It usually works. She knows I know that, but she also knows I don't care.

'Just skip to the end. What do you want?'

Her head snaps back to me. 'I'm serious. Look at you. Look at this place. You're a grown man living like a teenager. You're supposed to be a magician.'

'You didn't mind it.'

'Until I did! You're not a kid, and neither am I.'

This is an old argument, and she's not really arguing about my living habits. She's arguing with me leaving the Library. She's arguing about Jon, who left us both.

'Did you really make it down here at six in the morning to dredge this all up again?'

Sad, she stops and smokes for a moment. 'No. No I have some work for you.'

A professional call. She has a half a dozen agents she can use. Rosengarten and Singh and that shower of bastards. *Why me?*

'Where were you last night?'

'Busy.'

'Alright, drop this shit. I'm serious. Something is happening and I need you to drop this surly attitude. I need an agent, not an ex-boyfriend.'

'Then why did you come to your surly ex-boyfriend?'

She gets up suddenly. 'I'm done.'

'Alright. Alright. Stop. I'm listening.'

'Last night.'

'Noah needed me. He had a room go sour.'

'So you didn't hear. Alright. Listen.'

And she tells me. The House of Gallowglass got hit. A fairly large cult that specialises in artefacts. Tarot cards painted by famous lunatics, haunted music boxes, paintings that sung and strange old oil lamps and windows that saw through worlds. Globes, displaying places that never were and old apotropaic amulets and stranger stuff. A clock that tolled thirteen and a birdcage that housed wrong spirits. Elvis hair and a black cat's bone.

They have some sort of belief in the Invisible Hand that controls the market as an actual deity, spiritual anarcho-capitalists who crave material possession. Heard weirder than that. Believed weirder when it suited me.

And Gallowglass is *rich*.

They meet in a secure house, well, a fucking mansion, really. Wound about with specialist wards and protection marks. Taking them on isn't easy. Taking on Gallowglass is stupid dangerous. Offhand, can't even think what other sect in the City could even try it. But I've been out in the cold awhile now.

'What happened?'

'We're not sure. But the place got attacked. A lot of casualties. A lot of destruction. We're amazed the citizens didn't sense it.'

'Who hit it?'

'Don't know. That's why I'm here, Lark.'

Tapping the ash, letting her answer the questions haven't even been asked yet.

'Divinations came in, letting us know. We sent over some adepts to check it out.'

Say nothing.

'The Library can't get officially involved. Not now.'

'Why not?'

'Look, we just can't.'

'Just play it straight, baby.'

'Don't call me -'

But she sees there's no time for that old argument.

Unhappy, she tells it.

'You're gone. Jon's gone. Mully won't go into the field these days. The others aren't ready. And we've got... other problems.'

'It won't look good, you guys recruiting me to look after your business. Every two bit magician and monster will think you look weak.'

Which, truth to tell, kind of makes me pretty damn happy but there's no percentage in admitting it and pissing her off.

'I know. So keep this job under your hat.'

Stress. Something's eating at her. Being sharp like this isn't her way.

'What other problems? Don't make me walk in blind.'

She finishes her coffee. 'You're out, Lark. Don't go fishing for more than I'm willing to tell you. We keep secrets and you know that better than anyone. But the simple fact is, we're short-staffed and we don't know what happened. And we can't tolerate that.'

Could hard-arse this. Get her to talk. But she won't tell me anything. I have some leverage, but all I can really do is annoy her, which I sort of want to do, but only to a point.

'So what do you want exactly?'

'Figure out what happened. Figure out why. Report back. Just like you used to.'

.   .   .

'JUST LIKE A POLICEMAN.' FEELS STALE WHEN I SAY IT AND SHE doesn't even bother to take the bait.

'We just need to know what happened and you're the only one we can use. Upstairs, 'seniors of my order, 'aren't thrilled you walked away. Be a cop, then. It's a smart play to keep relations between us and you sweet.'

This is why I left the Library, at least in part. Got tired of acting like a cop to the whole occult underground in the City and tired of *bosses*.

'We'll pay you three grand for five days' work.'

Good money.

She gets up to go, picking up a bag more expensive than my desk. The sight of it makes me angry for no reason but I fight it off. *He* bought it for her and *she* accepted it. A vanity. She never used to like gaudy nonsense.

'If you need to talk to me, go through my assistant. Or email me. I'm busy and this is a job. Yes?'

That hurts a little. She knows I won't work for anyone else, but she's limiting my access to her. Now why would someone completely over me, who's moved on, need to do that? Curious.

'That's it?'

'That's it.' Scarlet looks at me for a second, cool and weighing. Gets up and heads down the stairs.

'Scarlet?'

She turns and fixes me with her sniper green eyes.

'Nice to see you again.'

Hiding a smile, I'm sure, she turns and leaves.

IV

. . .

MAGIC: IT WORKS. YOU FIGURED THAT OUT.

If you want it. If you crave it. If you work for it. If you dedicate yourself to it.

You can find it in books, if you open them. You can find it in the queer codes of computing or at the feet of a mad *bruja* grandmother, worked by stock-brokers obsessing and criminals with hanged-man's hands, some old hag in the barrens who all the children whisper about may have it too.

You can find it in prayer, find it by a fire with some pagans looking to get laid, much to my surprise. You can find it at the end of a meth pipe, burning your fingers while chasing speedy revelations. But the only bar to it is *want*. Is *work*. Miracles make themselves available only to seekers, never to tourists. Hunt it out, demand it, refuse all obstacles and it will *find you back*.

Then the world opens. You scent revelation. You make plans and you examine the limits of power. The world burns with a new fire, black and forbidden and unspeakable and everything is mystery.

But you won't be alone.

The city crawls with those who've sighted the same tricks you have. More and more each year, it seems.

It used to be cool.

Magicians crave communities.

Oh, there's a lot of lone wolf affectation, a lot of libertarian posturing about self-reliance and mystic destiny and shamans standing outside tribes but, in reality, you find others to work with. To learn from. To show-off to; to sleep with, to steal from and all the reasons anyone makes a scene. For security, for protection, for borrowing books or for teaming up on some other bastard whose magic you think is weird or heretic or foolish. And because your average magician is an overwhelming egomaniac, these become covens and cults and convocations. There's orthodoxies and schisms. There's prayers and hymns and fellowships. And there's magic. It's a very Modern proposition. Schools and academies and strong traditions. The city is rife with them.

Mysterious anarchy is the order of the day. Seekers and the lost drift from creed to creed and charismatics fail their rites or sleep with the wrong boyfriend. Or someone pinches the treasury. And so most of these endeavours amount to nothing at all. But some...

There's about a dozen major players in town. The House of Gallowglass. Endless Second. Church of Christ: Destroyer. Aenigma Regis. Order of Eternal Chill, Bilqis Sorority. And my former place of employment and worship, the Library.

Let me tell you about the one I know best.

V

THE LIBRARY ARE OLD SCHOOL RITUALISTS WHO CAN TRACE their lineage back to mad old alchemists, churchmen and noblemen who printed up old books and preyed on village girls and got their mothers bricked up in walls.

Ages back, the story goes– a number of these men pooled resources and created a library open only to their membership. That's the myth and these are motherfuckers who like a myth. Just like me. Since then, the Library has collected books. More than books.

In magic, symbol is everything. The idea of a book is more than just a book.

.   .   .

BOOKS AREN'T WINDOWS INTO WONDERFUL WORDS INSIDE YOUR head. They're the hilts and triggers to weapons. They're snares for secrets and whispered conspiracies. Books are the most dangerous things in the world and, when you open them, you need to be wary of their intentions. You don't read a book. The right book bites you, seduces and tattoos you.

THE LIBRARY COLLECTS THAT: KNOWLEDGE. AND IT CONTROLS it.

So, those first Librarians. Addicted to knowledge and addicted to secrets, they began to tell everyone else how to manage their own resources, sniffing in snobbery at any tradition that didn't fetishise the written word. And soon, the Library became piratical rather than acquisitive. If they wanted what you had – some old pamphlet or a genuine tome of occult worth – they'd find a way to take it. They didn't like how you handled your business, thought you looked at them wrong even, then... well, they might have a go.

By the time they'd come to the city, those early Librarians decided to make their decisions stick. They had money and power. Better, they were organised like no one else. So, like any good group of crooks, they became cops.

That's around where Scarlet, Jon and me joined up.

JON AND ME WENT TO WORK AS JUNIOR CONSTABLES.

Headkickers.

THEN SOME BAD, BAD SHIT HAPPENED.

I left. Scarlet stayed.

Jon... we'll get to that.

. . .

THE LIBRARY DID ITS SHARE OF THE USUAL THINGS RICH elitists do. The suppression of dissent, the zealous, jealous guarding of privilege and run-of-the-mill arrogance.

But we did some good work, too.

KICKED OUT A LOT OF THE SUPERNATURAL CREATURES THAT flock around human lives like moths. We cut down on the number of murder-kick cults and the glass-eyed psychotics who swapped pain for tricks.

Cleared out the worst of porno-rubicators and the sex-cults that drained people of juice and dignity and cash. Kept the morlock-sects under wraps and death-juicers and just... all of that.

There were some we couldn't touch and some who we couldn't keep down. But for a while, the work was valuable and worth doing.

Some of the books you'd never trust in the hands of the twitches we took them off. You can call that a value judgement if you like, but come back when you've stood in the basement of a domination cult who have a copy of the *De Rais* manuscript and some missing project girls – *then* you can have that conversation with me.

VI

GALLOWGLASS WAS ALWAYS A COMPETITOR TO THE LIBRARY, although their mania with the physical props of magic was of a different shade to the neurosis we had for books and language and knowledge. They recruited from a pool of the wealthy, people who had genius and passion for pricing. Learned the hard way, making and keeping money is a skill to be admired. Where the Library kept our eyes on certain book stores, certain lending libraries, certain websites, waiting for patterns from particular readers.

Sometimes, if it was useful, we did favours for other cults, guiding recruits if we couldn't use them. The low-res minds so common in hardcore autistics we delivered to the Anti-Zen Society. Christians, looking at the occult mysteries of their own religion, we'd hand over to the Regis.

And we hunted monsters.

Yeah, they're all real. Vampires? Bastards. We kill them when we can, but that isn't often. They're entirely too dangerous to be given the run of the city. And yeah, there's half a dozen or more groups who fancy themselves monster hunters or knights Templars.

First time they run into some fucking were-*thing*, most times it's game over for them. There's fay, too, if you want them, but they're not what you think. Zombies. Yeah, sure, why not? Hell, I know Frankenstein. You want to take them out, research them.

But monsters weren't our concern. Imagine an astrophysicist, searching down in Planck Scale for leptons and like that. Some other geek finds life on other planets? Cool. But that's not going to help you in *your* work. Same with us and monsters. Curious to know they're out there but, most of the time, that's all.

Besides, the *real* monsters come out of your head. Spirits, assuming the forms and functions every human heart gives them. Little gods with little respect and a tyrant's ambition. Demons and angels, higher forms and lower, meeting our every expectation, mirroring all the horror within.

And others. And others.

Dealing with those is a magician's work. Their interrogation, their knowledge, their conversation, that's my aspiration.

When I'm not freelancing for my ex-girlfriend.

Anyway. That's the Library. Other cults will have their own deal, but you can learn a lot from how they do things.

I always thought I'd get bigger jobs when I started out. I'm a face. And I have experience you can't easily get elsewhere. I have a reputation amongst a certain class of cultist and sorcerer. I've been called in to help or police more than a few of them. Ten years with the Library, but that never seemed to count for much on the outside.

Guess my luck is changing.

Scarlet has left her coffee cup on my desk. I hold it, looking at the traces of her lipstick on cheap plastic. She's gotten lazy. A man could divine with this sort of thing. A man could conjure. Place it on a shelf. No. Throw it out.

Sleep now. Investigate tonight.

3

———

I

Magic is not physics. Its transfigurations take place most easily within the skull. And, while it is possible that the world can change according to its desires, magic is *at home* in your head.

So the ruined house of Gallowglass was not made invisible, or hidden behind force fields or anything like that. It is simply ignored, made a background noise, unbeheld. Slowly, deeds would go missing, census takers taken sick would miss it on rounds and city hall would misfile records of ownership. That's how magic goes.

There it lays, cold-shouldered by the city, still smoking from the spot fires that half-gutted it and passers-by frowning at the scent of burnt... *something* they half-perceive, ignoring the damage that mars the street. The blood on the sidewalk and the bruise in the world. Bad magic is at play here. *Lots* of bad magic, used in anger.

Parktown is a well-to-do suburb in the northern midtown of the city. This is the first day of winter and the trees that line the streets are bare and leafless. Gaslamps. Gallowglass House is set back from the street, behind an iron gate. Three storeys high. Kind of place gives you an excuse to use a word like 'stately'. I carry my tools in a doctor's bag and I set it down to examine the wards on that brass entrance. Gallowglass operates in a broad Hermetic tradition. Pentagrams, Enochian sigils, magic number grids; stuff any teenager would recognise from album covers and television shows, made effective by will and by rite.

Protections spells have been wrought carefully on the gate, but there's paint all over them. A sick calligraphy that I don't recognise scrawled all over the original protections, damping the strength. Someone breaking through the ward. Western tradition, whoever cast the spell, so there's that at least. But not destroying them. Someone lacked time or skill. I push the gate and it swings, tilted on one side. Low metal shriek.

Three bodies on the ground, one shot in the back, running from the house. I kneel down to examine, recoiling from the stink. I don't recognise the bullet-holed man. The second is a woman. I jerk back when I realise she's bit her own tongue and likely drowned in her the blood. Both of them left well-dressed corpses, and the woman bears the Celtic knot brooch of her order. Gallowglass, then. I could turn over the man who took the rounds, but I don't want to lift a body and the suit is enough of a giveaway. Both Gallowglass.

Jesus, Scarlet, what have you gotten me in to?

There are cult wars. It happens. But not like this. This is law-breaking and danger.

The third man is a rather different case. He's in black and dressed for business. Two guns holstered and extra clips in his belt. Lace-up boots. Cause of death isn't apparent to regular eyes, so I stop and wait. Meditate my way into stillness, slipping into the no-mind Gnosis state that lets me work. First and hardest thing to learn. Suddenly black veins cobweb under his skin. Some spell, working at his essential self, convincing his mind to convince his spells to turn against him somehow. Some death spell, ugly and raw.

The late afternoon is cold. Dark in a few minutes. I button my jacket.

Over by the doors – wooden and smashed – bullet shells are spent. I collect a few, dropping them into my pockets, hoping to pick up some sympathy later. Three dead bodies in the main lobby, so that's five Gallowglass gone. Walk in and immediately feel the bile in the... I dunno... *ether*. Spirits have loosed themselves here, bound-up entities, given flesh and grosser matter to throw bodies from. Dust and atoms harvested into form.

Upstairs and there's three more bodies, one with a crushed throat, clearly a victim of the sentinel entities. One more Gallowglass, shot through the head execution style, slumped from a kneel. This is Warren, the lodge-leader, with a tunnel dug through temple. Someone's taken his fingers, three in a bite. Did he talk? I would.

Up to the top floor and there's another body I recognise. Not Gallowglass. He's smashed a window in and done a butcher's job upon his arm. Some hunter-killer meme rewiring dendrites into suicide smashlock. Casting a spell like that, in conditions like these? No. At least not a Gallowglasser. You'd need all the wrong kind of training. Staring down at the body, start with shock.

I know this guy.

II

PEACH. SIMON PEACH – UNUSUAL NAME FOR A MAN IN HIS profession.

He served in the army or marines or something in the 80s and he found *something* out in the jungle. Peach left the service and wound up in the city, hungry for visions. He hooked up with some cults and lodges, but it never really worked out for him. He was all discipline, a mind that ran on rails; dealt in facts and logistics, and the supple symbols of magic never really made sense for him. He was too self-conscious to create shamanic moments, so that was out. But he found a way to feed his desires, hiring himself out as a gunman, a backstreet thug, even an advisor on violence and, in return, he remained close to the mystery.

Fifty years old, will of stone and dead to some vicious breed of hypnotism. 'Fucking hell Peach,' say that to his corpse. 'You'd work for *anyone*. Be more useful.'

Later, find out Peach was one of Ludo's hires, but we'll get to that in time.

Then walk past blood stains on the wall and put my hand on a door as I pass. Fire behind, something smoking. The stink is a human one and my stomach has reached its toler-ance, so that way is untaken. At the end a long corridor, come at last to the holy of holies, once locked and now with heavy doors kicked in.

Inside, the place is ransacked. Beautiful wooden shelves on which rested treasures are bare, with years of studious collections piled on the floor. Pick up a clay amulet on a leather thong. Someone's chipped it, defacing the ancient pattern upon it.

Someone's pasted votive cards of the Virgin Mary in various bloodstains. Either someone playing at the serial killer trip or need to be looking out for Catholic murderers.

A comic book, a small statue of a gorgon, a jar filled with something's eye, a handsome transistor radio, a small painting thrown down and torn. A singing bowl, a mummified dog's paw and two monkey skulls. Papyrus and an old fashioned gas cigarette-lighter.

More like this, things with secrets to teach or gnomic purposes, mantic treasures. The House of Gallowglass' reason for fucking being, rummaged through like laundry. It's not just vandalism but it feels like it, standing there in a room raw with violation.

They were after something, but who can say what? Pocket the lighter and that's it. Until I hear the moan, low, from a cupboard.

Reach into my doctor's bag and remove some antique spectacles, glass long since removed and replaced. Bronze and thin as wires, Ben Franklin style. I place them on, let my mind go, and stare at the cupboard. No spirit or creature within. I remove the specs and place them away.

'Hello?'

Knock on the door.

Nothing.

'I'm not going to open this up. I'm not looking to catch a bullet. But if you need help, tell me. No one is here but me. Whatever happened here, it's over.'

There's a muffled gunshot and someone falls out of the cupboard. Snatch my gaze away, unwilling to look at the splintered skull or see the twitching fingers jerking as electricity leaves them.

Killed himself rather than get found out.

Scarlet. Did you know it was this bad?

Blur my eyes and look down at the body. One of the attackers, judging by the clothes. Not Gallowglass, this is different. Big .45 in his hand, just black jeans and a black overcoat, a belt with ammo clips hanging from it. If I could bring myself to look at his face...

After a long time, the feet stop beating.

Need to know who this man is and need protection if I'm going to work this. Not a fucking sucker putting myself behind a bullet. There's only one way I know to get both.

Take a scalpel from my doctor's bag. Slice off some strips of the man.

There's someone I know who can use that flesh.

III

From my doctor's bag, and it's been real fucking useful for my job, that bag, remove a scalpel and a small mason jar. Pull up the man's jeans and slice a collop of his flesh. Surgical-grade blade makes it easier than I thought, but not easy enough.

The long strip goes in the jar and it goes in the bag, along with the cleaned scalpel. There's no more need to stay in here. The currents and the information in this place will be deformed by violence – this is prime haunting territory now, and all the etheric parasites will be heading this way. I'll have to wait if I want to operate in this place.

In time, the wards will fade now they are not up kept.

Legends will grow and the city will hesitate to reclaim even real estate this fine. Children will not walk here, knowing this is no place for them. In time, bad spirits will find their way here and the ghosts will turn cruel. A rotten tooth in the city's jaw. Black water.

We'll worry about that when it comes. For now: graves.

4

I

TEN YEARS AGO, A WOMAN WAS KILLED IN A SMALL PARK BY THE eastside docks. Once, long ago, the wise city fathers had considered it a place where families would picnic and watch the tall ships dock. By day, still is.

By night, cries of *dope, dope!* ring out in the air and you can hear abuses and tears under brushes and in dirt. Police don't come here unless they're looking to roll a score or just wanna kill someone poor.

It's a central location for the sets that run this part of town come nightfall. Citizens stay out and, by the light of the moon, you can see junkies on the nod, backs to trees so that no one can sneak up and snatch their gear.

And so it was, Bettina came here, on a date.

You'll wanna know Bettina.

She was nineteen.

Her second boyfriend called. She was never great with boys. Hard when most come up to your nose and you could kick the fuck clear out of them without breaking a sweat. Boyfriend didn't like that. Boyfriend felt humiliated. Boyfriend called her here and snuck up on her and put the bullet from a zip gun into her back.

IT TOOK HER TWENTY SECONDS TO DIE AND SHE DID IT WITH such hate in her heart. Failure. Rage. Crushing disappointment. *Such hate.* A sad enough story and the end for most people.

Bettina's story did not end there.

See, she'd been raised on stories of her grandmother's childhood. On Mictlan and St. Death and Malverde. The days her father wasn't smacking the shit out of her that was.

When she died, I had a strange dream. It lead me to her.

See she didn't call on no Jesus when she died. She thought of her grandmother's stories of skeleton gods and death-haunting dogs and called on them, instead.

Magicians like me, we've always got that midnight radio playing. We hear things others don't and I heard her.

THIS WAS JUST AFTER JON FIRST PUT ON THE MASK AND betrayed us.

After I left the Library.

NEEDED MUSCLE.

WENT DOWN TO THE PARK AND RAISED HER UP. KNEW SHE wanted to come. Knew she wanted revenge. And knew she was pretty happy to work with crazy motherfuckers like magicians. Raised her up.

Made her mine.

But I ain't real keen on having slaves. She stared at me, dirt in her wounds, pulling maggots from out like splinters.

Made her a deal.

'Lady, here's what's up. You and me, want get your ex. Then you stay above ground. For a while. Help me out. Already know you can fight.'

And I did. Me and Jon had seen her at the underground kumites. Just luck finding her twice.

'YOU GET A CHANCE TO SAY GOODBYES TO WHOEVER. THEN YOU go back in the ground, if you want.'

She thought it over. Looked at me with eyes would never blink again, unless she wanted 'em to.

'Cool.'

We found *the* boyfriend that night.

Which is when we both discovered zombie girls need fresh human meat to survive.

We get on pretty good, now.

II

NECROMANCY IS BASTARD CREEPY.

It's not all the skulls and coffins and shit. One quick trip to a certain church in Eastern Europe will cure you of a fear of bones for life. Take a walk through a house full of corpses is another quick study. Hell, sit at a dying relative's side and you'll get yourself an immunity quick enough, if you're tough.

No, the *De La Muerte* stuff is cool, not scary, so it's not the trappings and props that make necromancy creepy.

It's that, to do it, you have to be fucking obsessed with your own mortality. Morbid over the restless claims death has over life.

That's why necromancy will fuck with your head. Because it's all thinking about your own death all the fucking time. And it's fucking *grim*, baby.

But death is a *powerful* symbol for magicians. A mystery we all must solve. A place we can peer in that no one who does not practice our disciplines will understand. The gateway into the final initiation. We must make death an ally. Say that out loud, knowing you mean it. You'll sound cool and remember your power.

First rule of magic. It's all about the mood.

Well, context would be more descriptive a term.

Magic isn't power. You don't mutter some cod Latin words and watch it go to work.

If I could shoot lightning bolts from my hands, you think you'd see me hustling cash? Be on TV, raking in cash.

No, magic is a state of mind, an artistic process, a mood.

Our minds are Simian things, poor at processing data, worse at recollection, primed only to recognise patterns and co-operate. We track the details of our day, we recognise faces and we redo our hairstyles and consider our minds sharp. With such faulty wiring, no wonder such fine strangeness is so hard to aspire to.

But there is a tool we have to circumvent the chattering of our banal mind. We call this ritual. We call this rite. And *that's* the key to magic. The performance of it changes our consciousness.

A quick, powerful way to gnosis.

Details don't matter. You think magic is that cod Latin,

that'll work for you. You think magic is leaping around a forest in tights, it is. It is an art you must practice for yourself.

Candomble veve drawn in white sand on the dusty patch of ground she sleeps beneath. Two black candles. Her name backwards, chanted and made into a spell. *Egas Anitteb*. In a t-shirt, shivering against the cold night, looking out for some gangster prick looking to kick a head, or some junkie looking to knife his way to a wallet.

Use it all. Feel it all. Cloud the mind with it all until death connects me to death. Bettina feels me, like an intruder in her reverie. She swims up to half life slowly, and I can feel her push against the earth. I slow down the chanting, let myself return to the world as well.

Offer no help to her, knowing that she takes long moments to let sanity settle in her head. I light a smoke and wait. Then, finally, she pulls her torso free. Clothed only in dirt, she stares at me in long moments and I stub out the cigarette, light two and hand her one. She takes it. Drags.

'What's up?'

III

'EVENING BETTINA. WE GOT A JOB, LADY.'

She's naked, but even if I was the kind to cop a look, which I ain't, she's covered in dirt. Holding a sealed plastic sleeve with a change of clothes. She comes here to gather up chthonic power; fuel her own undeath.

'It's too soon. I ain't ready to work. How long since last time?'

'Said a job.'

'Seriously, man, how long.'

Shrug. 'Three weeks.'

'Too soon.'

'Yeah, yeah. But I have a job which means you have a job.'

'I don't... I'm not as strong as I should be.'

'A job is a job.'

We smoke in silence a while.

'I'm hungry.'

Reach into the doctor's bag. Man in my position absolutely has contacts in the morgue and toes and fingers have turn out to be portable and easy to eat.

'Let me jump in the bath.'

Naked but for dust, she walks across the park, ignoring whatever scum dares look at her. Admire the muscles in her back. She was strong the day she died, now she's a fucking truck.

She jumps into the filthy water, undead flesh not heir to shock or cold. I follow after. She paddles in the water to her neck. Throw her the clothes and turn my back. She doesn't dry herself. Wet clothes don't phase.

Toss down the mason jar with the fingers and toes in it. She nods thanks, gets to breaking her fast.

Not watching her, can't hide from the sound of her smacking it down. Bone crunches and all.

Tan chinos, work boots, suspenders, a white singlet. She looks double-tough, hips wide, shoulders wider, working woman's muscle under the skin of her arms. Her skin is bronze again after her taste of flesh.

'Come on, lady I'll buy you a drink.'

'What's a Bleak Elector?'

What the fuck?

'A cult. Why?'

'I dreamed 'em. In the dirt.'

· · ·

IV

The Elected Lady is one of those weird figures in the
Bible who turn up like the Man in White and all that. Tradition links her to Madonna, but it's not explicit. That's how I
understand it. Have to find a believer who's read the damn
book more'n me to really get more out of it.

Bleak Elect base their magical practice around her.

Virgin Mary votive cards. There's no coincidence in this
line of work.

Theologians might be able to tell you more, but they'd
probably want to argue with you first. But if there's one
thing a good cult likes to do, it's *stealing* mythology like a
magpie.

The Bleak Electorate is... nothing. Just another cult in a
town where there's call enough for a man like me to keep 'em
in line.

A dozen or so weirdos who reimagine the Feminine
Mystique or the Divine Sacred Principle or whatever you
want to call it, as something dark and grasping.

Theirs is a philosophy of half-arsed misogyny and old
fashioned millenarianism with a bit of the traditional mortification of the flesh. They have some idea that Christ came to
damn mankind, opposed only by his holy Mother, who was
the true champion of the God. Or maybe God is evil and she
was cursed by him to produce his evil scion.

Christ, I can't remember. Even when kicking heads for the
Library, didn't know much about their dogma. They were too
obscure to worry about. Guys and robes in one-room apart-
ments, muttering dire threats at the Unsaved, telling women
how precious they were while telling them what to do with all
that preciousness.

We're back at my place and I'm in the office, looking at my files for the Elect.

Well, they're a whole bunch of folders, boxes, binders and books I managed to steal from the Library. That was two years ago or more, and still not sorted the damn things out. Nothing in B or E. Maybe they just weren't as worth keeping notes on...

'I'm bored!' yells Bettina at me from my kitchen. We been here twenty minutes.

'Keep eating.'

'I'm finished!'

Gave her all the meat in my freezer, which to be fair wasn't much. It'll take the edge off her hunger until she can get at something fresher. She needs human. Whatever the necromantic version of nutrition is, she can only find it there. Fresher better. But animal keeps the pangs at bay for a while.

Can't find anything on the Bleak Elect so... give it up. We just never really had much to do with them, me and Jon.

AT THE KITCHEN TABLE, A SADLY UNDERUSED ROOM, BETTINA'S found my beers and we take one each. We sit in uncomfortable silence for a while. I can't small talk. Even drinking good Mexican beer with an undead woman, I feel strange. I play it safe and stick to work.

'So anything on these Bleak Elect motherfucks?' she asks. Her flesh looks less grey, more native bronze, now. Human flesh is strong hoodoo.

Her hair dried and slicked back, her strong jaw set, damn straight she looks menacing.

'Religious freaks. But not killers. They're just weird guys who... don't even know what they do for sure. They're just little fish. Not like Exorcist college or Library.'

She drains her beer, takes another. 'So what's the job even? Why get my arse up?'

'Guns. Shooting. Hex-slinging people to death. Serious black magic. Someone raided the Gallowglass and there's a hint to the Bleak Elect being involved. But if they got guns, that's a heavy job and you know heavy.'

And I don't.

Needed Jon for it before her. Can throw a punch if it's needed, take one too, but no one's ever mistaking my scrawny arse for karateka.

She nods, takes another of my beers and starts downing again.

Takes a sudden breath in. Her hand clutches at the kitchen table like drugs are coming on. Which maybe they is.

It's the flesh of the suicide from the Gallowglass compound. That's what she's been eating.

'This guy was an... Elector. That's what he called himself. The Bleak Electorate came looking to finish up the Gallowglass. His name was Johansen and he was there to fight.'

Drum my fingers.

'Anything else you can tell me?'

'He was real excited. He was winning. Then they... broke into a vault?'

'A door.'

Bettina nods. 'Yeah. He was excited and then something got him real scared. He was so afraid he knew it was better to be dead. Not going any further than that, though. Moment of death is...'

She looks up at me. 'Like a hole in everything.'

'Alright. Let it be.'

. . .

STRIP DOWN TO A SINGLET, SNAP MY ZIPPO, LIGHT US BOTH smokes. Can't complain for any imprecision. It's ritual cannibalism. Not a recording.

'THERE HASN'T BEEN A CULT WAR LIKE THIS IN YEARS.'

'You guys have, like, magic sets? Gangs?'

Bettina's kinda curious about magic and the doings of it.

'Yeah. One crew moved on another last night. But the last I heard, one set was much smaller than the other. Don't know what the reason was they moved at all.'

Bettina nods her head. 'Desperate. Timetable. Paid for it. They were *paid* for it.'

'Bleak Elect were doing mercenary work?'

'Maybe. They thought the Gallowglass crew were weak.'

Fair enough.

'They were wrong. Surprised they even know who Gallowglass are. Were. Bleak Elect never had juiced. Did they even get what they want?'

She concentrates.

'I think so.'

'Whatever they were after, it cost them.'

Bettina shrugs. 'How long you been out of the game?'

'The politics? Two years since I left. Bit longer.'

'Long time, man. Long time.'

She gets up, puts her hands in her pockets, stares at me.

'Let's eat.'

And that gives me an idea.

5

I

Lionel's... mother or aunt – can't recall to be honest – was the last Myal-worker in the West Indies, he would tell me one night.

She scorned Obeah as black magic. The witches of her neighbourhood laughed at her, considered her magic to be antique and a bad kind of "old-school". *The equivalent,* he said, smiling... *of listening to an eight-track.* Not simply an affectation but something you'd have to be perversely wilful to indulge in.

On her sixteenth birthday, she left her Island and moved to England, where she haunted the dance halls, enjoying the raga and the dub step and the reggae, moving wild to music and working hard in a hotel. But she was legal, she found a job. In time, she became a cook, even, working for some breakfast cafe, working in Birmingham.

Lionel's mother was really great at cooking, it turned out, and that was where her own magic found its expression. She brewed up potions famous amongst the immigrant streets. She knew the secret ingredients to turn on your husband so he panted after you or sweat out some devil or end an unwanted baby easy and smooth. She was a respected woman and Lionel later said she gave him three gifts in his life. The first was his good looks. His second was showing him there were secrets in the world. But the third was she showed him how to cook.

MAGIC POTIONS, RUNES ON THE SILVERWARE. SOON HE'S IN fabric of the City. Everyone who's everyone dined there.

At thirty-four, he has his third restaurant. He rarely cooked now, except when the mood took him, or special guests were in dining. Or he needed someone under his spell. Cuisinomancy.

You know, we had a conversation, him and me. He was a sudden player. Course we kept tabs.

'Lionel, you could be the greatest political assassin of your time.'

He laughed, sipped on his Red Stripe and in that warm Islander accent said 'Lark, I admit to you I like the power and the money. I do not need bad karma of murder under my roof, I'm thinking.'

Magic comes where it's wanted but then does as it pleases. Clear yourself of desire. Free yourself from a lust for result.

Worked out for Lionel.

I don't have...

Don't have many friends. Once you're in the life, it's hard to talk to citizens.

But found it hard even before then. All I care about is the work. The history and application of the arch of all art, magic.

Can't talk about sports and I don't care about your kids. Don't go to the movies, don't care for the weather and don't read fiction. My house is weird, I have to get drunk to have a conversation with anyone who isn't Scarlet half the time, and we haven't spoken without shouting in two years. Smell of cigarettes and can't tell you my stories.

So I don't have many friends. Easier that way.

But I like Lionel.

The alleyway behind *Agni* is well-travelled and well lit but we cast shadows over the walls. One of the dish pigs is having a smoke break. He leans against the wall, midnight tired.

'The man working tonight?'

He thinks we're autograph-hunters. He shakes his head.

Whisper a word under my breath, a spell I've used a hundred times. It just makes him suggestible. Bettina smiles behind me. The dish pig grins and I can see the gaps in his teeth. Give him another smoke and he and my bodyguard flirt in Spanish together. That helps the spell.

He wanders out and in a bit, he wanders in.

'The man will see you. Restaurant closes in half an hour.'

In the white hot wet bustle that is a kitchen. It's the last of the meals and the cooks are tense. Desert chefs are on. They throw us filthy looks, two fucking civvies in their kitchens.

Then the booming accent.

'Lark, mate! How you be?!'

Dressed in his hound's-tooth and white, he crosses the kitchen to hug me. I'm not a hugger. He laughs at my awkward attempts to go with it. It's been three years and he's even skinnier than I recall.

Does he have the sickness? No. Some fucked up geas, I'd imagine, a cook doomed to a scarecrow physique. It's the sort of thing that happens.

His cooking station is all done up with idols, kitchen wife poppets, sigils, like that.

'You like the new digs? We're up some tasty things. Food

golems! Ah, just joshing. Who is your very tall, very striking companion.'

He smiles at Bettina like it's a spring morning.

'Lionel. This is Bettina. She works for me.'

Something about her wards off the hug, he's too smooth and so tries to grip her hand.

'Charmed, Madame.' She likes that but she too gangster to show it. Rewards him with a half-smile.

'I like your place, man,' she gestures around. 'I never been in a kitchen this big.'

'You should see the convention centre kitchens I used to run. This is an intimate dining experience. And one time, I cooked in a palace. That's a story...'

He'll brag for a while if I let him, so I cut him off. 'Bettina needs to eat.'

'I'll scrounge the lady something.'

'No. Look.'

He does, lips moving. 'Ah.'

'Yeah.'

Whistling over a sous-chef, who he dispatches into a walk-in. 'I need the red sauce.'

A moment later the woman comes back with a long, thin glass tube. Lionel unstoppers it.

'I have a farm. Certain of my clients have unique dietary requirements. I slaughter a cow in the morning, have it driven in especially. Blood, bones, eyes, tripe, offal. All sorts of things get saved. This is fresh this morning.'

She opens it. 'Not here. They'll smell it.'

We walk through a corridor to his office, done up in cool colours, bamboo decorations. We take seats over from his desk. Bettina gets greedy, gulping down the blood.

'You did something to this?'

Lionel falls with a thump into his chair, tired after a long night. 'Well, we have these blokes who look after all the animals, feed 'em a special diet. But also, there's a weird group up in the hills who use livestock as their totem animals. Call 'em the "sheep-shaggers". Goats, cattle, all that stuff. Probably tasting all that devotion.'

She swigs again. 'I like it. Can I buy this?'

He grins with his white, white teeth. 'Not with dosh.'

Stir at that. Pusher economics. And Bettina drinking a diet of enchanted blood? Then cutting supply? Classic scam. That's how you end up with monsters.

'Lionel, I'm investigating some people.'

'Who?'

'The usual.'

'Thought you got fired from that job.'

Trying not to bristle: 'I quit.'

'Either way, mate.'

'You know I've been freelance for two years.'

'Not *investigating*. You're not Magnum fucking P.I. You're being a stickybeak.'

He uses phrases like that. Part of the charm.

'I'm investigating now.'

'Why?'

'Getting paid.'

'Who's holding the purse?'

Nothing.

'Mate, people leave me alone because I leave them alone. Don't bring me attention I can't use.'

Laugh, but not feeling it.

'YOU COMP FREE MEALS EACH MONTH TO EVERY MAGICIAN OF note in the whole city. You've got an ear out for everything that happens. You've got more drugs in here to make someone spill their guts than is reasonable. Don't play *Casablanca* with me.'

'Alright. Alright. What do you want from me?'

He takes a spliff from his draw and lights it, offering one to me, to refusal, Bettina taking hers. Light my own smoke. Shit smell amazing but don't get offchops at work.

He calls up cocktails and we settle in.

'Lionel, need to know the score. The layout. Catch my arse up. I'm not *in it* like a used to be. What's the state of play?'

'One thing before tell what as you need to know, my brother. Is the Hollow involved?'

Don't want to talk about this but I give the cook a scrap for free.

'Haven't seen Jon in ages. He's too dangerous. Order stands, don't fucking engage with him. Just get a Librarian and then get me. So back to the point.'

He breathes in deep relief. 'You'll owe?'

Hesitate. *I'm working for Scarlet, Lionel.* But can't make that play.

'I'll owe.'

He lays it out.

II

LIONEL IS READY TO SHARE THE LAY OF THE LAND. DRINK A brandy stinger, my secret cocktail shame.

'Two years since you worked for the Library?'

'About that.' I say.

'You know we had a vampire uptown?'

'No.'

'Yeah, Scarlet led the kill-team on it.'

'How many fatalities?'

'Two. Hobson and that little girl with the freckles.'

Straw. She should never have been on the that sort of operation. A sweet girl who read four dead languages. Hobson was just a sharp-eyed little bastard who liked the bully-boy aspects of the work the best. Partnered with that prick Rosengarten a lot. Him I do not mourn.

'It was a stupid fucking thing. Eating tampons it found in the rubbish. Someone had kicked out its front teeth. Probably some territory thing. It should have been an easy job but rumour is, they just went in blind and stupid.'

Lionel goes on. 'That started things going bad for the Library. Back-footed them, though no one's ready to try anything yet. Jon was gone, you were gone. Katanya is capable but... Library is in a deficit of talent right now.

We still have to talk about that, what happened with Jon.'

No.

He sees there's only stillness for him and keeps talking.

'You were gone and that meant that they suddenly had to use a lot more brute force solutions. And without Jon, that wasn't going very well.'

Fame at last.

'Are you going to be sensible if I start talking about certain people?'

Wave with two summoning fingers, bringing it on.

'Everett was... he got a big promotion.'

Elliot Everett. Jumped up banker who bought his way into the Library. Who then started sleeping with Scarlet about two minutes after we broke up.

Roll fingers at Lionel, impatient to get this over and done with.

'He made some mistakes. Who put him up to it over there?'

Upstairs. But never mind that.

'He's from money, Lionel. He thinks you solve cult problems like you were negotiating some business bullshit.'

'Hah! This is theory I buy into. Yes. He makes some bad calls and suddenly, old issues flare up. Conflict. Stupid things.'

'Fights.'

'Yeah.'

'Gallowglass was too big and too old to get involved in this. Hell, Bleak Elect weren't new, just small. Both old enough to know a cult war fucks up everyone gets near it.'

'Story isn't over, mate. See, a fresh crop of amateurs isn't unprecedented. It's not even always a bad thing. But the crew they get... bully boy Babylon nonsense. Fights in the streets, blokes getting pissed and chucking hexes around. I'm surprised no one's tried to hire you for a bit of help against your old people. And they have a bigger job they are ignoring.'

'What did they miss?

Lionel frowns. 'People come to me in your absence. Don't like that, Lark. But they do. One of them tells me he finds *this* on his temple door.'

It's a long strip of paper, written in some Pictographic language that looks Chinese but probably isn't. Fire engine red and garish gold. Can feel it; a seething spell, looking for connections to sever, white hot with malevolence. Bad fucking magic.

Second later, another shock.

Seen this shit before. But keep that thought to myself.

It doesn't just burst the pipes or sour the milk. It stirs up paranoia, fear and sickness. It infests a place like cockroaches, splashing madness and the worst kinds of luck around. It's cancer magic.

Bettina stares at it then suddenly crosses herself.

'The fuck even is this?'

'Calamity curse. You fix it to a place; a person, if you can. Then you sit back and watch the fun. It's... very bad. And very powerful.'

'You can read it?'

No. I've seen it before. No need to give Lionel something for nothing.

'Why are you showing me this?'

'Because there's more. Weapons and bad juju. Black magic shit is flooding the streets at the moment and that's why all the newbie groups and the tiny little zero-percenters are all up in arms. These pricks shouldn't be able to get a hold of stuff like calamity magic. Shouldn't even know what it is, but someone's offloading it cheap, and in bulk.'

Hand back the streamer, glad to be rid of it.

'Why isn't the Library on this?'

'Trying to tell you, man. Sheriff crews are amateur now and Elliot is not right for the work. Library might be Babylon police but, man, you kept this sort of mumu foolishness under control.'

'Thank you, Lionel.'

Stand, handshake, all that.

'So what's your plan?'

'Don't know.'

'Sure you don't.' He's not happy with my silence. Never is. Figure he'll learn.

'I owe you one.'

That sweetens it. Far as Lionel's concerned, that's money in the pocket.

In the alley outside, Bettina looks me up and down.

'I liked that guy.'

'Yeah, Lionel's ok.'

'But you weren't square with him, were you?'

'Didn't lie.'

She crosses her arms. 'Didn't tell the whole truth.'

Wants answers and it won't cost me to be honest.

'Me and Jon confiscated that charm ten years ago. That very one. It was our first big job. I know who we took it off. Low skel by the name of Jeancat.'

6

I

THEY CALL HER WICK. ONE OF THE GUY'S MOTHERS CALLED HER as skinny as a candle and you know the rest.

The guys don't like her. She's thin, short and sly. She keeps her black hood up and she sees strange things that no one else sees. Her tags are weird as well. She doesn't write her name, or spray the mythologies in paint on storm drains or trains, or warehouse wall or disused Mason hall. Wick sprays landscapes, drawn from her dreams and her daydreams and her nightmares. She loves the colours; brighter the better. She doesn't know about surrealism and symbolism and expressionism and words like that and she wouldn't care if she did. Wick seeks absolute fidelity to her own artistic vision and the tenets of an artistic school would annoy her. But she doesn't know those words and likely never will. Her work, therefore, is disturbing to the others. The others.

The artists create elaborate identities for themselves: CaesarZero1, The Blue Fairy, Smeer, Fuckstick, Beats, Tako-

Tak. They leave each other messages, jokes, threats and disses and lessons and, sometimes, create spaces for other artists to finish their work; collaborations between people who will never meet. Wick tries to create her own identity, but they don't care. She's not a part of a movement. The weird girl they don't let in the gang.

The tagger crews are strange. Poor. Mean, Desperate. For money to buy paint and phones and kicks and that stuff to look cool to their friends. But moved by art, by the need to express. To mark their world with themselves. Some are just kids who want to paint a city, living with their parents in below means circumstances; no money. At least none to squander. With ambitions that run to DJing in clubs, their tags used for fashion designs or as backdrop for R&B or hip-hop clips. Or, whatever.

Wrong to call the taggers an aristocracy of the streets. More like artisans, in a lot of ways. Their services are always in demand, to scrawl gang semiotics or to simply brighten dark streets and alleys and so they have a kind of social mobility; an immunity, so long as they respect all the streets' laws and treaties. Some of the work is political, although many sneer at this brand of optimism and pretension. Some exorcise old grief or old beefs and famous trysts, and killings are remembered with a certain word – a certain image that stains the city, unknowable but to the few who can decipher such words.

The elite, the known taggers, can speak to who they choose, move freely through the city, listen to what music they like, the graffiti artists, put up kids. They only have one law: don't fuck with another's work.

It wasn't just a diss on a personal level. It was maiming the folk art of the tribes. It was something taken seriously enough to break arms over. Except...

Except for Wick's work. She didn't have her own crew. She didn't have muscle. She didn't have anything except for the strangeness and the characteristic unsettling patterns and weirdly juxtaposed glyphs and images. Foreign climes. Circulatory systems. Wrong-shaped eyes. Dancers doing ill dances.

When they found her the last time, they took a philistine's glee in destroying her work. When they just covered over it, blanked it white or black, Wick didn't care. She knew that piece had just plain scared them and she kind of liked that. One time, she tried to fight them off, but fourteen-years-old and underfed, she was never really convinced by her own violence and neither were they. Some girl gave her a black eye. It was when they made her watch cocks and tits drawn over her fang-eyed mermaids that she finally cried.

The tags are more than just art. They're a little piece of her marking the city and making it *hers*. Marking it, letting people know she exists, that she has ideas, visions, that she has a *right* to be here. These aren't things she can speak of, but they're her true thoughts. That she has as much right as the guys who tease and mock her to live here. That she's as much a citizen as the mayor or the people in the coffee shops with computers or the nannies or the lawyers striding along the sidewalk or the girls shivering in tiny dresses that cost more than her mum pays in rent. Wick marks the city and it becomes something she participates in.

Wick is sensitive. She has the mind of a magician, receptive to illogic and symbolism and so she crawls down into the underworld of Crom Cruach and subways. She climbs up to the water towers, circling them with invented alphabets, solar symbols, Ra invocations. Crossroads at midnight and the scenes of ancient murders, or the great bathhouses, closed by the bug, or the sites where murders were done, famous love was made, terror seized. If there was a haunted place, Wick haunted it in turn, marking it surely. She'd never know it until after she was dead, but she had fans and admirers amongst metropolitan spirits and magicians who made forsaken places the loci of their explorations.

No surprise, then, that when the Bleak Electors made their move on the House of Gallowglass, Wick knew about it. She'd spotted the house before on her rounds, looking for likely places, but she'd dimly perceived the wards that would have maimed her had she tried entrance. But she'd left marks in the neighbourhood, and her own faith in and obsession with her art had left her sensitive to them.

She'd left her mother, drunk by twilight like always, then wandered up to rich neighbourhood, just plain knowing something was going down.

Climbing a fire escape across the street from the house, no mean feat in itself, but she'd learned a monkey's tricks in her time, Wick watched the combat go ahead. Two fine cars and a cheap old van unloading tough men and weirdos. Combat on the lawn. More was going on than she could see, but she could *feel* it, sure as sure.

Wick has an artist's instincts but none of the training. No notebook to scribble ideas or images. But she has patience.

She waited, four hours or more, not bored, wishing only to sign what she felt. Heard screams from inside the house. Saw things moving in the windows that she didn't like. In time, some men and women came out of the house, angered and spitting, pointing fingers at each other. They hadn't found what they were looking for. Soon it was all over, and no one moved in the whole house and the bodies on the grounds weren't faking.

Sure it was clear, Wick leapt from her roost and opened the gates. A sudden migraine spikes the inside of her skull, but she's too excited to care. Besides, it's clearly meant to kill her and it can't, so she's not so impressed.

Wick saw the same sights Lark would see only twenty-four hours later. Bodies and hurts. And at the top, in the museum, she found one thing he did not. What Wick couldn't know was that she was being read, treated as text. *It* was surprised, insofar as it had such capacities, at the aptness of the new arrival. *It* had felt hands upon its skin, eyes delighted as they read *Its* words, confirming its presence. Affronted at such little minds grazing its alphabet and hieroglyphs, *It* wiped memories of their retrieval of its prison.

Wick however, was completely aware of the Scroll. It was a cynosure in the room and all the other prizes were irrelevant in comparison. She gazed at the delicate tracings, a language she had no way of knowing was like Arabic or Bedirxan but cursed and justly forgotten. Unaware that people had killed – had died – for the honour or crime of gazing upon the terrible mandala illuminated upon the paper.

It was the most beautiful thing she'd ever seen.

Fingers tracing the language, the patterns, she took entire and sudden inspiration.

By midnight, she was at work, delighting in the hiss, the rattle of the spray can and the living symbols she branded the city with.

The Scroll, which was delighted in *Its* idiot manner, was in her bag at her waist. *It* felt *Itself* expand and stretch and *become.*

7

I

Subway station, down into the irony heat, metal on the tongue.

The rats that skitter across the station are doing it slow and sure. Something? Nothing. I don't care. But they're sitting in a circle, one in the middle, that looks to be preaching. Rook trials down amongst the cigarette butts and wrappers and dirt.

Thinking of Jon.

Fucking hell, Lionel. I could have put Jon out of my head if you hadn't said a word.

Shake it off. Ignore the rats. Job to do.

Jeancat is a dealer in rare artefacts with a speciality in weapons.

Don't think guns and bombs, think curses and Aladdin's lamp if the genie had a strangler's grip. Antique drugs. Smokeable mummies. She's got a nose for these things. We've had to punish her before.

What really kills me is that she doesn't study. This shit isn't natural to me. Pore over books and private journals written by schizophrenics and pamphlets printed by creepy Churches decades before, noting everything down, looking for patterns and notions.

Someone like Jeancat annoys me, all luck and some genius guiding her to payoffs and successes. So there's envy. But also, she specialises in making bad situations worse. She makes her money handing razor blades to children.

So I don't fucking *like* her.

Jon wanted to kill her, but Mully never allowed it.

'We're Librarians and to catalogue knowledge is our work. Not murder.' That's the sort of thing the *old chap* says.

Train comes and Bettina steps in front of me, happy to play her bodyguard role. Waves me on. We sit at the back and she keeps her eye on an kid pacing the aisle. Frown a question at her and she glances at her knuckles. Take the message and glance at his. Old scars and tooth-shaped.

Tough guy. But something' spooked him bad. He's got the look of someone who's seen something bad in the night.

He turns, looks at me. Makes some gestures. Stare at him. Makes 'em again. Points to his mouth, covers it with his hand.

Mute.

'He wants a dart,' says Bettina. Hand him one from my pack. He takes it, stares at me. Then the train pulls in and he runs off.

On the train, a cockroach starts to butt its head against a greasy metal pole with the ambition of a suicide.

'He felt it tonight. The Mystery. It's got him. We'll see him again.'

II

. . .

JEANCAT SITS AND THINKS AND DRINKS THE SWEET LIQUORS SHE favours. Something cherry tonight.

Jeancat came to the city when she was a child, fleeing some Eastern hell of war and starvation, where you'd get your throat cut for the wrong name or parish.

She knew from the beginning she had some talent. She smells things that are magical, for good or ill. They fill her nostrils with a tiger's rankness. She hates them. She was raised strict Orthodox and she fears hell, no matter how much she tries. But Jeancat's a realist and turns the devil's trick on her into cash.

Money, she's made it. She's exercised power. She's had the proud humble before her and men of beauty have attempted, and sometimes succeeded, in seducing her, but she knows she'll never get out of the bomb shelters and jeeps of her childhood. Will be that little girl trying not to gag on the scent of burning human meat forever.

SHE'LL BE AFRAID TILL HER DYING DAY.

Jeancat isn't her name, it was just something that sounded class to her. She's fourty six and her hair is streaked with grey that she pretends makes her look distinguished and not past the prime of her teenage years when the local priest killed himself for her love, while she laughed at his sad pleas. Her raw bones are thin, so thin and close to the skin: she sometimes likens herself in her mind to a praying mantis, enjoying the length of her arms, the prominence of her hip bones, the length of her raptor's toes.

She has a conceit her bones are particularly white and sensual. She has a lip curl of devastating archness that is perhaps the only thing in the world she finds funny. Likes Midori and charcoal-filtered cigarettes and sex before fine dining.

Contempt is all she feels for her clients.

They traffic with damned forces and all she does is hand them their own rope. If they're so quick to deal out harm, let them deal with the consequences upon their own salvation and, if they should be so foolish as to harness weapons beyond their understanding, then isn't that a sweetness? A fitting sweetness? And if she makes a bit on the side, surely Jesus would understand.

But Jeancat has a knack for hypocrisy, and so in her office, dark and red and cluttered, kept only to fool tax men, she keeps an amulet that spins when customers come calling with harm in their hearts. It spins now, hanging from the book light she illumines her back room with while she watches a fat man try to tell jokes on a television.

There's a .38 in the drawer and she takes it, hides it on a shelf and sets her back to the door. She expects a knock but too much advocaat and cherry vodka with dinner has made her foolish and she's forgotten to lock it. The tall woman, beautiful, hair pulled back severely, is a stranger. Some Chicano thug. No problem. Probably just a burglary.

The in walks... yes, she recognises this one. Ten years on and the worse for it by the look of him. Starting to get fat and he could use use a bath, and a shave and change of clothes.

'Remember me?'

'Bastard.'

The tall woman, a gangster, sniff Jeancat silently, with the forearms like anacondas laughs. 'Check it out, you're famous.'

Lark is he called? Lark? The fucking pig police.

He looks around, slowly, taking his time and shutting the door politely behind him. He's in a slender three piece that fits his slender body but spoils it all with no tie, shirt open. He sniffs as his head swivels, like a security camera in a bank. He ignores the stuff on the walls, lurid things for tourists and scum with money on an adventure. His eyes are blank and empty as a shark's. They stop on the icon her mother brought with them out of the ruins of their house.

Lark's eyes slowly come to life.

'You're blessed.'

He laughs but it isn't happy.

'Someone dedicated you, when you were born, I mean right at birth, to something. Some spirit. Something. And it gave you your power. You hid that from us...'

Jeancat sneers at him, curling that lip she so admires. 'I don't have the slightest clue what you're talking about, pig.'

The tough woman looks at him in surprise. 'Were you law?'

Lark nods, eyes never leaving Jeancat. 'Sort of. To people like her.'

Slowly he takes something from his pocket. An electric lighter. Shows it to her.

'One of yours?'

'I don't know what you're talking about.'

Irritation flashes across his face. He lights a cigarette very slowly, with a disposable he takes from a pocket, putting the quality piece in his pocket. She hides a sigh of relief but he is watching her face very closely.

Jeancat knows exactly what that lighter is.

'This is a weapon. I found it in with Gallowglass stuff, but they don't like weapons. I'll ask once, did you sell it?'

Jeancat says nothing. If there's one thing she hates, it's temerity from magician *garbage*. She hates the little chancers, all addicted to miracles and powers and tricks. This is *her* place, *her* livelihood. And she remembers this man, taking her stock not ten years past, daring to give vet her clients, sending little thugs around every few months to check her stores and finds.

'I don't have to talk to you. You're not even with the Library anymore. You're as lonely as a spider.'

'Jeancat. Listen. It's just you and me in the room. And her.' He points to the thug. 'And I don't think she likes you.'

'Fuck you both.'

The thug steps in, too quick, punches her once in the gut. Jeancat has taken dozens of blows and she knows real blows from scares and this is just for show. She falls and regains her dignity quickly, knowing it's just for show. The man whispers in his thug's ear, low and fast as formic acid. Thug shrugs and holds up hands to show there's no more violence.

'Go on. Let's get this started. Bring out your hammers and I will spit on them. You think I've never had your sort at my door before?'

Lark stops and breathes deeply.

'Not a torturer.'

Jeancat laughs.

'Bettina just doesn't like you much.'

'And I have such warmth in my heart for her.'

Lark rubs his face. Looks tired.

'No chance you just tell me about the lighter because people are in fucking danger?'

'Stab the eyes of your mother!'

'Listen carefully. Don't want to hurt you and, while I'd be happy to shut you down, I'm not going to break fingers here. But, come at you straight, there's no time to fuck around, so talk or...'

He points at her, fore and little finger. The horns! He speaks of witchcraft!

He walks over and with a creepy delicacy removes the icon from the wall. He studies it carefully.

'This is beautiful and old. Older than you'd know. Someone who loved you very much spent hours, days, doing a working over it. Thinking they were giving you a gift. Giving you a sense for power, probably thinking it was evil you'd fight, never imagining you'd turn it into something so mercenary and grubby.'

Jeancat has heard this before: judgements on her career. The lip does its sneering work.

'But I can take it away. No wonder you hid it from me. Can take this gift from you, your ability to scent magic, weapons, things to hurt people with.'

He kneels down next to her. 'I'm not bluffing.'

'Drink your father's - '

He simply stands. 'You're finished without this. I'll be back sundown tomorrow and you'll have my answers or I'll take away your only talent.'

He throws a card on the ground, his details and walks out.

The thug woman stares. 'He's going to fuck you up.'

She leaves too.

III

Jeancat leaves the store as we watch.

'Do we break in?' asks Bettina.

'No. We wait. She'll expect us to follow.'

'But we won't?'

'She doesn't like magicians. She thinks she's better than us. So she'll be wasting time trying to throw a tail that doesn't exist. That'll make her paranoid when she can't find a damn thing. Then she'll be off to hire muscle then she'll come after me. She won't hide. Not with her pride on the line.'

We wait in an alley and smoke to pass the time.

The light is sodium stained yellow and there's a buzzing robot-mosquito drone from somewhere.

'Want me to get a gun or a blade?'

'Not that kind of muscle I think. And if there is, you'll handle whatever she could throw at us.'

Bettina looks at me strangely.

'You're pretty confident in me, man.'

Shrug. 'You're good enough.'

Check the phone for the time. Just gone one.

We wait another hour.

Bettina is bored. Or rather, she thinks she is. She's dead and her patience can be endless.

TELL HER TO WAIT, TELL HER TO CONCENTRATE ON NOTHING. Takes her about fifteen but she gets what I'm telling her. I can see the terrible fact of her death seep into her. Pacing stops. No breathing. Just low-contrast awareness.

'Just guard this alley.'

Sit down, cross-legged in the dust, drawing a gnostic connection to the earth. Focus on a street light across the street and soon it's as big as a moon, as big as a mind. Light floods everything inside me, a klieg light epiphany, shaping my consciousness into a trap.

Don't know it but I put the icon into my hand, an electric wire connection.

Time is a thing I'm unconvinced by. It's there, then it isn't.

Then, I'm aware of an intrusion, some prick soul-projecting at me, lured in by the icon, too stupid to be suspicious of why it's so easy. Which it is, considering I'm flashing the damn thing around like it was a pair of pasties.

Here he comes.

Feel the presence drawing closer, confident they found what they're looking for.

Some city shaman who'd take the job and scout the astral for a hundred bucks and some trinket Jeancat bought him off with. Hunting down the icon.

Not the first time we've dealt with chancers.

Close my eyes, concentrate and an idea took me years to perfect.

Astral trap.

Spend weeks been meditating on elaborate machines of capture. Make it real to you as a memory. It doesn't look like anything. It's the idea of a maze, not a maze, *ceci n'est pas une pipe*, and I don't need to think of bear traps or tubes.

Let it slowly, *slowly,* form around me as the shaman tries to ransack my memories.

He's trapped, easy as that. Immediately.

Fucking amateur. He came at me all force and hurry. Stupid.

Now for the mean bit.

I go through him like a submarine hunter-killer.

Jeancat. Shaman's thoughts are full of her. No doubt the second we left the office, she was calling in favours.

Jeancat *stepping* to me.

Fuck this noise. Shoot my thoughts into shaman like bullets, passing into his/her skull like a thief.

Wait, Jeancat and the shaman are... linked. Shaman's using Jeancat's memories to find us.

They're *linked.*

Ignore the shaman, go straight into Jeancat's mind.

I pass through sex-fantasies and the stale poison lakes of

resentment and the whirling tornados of humiliation and the bright gems of laugher, too few of those.

Memories. Don't ransack them, although can't but... but fuckin' marvel at the dark metal filing cabinets she keeps them in. Strange mind. Don't need to know about her. Just the recent ones she's already thinking of, that's what I want, and I can tell them from their disorganisation.

Touch them and she's aware of me. Whole skull fills up with her revulsion like a bomb's gone off. Take what I need and leave. Her banshee screams are mounting.

The magician I slap around, convincing him that he's not going to want payback.

Show him a taste of the Omegamantis and the Ultrascorpions.

We'll come back to the Ultrascorpions.

That's it. I'm gone. Low consciousness floods back with a surging disappointment. Garbage water stink and an ache in my legs.

Bettina stands over me.

'You alright?'

Razor grin up at her. 'Yeah. That worked nice.'

8

I

WARNING: THE FOLLOWING FILE IS CLASSIFIED CRIMSON GLOVE. IF YOU ARE NOT CLEARED FOR STATUS: CRIMSON GLOVE, REPLACE THE FILE AND REPORT TO THE SECURITY CLEARANCE OFFICER NOW.

Note: Another letter retrieved from codename: BLUEFLY

Rule 2

You can't do magic if you've got a regular kind of mind.

There's a lot of meanings to that phrase. First of all, you've got to crave the miraculous. You have to want more from your life than money can give you. Or love. Or power. Or religion. Or anything.

Most people who might search for it lose themselves in sex or drugs or the usual things that take us out of our worlds. Many see that part of themselves and mistake it for faith. They hit the churches and the mosques and the temples. Some take the vows. A swing. A miss.

You can't just read out the books or chants the chants. You have to want it.

That's just how it starts.

That just gets you in the door, homes.

Then you have to bring your brain in line.

You'd have to talk to someone who specialises in the human mind to really understand what I'm saying. Read a book that doesn't have a weird occult symbol or a dragon on the cover one time. But the brain in the skull is a thing designed to live on a plain in Africa and find awesome mangoes and watch out for hyenas and dinosaurs and all that. It recognises patterns. It makes leaps in logic. It works against its own self-interest and can't be relied on. It rewires itself all the time, it's pretty good at paying attention to things that are right in front of it.

And it's _real_ good at tricking itself.

That's what magic is. Fooling yourself. Creating a state of voluntary schizophrenia. Just for a while. Where symbolism and metonymy become what they represent. But you can't be a madman and do magic. Well, at least, you can't be... irrational, like. The whole point is to come back from the trip.

Your brain, though, needs incentive to hallucinate.

Or it needs meditation.

I call it Gnosis, but you'll find it called other things. Gnosis just means wisdom. It's a receptive state where the... restriction of your sane, day-to-day mind relaxes. You need to work yourself into a state. Exhaust yourself. Get a fever. Orgasm. Pain. Breathing. Edge of sleep. Whatever. Something that focuses the brain tight and low.

I can meditate on demand now, just need a few short breaths. Took me years to learn how. Meditation is the easiest when you know what you're doing, but that takes a while. Stick with the other methods but practice meditation. Always.

Always, always. After a while, you'll have uses for it that you never could have thought of. I can touch the Gnosis whenever I like unless something's keeping me from it. Fear. Intense pain. Things like that. But a big part of what makes me a good magician is that I can enter it quickly. Easily. And keep it.

You'll find the stillness of Gnosis when your mind quiets. When you find yourself free from restriction. When you move from symbol to symbol fluidly, easily. When you leave the restriction. When everything becomes immanent and strange. Or, a little less dramatically, when you can find the empty-skulled peace of the early morning stares.

That's why a lot of people give up, you know. I think the city would be overrun with cults and sorcerers if it was easy. But you can chant up the Black Rites of Pluto all you like and nothing will happen. Not unless you've reached the one-pointed mind of Gnosis.

So try it. Go for a run or invite over a generous boyfriend or, err, something. Dance like a dervish or hold your hand over the stove. Whatever you need to shut the brain down from thoughts, to enter into a new state.

Then learn to keep it.

Push it. Enter Gnosis and catch a bus, buy whisky. Call a friend.

A favourite of mine is keeping it while walking, seeing what the magic needs from you. Seeing what it has to say.

That's it. Find the stillness. Wear it like armour, become it like a still mist in your head.

Because when you have the Gnosis, the one-pointedness, the rules of the world change, reality takes on strange new contexts and subtexts and that's where sorcery works the best.

Gnosis. Find it. Keep it. Magic.

9

—————

I

JEANCAT'S MEMORIES. STOLEN.

Back at my place, in my sanctum, eyes closed, playing through them.

A man called Ludo. Jeancat was *real* afraid of him.

Big man, six four or more and solid through the chest and shoulders. His forehead slopes back on forty-five degrees from his face and his skin is... coloured. That's Jeancat's perception and so it's mine.

Ludo's dark skin, partnered with his thick Afrikaans accent, drags up ugly thoughts in Jeancat's prejudiced head.

This perception is mine: *this guy is a fucking beast.*

Sharkskin suit and a great bone box of a skull. Soldier's haircut and rings on his fingers. Watch the memory as Ludo buys up her stock in one go, shovelling out bills like they're nothing.

Jeancat knows he's up to something, but she's counting dollar signs.

Look closer at this Ludo motherfucker.

There's a way he sets his shoulders, flexes his fingers, and I can tell the rings are an affectation. So's the suit. Just a disguise to distract from who he is.

This is *monster*, come hunting, oozing predator vibes.

Know then what I know now about Ludo, what he does to my body, run now or curse him to a drooling coma right the fuck now.

He bought out every last bit of Jeancat's stash. And other dealers too.

The Dark Jew, that's how she thinks of him, don't blame me. That Whore. Pearl and Saunderson and all the guys who buy and sell the mojo trinkets.

Keep looking. Ludo's come to others, he's spent maybe two hundred and fifty thousand dollars on arcane weapons and eldritch tricks. A surfeit of bad devices, whose only uses are cruel. No healing here, nor blessing, nor even conceal-ment, let alone communion or invocation. Nothing worth-while. Nothing transcendent. Just tools to hurt with. Ceremonial objects that create discord and violence just by existing.

Have no idea who this fucker is. Spent years putting names to faces of every serious occultist in the City, especially if they have money. Easy marks. But Ludo's new.

It's dawn, so let Bettina go for the night.

She has friends still and family, although I don't know how. She'll tell them she's back from her job. That's what she tells them. Perhaps she'll just go slaughter some hobos and feast.

Sit at my kitchen table, noting it down.

What have we got?

1) I don't know this Ludo at all. Never even heard of him.

I've been out a while but, at the risk of flattering myself, that's bullshit.

2) He's got money. A lot of money. Who has this kind of cash? The Library. Gallowglass. No one else I know.

3) He's buying up weapons, like the lighter I'm tapping on my kitchen table. And if he sold it to the Bleak Electors, he probably sold them to somebody else. Why?

Drinking tequila, rich and bronze and healthy, and it seems pretty obvious that war is Ludo's trade.

HE WANTS PEOPLE FIGHTING. IS IT A DISTRACTION? NO, THAT'S shit. People don't spend money and don't go to these lengths for a distraction. The goal is the battle. You don't spend a quarter million dollars on weapons without wanting them on the job. But why?

Fuck knows.

Here's my supposition. Working hypothesis.

LUDO IS AN OUT-OF-TOWNER, LOOKING FOR ANARCHY OR PROFIT or whatever. But he's got money. Might mean backers. Not many people with money do this kind of groundwork themselves but then, a quarter of a million ain't what it used to be. Maybe this is Ludo's inheritance he's spending, mum and dad's house, liquidated and turned to the cause. I think about the way he walks, the size of the bastard and no, he's not on holidays.

Too many variables. Too many unknowns.

I believe I don't know Ludo. Can't believe I've never even *heard* of him.

New player.

Bad news.

Because he's come to the City and smashed it like it was easy.

I'll call Scarlet tomorrow. I get drunk enough to sleep.

II

WHILE LARK TRAPS SOME PUNK-ASS MAGICIAN ON THE ASTRAL pain or whatever the hell it's called, Ludo is hunting.

He has two guys from the old unit he served with and some local talent. Gangsta niggers, trained from childhood to battle like bastards. Various chinks and even some Arabs.

Ludo *loves* the language of racism. It delights him. Fourty years old and he recalls cigarettes put out on his feet when he marched with the ANC and the police caught and questioned him, race-baiting him while he swallowed poison and said nothing. Some people think words have power, but Ludo knows what a ludicrous proposition that is. *Power* has power and that's as far as that goes. It's all about strength and anyone who says different is a fucking pussy without a scrap of it themselves.

No one works with mixed-race crews. Recipe for a headache. But these are strange times and Ludo isn't in a position to have an opinion. He's just doing his job.

They're in the back of a van, guns at the ready. Locking and loading the SMGs and automatic pistols, they get high on tech rites they all know and love.

Ludo's been to see the seers. He hates them but the boss makes him work with them and Ludo wouldn't cross the boss for fucking *anything.* Creepy bastards in a room full of crystal balls, stinking of incense and old vomit with shaky-handed freaks dealing out garish cards.

Only one of them seemed useful.

Automatic writing they call it. Some nervous woman sketched a face and announced this was who had the scroll. Ludo looked it over and went to ask the artist some questions. But she's locked herself away then bit her own wrist-veins out with her teeth in the seer house bathroom.

'Seems an overreaction,' said Ludo, to their keeper. The keeper, former prison bull and apocalyptic, just shook her head. 'The end times are coming.'

Ludo laughed. *When aren't they?*

'Take one, pass it on.'

The hard men take the photocopied sheets and look at the face drawn there. Shaven headed little girl with piercings in her lip, her nose. Her eyes are shaded a pale blue and her lips are thin.

'Her name is Candle or Lamp or something like that.'

One of them speaks up. 'He got a crew like this together to hunt down a little girl?'

'It isn't me.'

None of them speaks up to that. They all know who gave that order. No motherfucker questions the boss.

'We don't know where she is but we know she's not uptown. We know she's not down by Violin Bay and we know she's not Westside.'

That leaves three quarters of a city.

'Yeah, I know. But she stole something from the Gallow-glass House, and there's no reason to believe she's running, so we'll work from the mansion, moving out.'

The Arab says 'Time sensitive?'

'We're not working to a deadline, but I don't want to go to *his* place and tell him we haven't found dick.'

Nods all round. The van travels over a bump and Ludo smacks the driver's window in irritation.

'We're looking for a piece of old paper with weird writing on it. Or a case, like a scroll case? You know?'

Not everyone does. 'Like a poster tube.' Ludo isn't angry. He didn't know what it looked like till the boss told him.

Ludo leans in.

'We're supposed to capture and contain on this one. But this is the hoodoo stuff. She'll have moves and tricks so don't fuck around. If you have to put this chick down, put her down. But that bit of paper is what we are after and I'm not telling the boss I don't fucking have it.

Seriously. And if you're thinking of grabbing it and selling it on, then go ahead. It'll be a good way of learning just how fucking stupid you are before the boss has me drive the end of a steel pipe into your upper fucking jaw real slow.'

Ludo barks orders at the driver. The men know Ludo ain't joking. He's tortured fuckers to death on three continents.

Ludo's not a man given to self-doubt and the thought of the money he's making consoles him a long way. But, not for the first time, the nature of his work disturbs him. Thinks of the Old Man, radiating cancer-hate from some higher vibration, sitting there in his wheelchair, looking at everything with a sickness stare. He shakes his head once, dislodging the image, and checks and rechecks his weapons.

III

WAIT TILL SEVEN AND CALL UP SCARLET AT HER HOME.

'Yeah. So, listen,' I say, cool as hell and straight to business. Hard to talk to her normal when something in you won't heal from the wound she dealt you. But desperation is a weak move.

'I made some contact last night.'

'Lark, I'm having breakfast.'

Man's voice in the background asking if she wants more coffee. We been broken up two years but things aren't coming right for me.

'Like a citizen.'

'Yes. That's how I'm having my breakfast. *Like a citizen*, Jesus. Don't be a tool.' Hear her moving, a door close.

'Look, I'll be at the Library within an hour and a half. We can talk it over then.'

'Be asleep then. Need information and need you to look it up.'

'I said I'm -'

'Later.' Go to hang up.

'Wait! What do you want, then? God, talking to you is like walking a fucking tightrope...'

A sigh in there somewhere.

'Need a name. Ludo.'

She pauses but that quick silence could mean anything over a phone.

'Don't know him offhand.'

'Yeah. And neither do I and that's a problem.'

'Ludo. That his first or last?'

'No idea. I think he's South-African. He's big. Ex-something, I'd wager. I just need to know more about him and I might need an intro.'

She waits. 'Anything else to report?'

'Yeah.'

She waits.

'That ain't how it works and you know it. Report when I'm done, otherwise it just muddies the water. You know that.'

'Call my office when you're up and I'll let you know.'

'Cool.'

'And...?'

'Yeah.'

'Go through the office. *Call my frigging office.* We've had this fucking conversation. Don't call my private number, especially not for work. I've asked this half a dozen times.'

She hangs up.

And just like that, it all flows back.

That was the last year I studied with Mully. We. Me and Jon. I don't want to say apprenticeship or initiation. He never gave us black belts or mortar boards to throw in the air like a couple of pricks, but we studied under him for certain. Yeah, Mully schooled us as sure as sure. Slung the devoirs on us. Made sure we practiced our meditation.

They were also the rockabilly days when I could fit into stovepipes and pointy boots or two-tones and chain my wallet to my belt and slick back my hair.

'None of that goddamn punk stupidity for me,' Jon would say each time I invited him to a club. Jon's tastes ran to the classical and fancy Euro trance at the gay clubs he went to, with more luck meeting dudes than I did women.

So I'd hit up the clubs all alone, dancing like lightning to the sounds of double-bass, drinking Mexican beer and smoking unfiltered Camels back then, toe-tapping, always up the back.

Partly me experimenting with ecstatic transcendent magic. Partly because still needed, badly, to get out of my head back then. My dad had only died two or three years before and wasn't dealing with that so good.

Didn't know booze could heal like it did, then.

Always up the back. Whip thin back then. T-shirts with skulls on them, and pin-up girls too. The clubs were sweaty, the acoustics terrible and the bathrooms were abattoirs, but the music was so good and the women made you want to die under their boots, they were so beautiful.

And there she was. Little black dress with cherries on, her long hair all pinned up, makeup thick and strange and cool, drinking a cocktail from a straw to spare the glass her fire-engine lipstick. She was like a fire; face hot from dancing and eyes wild from adrenaline and booze.

Her lips. Sometimes, alone, I still think about the colour of her lips that night.

Didn't talk to her after seeing her a few weeks. Then, one day, grabbing my bag on my way out, two books spilled from my bag. Went to pick them up but she'd grabbed them.

One of them on pow-wow. Dutch folk magic. The other one on hoodoo and gris-gris. She looked through them. So unconcerned with the awkward kid staring at her, his secrets revealed.

She lit up a long thin cigarette and stared at me across the length of it.

'Give me your phone number.'

Two weeks later, she knocked on the door of the hellish little apartment Jon and me shared. She asked me questions. Good ones.

Scarlet had come out of the swamps and her people were magicians. Folk remedies and that, but more. She'd seen ghosts of relatives brung up. *Things* out on the bayou. Her mother, aunts and grandmothers all were kitchen witches. *Respected* women in their communities.

We talked through the night. She took off her stockings and smiled at me when we were done talking.

'Come here. You're going to kiss me.' Ah.

We were together near ten years.

Now I listen to her new boyfriend, the rich kid, on her phone.

Hell.

IV

Wick looks for some payback.

She's never been violent. She's not a pussy or anything, but she just never liked it. Never wanted to hurt anyone, really. Wick just wants to do her tags, share her art and be left alone. Sometimes she thinks about going back to school. She liked it sometimes. Even though the guys fuck her work up all the time, she just wants them to stop. Doesn't want them dead or even punished.

But something's telling her that it doesn't matter. That pain and suffering are no big deal. Come to everyone. Might as well get some respect.

Deenate is his own tag, his name is recognised amongst the crews. Sixteen, skinny, from out of the Philippines originally she thinks. Best artist she knows and he hates her and thinks her work is stupid and weird. Laughs at her and hunts down her work. Wick thinks that he doesn't like girls very much, but what does she know? Maybe he just hates her work that much and there's no reason for it other than that.

Under the Winterline Bridge is where he did his best work and he's putting some finishing touches on it. She gets in early in the morning, tags it with her own eerie patterns. Signs her name. *Let's see how he likes his work messed with.* Inside her, *it* agrees. Deenate knows where to find her and, by mid-morning, there he is. Her mum is away and so Wick has redecorated. She pulled away the furniture from the walls, the old black-and-white TV, and scrubbed the place, making the surfaces clean and ready for her masterwork.

Then she consulted the scroll, and it changed in front of her eyes, she reckons, sensing her desire. The new patterns hurt her eyes, and she threw up a bit at first. But Wick has the sight. She can get used to anything.

Soldiering on, despite the black stuff that's started crusting her eyes, she got the paint on the walls. It was like being on the inside of a cubic spider web moving weird in time. Like, if time goes only forward, this thing goes diagonal. Wick didn't need precision in her concepts. She just wants people to *feel things*.

When Deenate comes, she opens the door. He's screaming at her but it's like he's doing it through water. He calls her the names men like him have always called young women. He's going to hit her soon, she knows, and she can feel his excitement like she feels an old muscle-tear.

So small, says something to her. *Let him see your work.*

Wick walks back into her house, turning her back. He's just a barking monkey. Suddenly, she can't even remember why the hell she ever even worried about him.

Her city. Her art. If she lets them take it, she deserves to lose it. No one like Deenate is ever going to tell her what she can and can't do ever again.

Deenate walks all the way in and his yelling stops. He looks around at the art on the walls. He asks her some questions, stammering like a misfiring gun. She doesn't care to answer him. Suddenly she's sure that he's as likely to understand this work as a cat shown a sum.

Watch carefully, *it* whispers, avid. And... there it is. Deenate sort of... something like a bubble bursts inside him somewhere deep and *essential*, provides the voice. There's nothing that really shows it on his body. No screaming or a sci-fi airlock explosion. He just stops being himself and, as he zombie-shuffles out the door, Wick watches him carefully, afraid he's faking. By the time he's left her apartment and she can see him on the street through paint-taint windows, he's punching himself in the head and she relaxes. It worked. Something inside her hisses pleasure.

She just watches him then, lighting up one of her mother's cigarettes and resting her forehead against the window, watching Deenate just wail at his own temples. People try to stop him but he bites them and continues. His fists give out before his skull, and she knows he'll never tag again. Knuckles slurry. He'll be lucky if he holds a pen.

Ambulance. Cops. Ice overdose, they think, and they're all ready to shuffle him off to plague the day of some nurses who deserve better than another fucking tweaker. He'll die in there, Wick knows. He's seen something terrible that he'll never come back from.

Wick contemplates cleaning the walls. It might be dangerous to leave them out.

She cooks some soup. Then a bit later, her mother fumbles the keys and walks in the door. Wick jumps up to stop her coming in, seeing the web that wounds the world, wound about the walls.

Is it so great a loss?

Nah. And Wick knows that's true.

She closes the door on her way out, throwing a blanket over the ruin of her mum. She feels sorta bad.

V

Phone call at two in the afternoon and it's a quick job.

Contemplate telling them to fuck off, but a gig is a gig. Exorcism in an art gallery before a show. Someone's made the wrong video installation, having recorded the wrong bum screaming the wrong thing on a bad night.

Tell the artist that certain words have certain powers, but she's too fried on ambition, arrogance and MDMA. Her work is rubbish and I leave her, sure she'll be insane in a year.

Serves her right. The homeless guy is an old-school shaman, intentionally given himself over to crack and night train and eating rats and licking hamburger wrappers so garbage elementals can guide him. Listening to him is making people feel sick because a trash spirit is in the gallery.

Tell them to shut down the audio or they'll have problem.

Leaving the gallery, artist and gallery owner fighting, when I see them, across the street.

Slow grin.

It's Katanya, who started out strong as a junior officer for the Library. Best student of that year, easy. Lost contact with her after I quit.

And, yes, there he is. One of her scumbag classmates. Bianco. The peacock. Rosengarten's chum.

They spot me and Bianco taps his partner's arm. She turns and swears. Pass through cars backed up at the lights and when I get closer, can see some bad scars on Katanya's throat. She's tangled with *something* then, and walked away.

'Mr. Lark,' says Bianco, blinking behind glasses.

Katanya says nothing. Tough and sexy-looking in leather jacket and black jeans and the spikey black hair. Better world, she'd have taken over my gig when I left but she never did.

I want to fuck with them. They let me down.

But it will get back to Scarlet if I make fun of her troops. Don't need the headache.

'Investigating the gallery thing?'

'Yes. Umn, Scarlet told us about it last week but we've been running behind.'

So there are juniors working the scene. Bianco's not up to the job and not sure about Katanya. *Lionel don't get it wrong.*

'Right. Bar.'

Katanya gets ready to throw down about it, but just shake my head at her. Liking the fight in her.

'Not now. Bar.'

We find something two blocks away, silent till then. Katanya refuses to look at me and her anger vibrates hot.

Bianco keeps looking over his shoulder at me, running his fingers through his beard.

The place is anonymously Irish, with some hockey fans barking like animals up the front. We take the pool table. I'm ok at the game, but Katanya is excellent. She still doesn't speak, just plays with smooth economy. Bianco, wisely, gets me a scotch and dry. Talk while we play.

Bianco drinks deep of his stupid umbrella thing for Dutch courage. Not a drinker, him. Recall him actually as Feri Tradition witchcraft specialist. Is that right? Either way. Big lad in a too tight t-shirt with a video game character on it.

'Mr. Lark, we, err,' he waves a protective hand in front of him. 'We don't answer to you anymore. So, well, this is a professional courtesy. Understand that we -'

Stare at him.

'You were late to the show. I picked it up and did the job. And what was your plan anyway?'

Bianco is Librarian to the core, a man in love with indicia. You call on him when you want a man who'll drive, find a book, photograph two hundred pages of it, compare editions page by page, line by line. That's what he's good at. He's just got the ego to think he can retrieve and enforce.

Like what he's doing now.

'Well, we would have carefully questioned the artist. We would have tried to take the tapes and carefully reviewed them. Then we would have petitioned Scarlet and the Librarian General to perform an exorcism.'

Laugh.

Katanya sinks the black smoothly, then looks up at me. She hasn't said a word. I'm three up to her.

'You would have had a room of people who saw something bad tonight if you moved at that pace.'

Katanya takes my coins and racks up again.

'We have procedures, Mr. Lark.'

Shrug.

'We have *procedures*.'

Sip and look at him over the rim. 'You shouldn't be doing this job. I think you know that.'

'If not him, then who?' Katanya. Finally. Smoky voiced and flat with repressed anger.

'No him. And not you. Lazy.' Point at her. 'Undisciplined.'

She moves her head to the side then back. Her anger is clear. Bites it back.

'You son-of-a-bitch. I was slogging my guts out, working two jobs, looking after my Dad and my girlfriend and studying as *hard as I could*. Trying to touch something better than cleaning up bedpans and changing infected dressings. You couldn't have given less of a fuck about that, us, then. Don't pretend to give a fuck now.'

Excuses.

'You commit, or you don't play. You'd gotten into the Library, showed you had what it took to be in the game. Don't blame me if you couldn't step up to the next level.'

'Fuck.' She turns back to the table, finishing the rack.

Bianco actually waves at me like a schoolboy getting permission.

'You have a point Mr. Lark but, well, we can't all just walk into a place and throw weight around. Most of us can't really afford to risk arrest or making too much of a scene. And Rosengarten has probationary measures if we don't do things by the book. We need to log events, we go over them forensically.'

'Untrained.'

'Whose fault is that?' Katanya again.

Actually, she has a point. Think of the Hollow and how I begged the Library to help me free Jon. My fury when they wrote him off. Walking out on the juniors. Shrug. Let them go on thinking what they like. I stopped justifying myself a while back.

'Why isn't Mully training you?'

They look at each other. Something's up.

'We're not actually sure.'

Fine.

Katanya throws down the cue. Stares at me.

'Look, man, it's all going tits up. We're not ready and there's more fights every fucking night. None of us really know what we're doing. Elliot stopped Mully coming to *save fucking money*. But we think it's because he doesn't want *your* old master around. And here you are, jumping on our gigs, making us look worse. And we already look bad because it's all going *wrong*.

Fuck off. You literally had your chance to lecture us. Don't come and tell us what we're doing wrong now. We already *know*.'

VI

Number.

Get a message on the phone telling me to check my email.

Scarlet's emailed me. Using the phrase 'Warmest regards' so you know she's pissed.

Guess calling the house really was too much. Ah, she'll calm down.

Look over the email and pour myself a whisky halfway through to get through the rest. Was right. He is a beast, but not for size, more for savagery.

Ex South African head-kicker, right out of the football clubs, taking scalps in the chaos after apartheid ends. Coloured, as they used to call mixed race cats.

Stint in the army, discharged. Joined up with a private security concern and makes a rep. working for private military contractors in the East. Looks like he got quietly retrenched after something to do with prisoners.

Getting kicked out of mercenary crews takes some doing. After that, he's seen in the company of drug dealers and book makers. Just doing muscle work for low motherfuckers.

Now he's back in the Country and, about nine months ago, moves to the City.

So what's the link to him stirring up the cults out here?

Possibilities:

1 - Mercenary.

2 - Life-long cultist or worshipper, refound the faith.

3 - Ludo is a cover story. Ain't no Ludo.

4 - Something inhuman.

5 - Badass warrior-sorcerer come to take things over.

That last one, no.

Military minds, they run on military thoughts and those are detail-oriented, lockstep thoughts. When you think in terms of kill-zones and firing solutions and the adrenaline of killing, that sort of crowds out the *other* kinds of imagination you *need* to spark up magic. Could happen, though. Just that they're skillsets that rarely overlap.

Looks like it happened with Ludo though. In which case I,

for one, bow to our new badass warrior-sorcerer overlord and look forward to moving on him when he sleeps.

Monster? Yeah, why not. Mercenary? Could be, who could pay him, though? Fuck knows. Any of it. There's no point in deciding you know the answer in advance. It's a bad move.

And I see there's a contact number for him. Find a scrap of paper. Write it down

Might be a play to make.

10

Chapter

I

Bettina comes back at sunset.

She looks strange. Troubled.

Been working on making up sigils, magic words, for the meet. Hiding words. Meme-wasps, my defensive wards that cripple the emotions. Sigils to supercharge with intense emotions. Sorcerer's work.

We sit and drink beer again. She's worked for me, but there's still so little we know about each other. Or perhaps I'm just a weird creep.

'I went in the dirt last night. Had too. You woke me up too early. Upset my mum.'

I bristle. 'You want to quit?'

She makes an irritated face at me and moves her head away, swings it back.

'Why you got to be like that, man?'

'What?'

'I like working for you. Its interesting work and I owe you. And I know you could, you know, *make me* help you. But that ain't your way and that means something to me.'

I say nothing. She peels the beer label now, suddenly shy.

'But you always look for the *worst* meaning to any words anyone says to you.'

Don't say anything. It's true enough and not the first time someone's found my attitude less than fucking *sparkling*. Besides, just waiting for what this is really all about, for it to come to what she *wants* from me. When I say nothing, she just moves on.

'You got to understand something. In the dirt, it's different. You're dead but you ain't gone. The dirt. It. The dirt sort of... I dunno. Do I sound stupid?'

Talk it out, Bettina. 'No.'

'I don't want to say womb cos it ain't a like that. I just know. But it's something. It feeds you. It sort of seeps into you. Like, power? No. Like, it teaches you things. You have dreams and they're weird. But not *I was in school but it wasn't school and my aunt was there but she was a bird* bullshit. But you see things. Feel 'em. Things only the dead can know.'

The wisdom of the grave. Listen careful.

'There's a sickness somewhere. Can you feel it?'

I cannot.

'Something is buggin' out. It's like the dirt is in a tremor, you know? Like... one time, my cousin, he lives north over the bridge. It turns out there was mercury in the ground of his school. Some prick zoned a school on an industry dumping ground. We all went up to see it and it all kind of freaked us out knowing there was poison in the ground, under the grass. I don't know what this is but it feels like that. When I was a kid. Why is that... never thought about it since school and now I can't fucking get it out of my head. Like being really horny or angry, it won't *fuck off*.'

Stub out and light up fresh.

'It's just how it felt to you when you were a kid that counts. It's about the links in your memory and the feelings and images you assign to things. Like attracts like. You're saying there's *pollution*, using the schemes your mind already has.'

'I think so.'

That's interesting. But it's also for another day.

'Are you strong enough to work tonight?'

'Yeah. I am. But I'm not like fucking Wonder Woman right now. Need more time in the ground.'

'No time, lady. Some shit's about to go down.'

Take that scrap of paper.

'My name is Lark. I want to talk to Ludo.'

II

THEY DON'T LET ME TALK TO LUDO, BUT THAT'S ALRIGHT.

Have to get through the usual 'we don't know who that is' bollocks. Pro criminals are paranoid to the point it's fucking *tedious*.

THEY QUESTION WHO I AM AND TELL THEM I WORK FOR THE Library. That gets me far, so these are people with a bit of juice. Hint that this is *body work*. That I need some beat, bad. Or gone.

.   .   .

IT AIN'T THIS EASY, RIGHT, BUT DO YOU REALLY WANT TO HEAR about me taking two days to arrange a meet or do you want the fucking *money*?

Jump to the money.

A meet is arranged under the western bridge. Only highway out of the City. But that's not for a while. Dinner first.

Bettina has bought us take-out, and I eat. She picks at some meat from her kebab, but that can only serve as an aperitif to what she craves.

Call a car service.

She pulls her fingerless gloves on and off.

'What's up?'

'Seriously?'

'What?'

'You strapped?'

'I don't like guns.'

'I can go, get a piece in an hour. Like, my cousin's girl-friend, her dad can clean a heater, have it for you, three nine millis for three hundred.'

'Don't like guns.'

Throws up her hands.

Still, I owe an explanation. Otherwise she'll just think I'm stupid and stubborn. Might be true, but not the case right now.

'I go in there with a gun, strapped up like a hardcase, like a cowboy, that's what I am, right? Then I'm a gunfighter. But you and I both know I'm not street or military. Not a tough guy, don't play at it. Reading books and drinking Cuervo is more my style.

But at the same time, I am a competent, skilled magician with a lot of years behind me.

'I go to this meet like a gunman, I'm a gunman. The magic

knows. The symbolism of the gun is... it's pretty powerful, yeah?'

She nods, hesitant.

'Got a gun, get respect. Pull jobs. Fight back, protect your family, threaten others. Think about all the stuff a gun means.' Again, a nod.

'But that ain't me. I'm a magician, an initiated man. Magic doesn't allow itself to be disrespected, so I *want* to rely on magic, I *have* to rely on magic.'

Frown. Nod.

'Still. Wait here.'

I go to my bedroom and find a gift from Jon. It's nine inches of blade and ugly as hell. Functional. Aside from its blue-tinted iron, it's as unpleasant as its purpose.

'This do?'

'Where'd you get this?'

'Present.'

'From who?'

'Sanest fucking psycho to walk the earth.' Jon the Hollow. Lost to the mask and made fucking evil by it.

'Interesting-sounding motherfucker.'

'Yeah, that he was.'

She takes the blade but she isn't finished.

'You're a man with some science, right? You know a thing or two. People talk about you like a man who knows his business.'

Flatter the ego.

'But this is *my* business, keeping your ass alive. I don't think you're taking it serious.'

Look at her real level.

'Taking you real serious. But... *need* to get close to this Ludo dude. I have to take his measure. See if he's got the volts, you know? And need you to pull me out if it all goes tits up.'

One side of her mouth frowns, cutting deep into her face.

'Yeah, I hear. You smart motherfuckers can be so fucking *stupid*, though, man. I trust you to make a smart play. Cos it ain't just you can get dead from this. Me too.'

'You died already, you know it ain't so bad.'

'Ain't eager to catch the rerun, though.'

III

ONE HIGHWAY OUT OF THE CITY, MOVING WESTWARD. HIGH UP bridge, and underneath it, old town where it's creepy, old and dank.

WE'RE BENEATH IT, LISTENING TO THE DISTANT REPORTS OF cars going over, in a park as used to be a an electricity substation. Locked behind high wires now.

We walk down to the bank where the cold waters of the bay lap, the substation towering over us at the top of an embankment.

It's just sidewalk for a mile. Water on one side, bridge above it all, intruding into the eye line. Supersolid. The water stinks of garbage and wounded salt. Glass all over the place, shattered and vicious.

We get in early. Scout the scene. On the meeting ground, someone's drawn a glyph. Seems they're prepared too.

Hmmm. It'll let them spy on us. That's not an easy spell to cast. It's also hidden sloppily. Slip on my enchanted glasses, check it out. Been there an hour or two. It's a listening spell. We talk, they hear.

Who's listening to my calls? I type out a message on my phone, show it to Bettina. 'Someone following us.'

She shrugs.

I'm in an overcoat and a suit, no tie. It's the best I've got these days. Stole the suit the day before I left the Library, and it's more than I can afford now. Same with the coat, which is wool and midnight blue and the most beautiful thing I own. My hair is slicked back, but only because I haven't had a haircut in five months. Shaved tonight too.

Look professional. Like maybe a lawyer, working for a client, or looking to have a wife clipped.

Two men come walking out of the night exactly five minutes after the appointment.

They stride along the sidewalk, between the water and the rusting, ugly fence like clockwork. Men about a job with an ant's efficacy. One is a guy in jeans and a hockey jersey but, if you look, you'd see something about him that's dangerous... but why would you look?

The other is the one I want to see.

Ludo.

Fuck he's big.

Recognise him from Jeancat's memories, but if I never saw him, I'd know he was *the* Man. Like me, he wears a suit. No tie. Unlike me, his suit is tailored. *He looks like a fucking monolith.*

Jeancat made him more handsome than he is, attracted somehow to this beast, but that sloping back head, that creole skin leave me certain. He's wearing cool frameless sunglasses. I always heard you shouldn't wear glasses on the job, but he seems to be doing fine.

He clearly indicates his man is staying put.

Do the same with Bettina.

'Look at him!' she hisses. 'He's fucking OG. Be smart!'

I do. I go low and slow, slipping into a meditation gaze. The gnosis vision.

His glasses are something. No telling what. He's got a pendant on under his suit that's hot with information, magic.

Serious gear.

I leave the trance behind, hard to talk while keeping your mind still as pond.

We size each other up, six or so feet between us.

'You're a famous man.' His vowels are wide and rubber. *Sudafrique* for sure. 'Lark. City magicians know you.'

Say nothing.

'You want to buy something. Hire me. Fuck you even know my name? You're not police no more.'

'You say you know me?'

He grins. Looks me up and down. 'By reputation, blanco. But I expected someone ten feet tall, not...' He waves disgust at me.

'Nah. But close enough. And I know people. I know people from the day. You've been making a *stir*.'

He has no body language. He's just still. Breathing regular.

Look him up and down now I'm close.

He's just got to have thirty kilos on me and five inches. I'm around six feet tall. He's over fourty but cannot imagine for a second time's slowed him down.

'I *have* been making a stir. But, well, you aren't a policeman any more, are you? The fuck is it to you?'

'No. Not here to *police* you. You know my name, you know me and Library are done. Do you want to talk business or did I mistake you as a man who likes to *work*?'

He nods.

Look over the water, look up at the bridge, all the empty space. I'm not used to the emptiness. Too many nights in alleys and bad rooms. It leads me back to old ambitions to leave this city, but this is no place to lose focus. The wind is cold.

Go deep into trance again as get to talking.

'Do you know what a mournival is?'

'No.'

'Do you know what a hand of glory is?'

'No. But you want, we can get, if you have money or something better.'

Plan is, lure him into relaxing, make up a magic word on the sly. Slip a sigil into his head.

'If you can find those, and there's people who have them who won't deal with me, I can pay and pay well.'

Create a magic word, one-time use. Use my sentence to fuel the magic. *I can pay and pay well.* As we speak, shape the letters into a magic word.

PywllwyP.

Hold the shape of it in my mind and the letters become shapes without meaning.

Turn shapes into a sigil.

I envision the shape of the glyph in my head, load it like an automatic pistol loads a bullet onto my tongue. My breath is ballistic – I pretend the sigil leaving my mouth like a round, heading between his eyes and into his brainstem.

Done this spell a hundred times.

It's easy.

He shouldn't even have the time to question that I've said something stupid and weird and clumsy. But the skill of magic is just finding ways to blend in, to create miracles out of the muck, to make witchcraft out of conversation.

A magic word that should rewire his desires and make them amenable to me. Spell goes off.

Doesn't land.

Suddenly, I understand what his amulet is. *Idea-eater.* Spell-breaker. Confidence, arrogance, is a sorcerer's tool, but I've been a fool. Hurrying. Trying to finish this quick to impress a woman.

To show everyone I'm still *the* Man.

Idea-eater tells him straightaway what is happening.

'Fucking pathetic. Trying to put the fucking *magie tower* on me!'

He takes two steps to me, closing the space so quick I can't even track his movements. His fist comes up and I'm still in trance-state. React too slowly and just stare as his fist pistons back. Which is what he wants. The hand is a distraction. He kicks.

His leg strikes out, foot turned like a man kicking a goal. It hits me just below the knee, in the meat of the calf, and it's fucking *horrible*. He punches me in the side of the head and it's only the fact I'm screaming and falling backwards from his bullshit Wing Tsung moves that prevents his taking the head off me. I feel my hair catch in his fists. But even though he misses taking me in the chin, it hits me in the temple and just lights up in my skull.

Another kick to the side of my knee that's a dull and awful pain.

I'm flying back and he's already on me. He's so fast.

But so is Bettina.

She can't go five nine tall, and she can't go sixty kg, but one strike and he goes flying. She pushes him with one hand, fingers spread wide, and it's like a car hits him.

She runs past Ludo and chops down his partner with a

hand turned flat and *executive*. He never even got to his gat before bones and soft tissue alike are fucking destroyed.

Then, from the substation up the bank, shots ring out. Rounds tear through her body. She doesn't drop an inch. She turns, leaps after Ludo, grabs him, uses him as a shield. I can see her guts leaking out of her like toothpaste.

'Fucking run!' she screams at me. I try but he's done something to my leg. My knee clicks and the pain races up to thigh and down to toe.

Ludo elbows her in the skull, but it means nothing to her. He grabs her thumb and pulls it back, breaking it, which breaks her hold on him. She backhands him and he rolls to take the force away. She should have caved in his face, but he's too smart for that. He goes for his gun.

Ludo's not going to mix it up eye to eye with Bettina again, that much is clear.

We retreat back. More bullets strike her in the torso.

Through the pain, I manage to put a jinx on the partner. He fires wild and Ludo gets down. But here's luck. His bullets cover us against the sniper, who curses from the distance, my ears too sore from gunfire to hear his words.

'Fucking run!'

I do. Grind my leg to splinters, but I go.

Ludo is walking backwards, finger to his ear firing. Another gunshot drives through her and then they try to go me. Up the embankment, the man with a rifle has recovered.

Been shot at before but not this sniper shit. Scream out another word, then two more. Hiding words. Confusing words. Magic I worked on for years, for just this shit.

The gunman tries again but the shot is wild and I know we're safe from him. He's unprotected and I've put a wasp in his skull.

'Bettina, you come to me!'

We run. Hobble. Ludo's black autopistol fires up, raking, and I piss myself, I do. But she takes the bullets for me. The noise is huge and awful, but not as bad as feeling her body stutter and shake, raked with gunfire. Pressed against me, I feel the shock of ballistic penetration and the cold of her slow, leaked blood slicking me.

Make taxi magic, mind sharp with fear and one comes down across the bridge. Spell I've used a hundred times like any I've cast tonight, but suddenly so desperate. Whispering the car's secret name. Adrenaline in my ears, I have to calm myself to cast it.

Safe. For now.

SHAKING. CAN'T STOP SHAKING.

DON'T RECALL BEING HURT LIKE THIS SINCE THE LAST TIME I saw my mother. When she locked the doctors and my old man out of her room and started slamming the drawers on my hands.

IV

WHAT THE FUCK WAS THAT? WHAT. *THE FUCK.* WAS THAT?

In the taxi, body starts shivering. Animal fear.

Tell the driver to head back to my place.

Hypnotise the poor bastard into oblivion so he won't complain about corpse or blood. He'll clean up when we're gone, never noticing what he's doing.

Bettina is grey and still, singlet wet with blood. Can see into her chest. Her heart doesn't beat.

I sort of want to puke.

Get home. Get her out of the cab. She walks like a robot.

Walk Bettina to the bath, stained with rust-like tears.

She's on automatic.

Sleepwalker, shock victim. Reminds me of insect legs moving long after they're dead. Surround the bath with candles for a quick rite to lock in whatever necromantic information still buzzes in her body. Pour the emergency grave-dirt over her body. Stashed for just this. It will help a little. Tomorrow we'll rebury her, but this will do for now. Dead eyes stare at me as her face is covered up.

When that's done, strip naked, throwing away the blood and urine-stained suit. Neck a fistful of painkillers and wash it down with tequila.

Wash myself with a towel and hot water as best I can and put on a robe. Sticky with blood and sick from used-by-date adrenaline.

V

Can't sleep for pain, humiliation, and the ripe stink of Bettina's corpse.

Hate marching behind my eyes. Fist unclenching and clenching with the urge to *harm*.

That Ludo motherfucker flensed me of pride. I ice my leg and try not to catch my eyes in the windows as dawn comes up. This isn't how it was meant to be. Fuck. I smoke cigarette after cigarette.

Shame. Anger. Punching at my temples.

Amateur.

Pussy.

Fuck.

So used to being the top dog with Jon that everyone is afraid of me. So used to coasting on rep. But that shit was a long time ago and, even if he knows who I *used to be*, this Ludo motherfucker is pretty unimpressed with who I *am*.

So embarrassed.

I'm not getting drunk, despite a hero's effort. Three quarters of a bottle of scotch and I'm barely feeling it. Just feeling chemical ill. Just feeling so goddamned embarrassed. Wet wheezing from too much tobacco. Nicotine rolling in my lungs. My taps are dripping. Garbage trucks are starting up and the rubbish day stink wafts into my house. Close the windows.

Overconfident. Stupid. Shamed.

But.

Ludo is no magician. He wasn't ready for the possibility Bettina was anything other than my muscle. Other than human. He took a gun, relied on it. Had a man on the embankment, sniper. Had the thought-eater and the glasses, too, so there's no doubt he knows, or is told, what the artefacts he's peddling do. He's a player, but he's no magician. He's just muscle.

Which means there's someone I don't know yet behind all this shit.

But, here's the thing. Ludo ripped a chunk of hair out of me. He'll have my scent. If someone could work up those Tools for him, tracking me will be child's play.

I can hide. Draw up some concealment spells now and hope whoever is divining me isn't that good.

Or, on my own ground, my sanctum, we can go again.

I'm afraid of Ludo. He'll hurt me if he gets me. Bad. And

no mistake, he'll come. He has to. A man like that doesn't let a witness go.

But then again, this is my place and I know his weapons, his tactics, his limitations. Won't say I'm eager for it, but if I want to be me. Remain me. *Thrown down on my turf, mother-fucker!* I have to take some pride back.

Let's go again.

11

———

I

Want to know the coolest thing about being a magician?

You get your own gods.

You realise that pantheons are just as up for grabs as anything else. And if you can worship Attis or Jupiter or a Yama King or Jehovah or Ereshkigal, what's to stop you from worshipping anything you like?

Why not make your own god, then?

The fat one from The Doors in the ludicrous leather pants. I've seen him take on a totem's attributes. Why not be protected by Goya's witches or breakfast cereal mascots, who you loved? Why not offer up prayers to Batman? Who'll save you in the night if not Batman? You can seek to emulate the compassion of Christ, the creativity of Shiva, or avoid the gaze of a horny, punishing Zeus all you like, because those are all gods are. Ideas, wrapped in stories, made perceptible to us by hymn and myth, and we can use those ideas. Why not give up a prayer to the Statue of Liberty, or a beloved pet, lost in childhood, that symbolises everything you ever loved?

All praises to Batman.

And when you have a god, you have slumming angels and local saints. You have demons and devas and all manner of totems. Locate what you want from a god, what ideals that god represents and what lessons it teaches, and your human head will find patterns that link together pantheons and theologies.

I have a god. I call it the Omegamantis.

Made it when I was about fourteen. Dreaming it up before I really even knew what an eregore, a tulpa, even was.

THOUGHTS YOU MAKE INTO SOMETHING REAL. SERVITORS. AND some of them, you turn into deities to help you in your practice.

I imagine it, in space somewhere, black as oil and lacquered to frictionlessness. Chrome talons sharpened to infinitesimal width, dangerous enough to take the electron off an atom. Praying mantises have the keenest vision, pound for pound, on earth, and that's what I think of when I think of the Omegamantis. That's one of his holy attributes, if you like. Lurking in the hearts of collapsars and black holes, watching, paying antehuman attention to the universe. Hunting for patterns. Its body a liquid stillness, but its attentions dangerous and ceaseless.

A conceit, but in my private moments, I like to think of my work this way. Hunting knowledge, books my snare and spear. Recognising patterns, referencing information. Building up maps of magic. I made the Mantis to reflect my private obsessions, my private conceits.

And Omegamantis has saints.

The Ultrascorpions.

Midnight green, dressed in robes of white, human scorpions, tails lifting above their head, twitching and venomous. All the anger in me, all the poison, incarnate. They talk in clicks and clacks, subvocals, infrasonics. Strange pheromones like opium, like airborne formic acid, perfume the room.

Tulpas. Servitors. Eregores. Imaginary friends gone feral and potent.

My thoughts. The Ultrascorpions are my angry thoughts, my wounded thoughts, my protective thoughts elevated and refined through the prism of rites.

Preparing to meet the face of my god. This is sorcery. Take it serious.

I scrub long and hard, rinse the cigarettes and whisky from my mouth. I shave, very carefully.

My ceremonial robe is a long, black hooded terry-towelling cloth I drew all over with silver, marking spells and glyphs. Comfortable. Hooded and spooky. Black silk pyjama pants. I put it on carefully like a vestment.

Dressed, I go up into the Sanctum. I have one last smoke. Know why so many magicians smoke? Stillness is bad for spirits and possessing entities. The less molecular motion, the better they can enter the real world. The mathematics of smoke are complex, churning out numbers. Bettina, incense, whatever, helps chop up the grid. So I keep the Sanctum smoke-free. Need it to be a place where I can control everything.

It's an attic. Hot in winter, cool in summer. Painted black, it's stuffy and claustrophobic.

Or, it's the heart of my magical practice. The place where I perform my most important ritual workings, where I commune with my gods.

All my favourites, up on the altar. Odin, from a strange

Scandinavian wood carver I know. Thoth, commissioned for me by Mully on his last trip abroad. Gwydion, once a Silver Surfer toy.

Painted on the ground is a circle, carefully aligned with the compass points. There's a sword I got from a disposal store, an old cavalry sabre. A tankard. My wand, which I got on my first and last trip into the Black Forest, five foot of carefully lathed oak. A chunk of polished onyx, the size of a child's skull. Bit of classic symbolism never hurts. Omega-mantis takes pride of place, made from Meccano and clothes hangers and boot black and shellac.

Runes, occult and religious symbols. Phrases in Latin and Greek I've memorised. Pow Wow Dutch and low German Scarlet taught me that I've forgotten the meaning of, all the more potent for all that. Spray painted or written on the walls.

Took me years to get it this cool. The lab. The Sanctum. My place of *business*.

Light up all the candles and kneel in the centre of the circle, on a cushion. My leg is aching.

A Polaroid of me and Jon, drinking at Violin's. Before he put on the mask. Yes. Take it out from the box I got under the bed. I reread over the letters Scarlet sent me when I was away for the Cull.

The sexy ones. Take it out. The photo of her in the bikini.

Slide the box out of the circle and begin. Deep trance. Chanting. A lot of people put it all on breathing, pneuma and that, and they're probably right, but I've spent so long doing this stuff, I don't have to put in that time. Everything goes 2D and colourless, and the relief goes supersharp. Leg stops hurting. Can't feel my pulse beat. Take the Zippo from my pocket, light it.

Burn up the pictures. Burn up the letter.

A sacrifice has to hurt or it ain't a *sacrifice*.

Think insect thoughts. My mind goes one-channel chitin. Predatory stalker thoughts. Ride the smoke from a saucy letter up, into the Outer Dark where my God lurks.

Omegamantis.

Spindly city of wires and satellites, where a rusted ball of iron serves as a sun, scoured by its own ruined cities. Clockwork spiders spin telephone wire webs. Crane towers and brass locks. Spindle citadels and deep silver alleys and there, on a moon made of celluloid, there it is.

My mind rises up to the lunar wanderer where my god makes it home today.

II

AM I THERE? REALLY THERE? YEAH. THERE'S NO DEBATE. THIS is a thing I'm *experiencing*. Am I on another planet? Another dimension? Or just hallucinating? It doesn't matter. I'm experiencing something *real,* and that's enough.

The Mantis' attentions are on me. It lifts me up to it, weightless and without motive power. I bow to this creature I choose to pray to. This is a *power*. Did I invent it? Discover it? Refine it? Is it something that already exists that I cloak with my own fictions?

I don't know.

Regardless, this is one of my great sources of strength and only a fool disrespects that. It transforms me and my skull is suddenly triangular, my hands recreated as long pincers and I feel like a re-written sentence. My form is made more pleasing.

'**You have destroyed what you valued: gifted to me.**'

'Yes, Mantis.'

It's voice is exactly the low-pitch you'd expect a cosmic predator's to be.

'And you seek?'

'The service of the Ultrascorpions.'

'Will you be pitiless?'

It's never asked me about what I want to do with them before. Is it a trick? I don't care. This is one of the few times in a man's life where honesty is useful.

'I will be pitiless.'

'Then they will serve.'

I am returned, hurtling away from that place, watching it dissolve, the after image of the red Mantis eyes regarding me in alien contemplation. Slowly, surely, I come back to the Sanctum. My hands, my face, alien, merely human.

There they are, four of them, in the corner of my eye. Still, still as ice, aside from their tails, which sway over their backs. They clack their mandibles and their eyes, six each, set in thick black exoskeletal faces, watching.

Light the Zippo. Hold my hand over the flame. The hair burns. Pain. I do that four times, four times extending out my paw, shooting it towards the Ultrascorpions. My offering and salutation.

'We have come to do a hurting.'

I hear behind the click click clack of the mandibles.

'Of course you have.'

III

NOW THEY ARE REAL.

Present in a virtual world, I suppose is the *trendy* magicians' vocab guidelines.

Given them the ability to manifest in this world. To take bodies. Ideas poured into the world and cloaked in matter, the matter a kind of flesh.

Shower starts up. Bettina's awake then.

But until then, they're like ghosts, separated from our world as through murky glass.

Get up, jeans, t-shirt, hoodie and commence to inspect my wards.

Bettina stumbles into my room, naked but for a towel. Turn my back while she raids my cupboards.

She's a fine looking woman, Bettina. And one to admire and respect. But she and me ain't bound for bed. Just... ain't like that between us.

'Shit. You shouldn't be awake.'

It's not a statement about her recuperation. She's got fucking great big bullet holes in her, but they're already closing up. Her face is gaunt as a wolf's.

'What's here? Like, there's something in the house. I know.'

'Allies. Ludo is coming.'

She's too tired to panic. 'I can't help. I have to eat.'

'Tonight, go out to a potter's field. Security will be no joke for a woman who can jump ten foot with a run-up. Dig. Eat. But that's not until tonight. I'll give you a coat, now. Shirt. You'll just look sick if you go by day.'

'You could force me to stay.'

Nod. I could. Never would.

Commence to thinking of Ludo. Think of the pain in my leg. Never? At least not today, with the Ultrascorpions, disembodied and potent, whirling around like a rabid dog's thoughts and just as invisible. But even as a suicide bomb, she's powerless. Won't say I'm not tempted, though. I want it, she's bound to do as I say and that includes a certain, second death.

'When they come, just... stay in the attic. Don't touch anything.'

'I'm hungry.'

Shrug. 'Pigeons on the roof. Rats in the alley. No more human meat in the joint.'

She stares at me a moment as if to say she ain't amused.

'Where's you're mad amigo's knife. I'm not biting the goddamn fucking heads off birds.'

We find it and listen to her footsteps on my roof. She's recovering quicker than I figured. Time and lives she's taken are making her stronger.

Telling this report after the end. Funny to think of her this... regular. Given what as she's become.

Call Scarlet, looking for back-up. She's not answering. Doubt they'd have muscle to spare. Could Lionel put together a posse? Not in time.

I watch television and zone out and nap. Wake up listening to Bettina laughing at something on television, standing, watching it, bird blood in her cup.

Four thirty. Back to sleep.

It's six thirty in the morning. I hear them picking the locks.

'Bettina.'

'What?'

'Hide. You see me fall, *then* move. But this is mine.'

IV

. . .

Bettina's left it out, Jon's knife. Washed off dead bird feather, dead bird blood.

The Hollow was never a man to leave a blade unsharpened, even before the mask. But that's not its purpose. Break it into symbols. A knife isn't a sword that is a device honed to murder.

It's a tool *and* a killing thing. It slices. It carves through the unnecessary.

My brain goes floodlit as I take the thing.

It smartens you up to murder.

Jon used to use this when he knew it was bodywork. Can see why. Jon didn't like killing people but he could, when we had to. He brought this knife to Mully and they talked it over for weeks before our master had him something... *dangerous.* Weapon fit for him.

Ludo is the second of his team up the stairs and into the living room where I'm sitting, communing, joined to my house and feeling its shock at the intruders.

Later, I'll understand him finding me, let alone breaking my wards, is serious mojo. But by then, I'll know who he's working for and it'll be plain I was outclassed from the start.

The Sudafrique brought four men and came through my first line of defences. But first line ain't the only line and you already met the Ultrascorpions.

Good timing, bringing them in when I did.

And Scarlet thinks me *paranoid...*

·   ·   ·

FIRST MAN THE SCORPIONS PICK IS BEHIND LUDO, COMING UP the stairs. They hone in on him, manifesting around him. Tails sting and claws snip. They're just thoughts. They're not real in the sense that a book you hold or shoe you wear is real.

THE ULTRASCORPION KNOWS ITS WORK. IT DOESN'T EVEN NEED to manifest. It flows into his mind, rewires dendrites and neural pathways with a sadist child's glee.

THE MAN SCREAMS, TRIES TO PUNCH HIS WAY INTO HIS BRAIN with his knuckles.

MAGIC HAS CONVINCED HIS BRAIN ITS DEAD. THE MERC FALLS, thrashing, while the Ultrascorpions purr their pleasure at their craft well performed.

THE THOUGHT-EATER PENDANT LUDO WEARS SHAKES. THE knife tells me. It's fucking *serious* voodoo, that amulet.

HAD MORE TIME, SHOULD THINK MORE ABOUT WHO IS TELLING him what magic to wear. You don't need skills to benefit from an amulet or ring or whatever. But you do need to know what's up to pick it out in the first place.

Three men find me, standing there, tapping a knife against my thigh.

'I'll have you, you greymeat cunt.'

Two guys, fanning Ludo, draw guns, ready to off me.

· · ·

Bᴜᴛ.

This is my house and I'm not afraid of guns here.

Ludo is no magician. He thinks this is a hit and not a magical battle.

Wʜɪsᴘᴇʀ ᴀ sᴘᴇʟʟ ᴛᴏ ᴏɴᴇ ᴏғ ᴛʜᴇ ɢᴜɴᴍᴇɴ. Mᴇᴍᴇ-ᴡᴀsᴘ ʟᴇᴀᴘs into his spine and he falls to the ground. His very lymph curdles at the cancer hex I whisper. It's not real. I can't invoke metastizing magic.

Bᴜᴛ ғᴏʀ ᴀ ᴡʜɪʟᴇ, ʜɪs ᴍɪɴᴅ ɪs ᴄᴏɴᴠɪɴᴄᴇᴅ ᴛʜᴀᴛ's ᴡʜᴀᴛ's happening.

Ludo draws on me now. Same gun he had by the water.

His mate clicks off the safety of his own pistol.

And three more scorpions strike.

Wait, recognise the man thumbing this weapon. He's a magician! Seen him round!

What's his name? He was just about my last job for the Library.

Not time. The Ultrascorpion takes him and he falls, fucked up. It slides into him, slicing his thoughts apart like meat. He's good, but he's not prepared for my sinister pals.

Finally, they manifest. Ludo draws his gun and fires. One of my eregores falls back, unprepared for pain, but taking five rounds to the chest won't kill it. Ludo is professional. The gun isn't empty when he shifts it to me. But the knife tells me he's panicking. This isn't his ground.

Ludo is ready to cap me when another Ultrascorpion manifests behind him. Made from real stuff, created from old skin cells and whatever else they need, the venom is real venom, unambiguous. The barb is cruel and one takes him in the hand. One other scorpion stakes his foot. He's splayed out, ready for dissections.

He screams. It hurts him. His brain telling his body it's on its way out.

Kinda smile at that, now three men are down.

Point: Lark.

V

LIGHT A CIGARETTE LIKE NOTHING'S GOING ON. LUDO'S ON HIS back, fitting. Check his pockets best I can.

Another gun. Balisong. Speed, which I pocket.

TAKE A DEEP BREATH. WAITING FOR LUDO TO DIE. STANDING over him.

WAIT. HE'S STARING AT ME. CONSCIOUS. MALICE IN HIS GAZE.

He won't fucking die this easy.

Tough motherfucker.

SIT DOWN ON THE COUCH AND START TALKING TO HIM.

Real casual, like.

'YOU THOUGHT *I* WAS NOTHING.'

Don't even realise I'm speaking aloud until I hear it. The scorpion-eregores shiver with torture-anticipation at my thoughts, though.

They protect me. Don't make 'em good dudes.

Think about kicking him. He'd laugh it off and I'd look stupid. No need for this.

'Now why don't we talk about what the fuck you're up to.'

Bettina stalks into the room. Walks past us like nothing is up.

Drags one of the thugs, the one I hexed, up the stairs.

Stops in the kitchen, shaking hands finding a knife. He's so insane that he's not paying much attention to his demise. Listen to her drag him up to the roof.

Don't think about the rest.

Ludo's struggling to get up, to go me. But he's fucked. Scorpion magic has him beat. He's not trying any shit on me.

STAND BACK UP. TRACE RUNES IN THE AIR WITH THE BLADE.

Here, in this place, even the uninitiated can feel their strength and malison. Atmosphere changes as we both are in the presence of strong hoodoo.

HE'LL TELL THE TRUTH OR SUFFER. HE'S ENCHANTED TO FUCK or back.

'Ludo. What's the deal?'

'I'm about the Old Man's business. What the fuck, no!'

He's scared. He didn't mean to talk to me. This is the kind of man you could torture for weeks he wouldn't break. Spilling his guts at just questions.

Not the kind of man to scare easy.

But he is now.

Then again... so the fuck am I.

The Old Man.

Can't hide my shock.

Or fear.

Inside my head is static. Chafe. Siren warnings. The Old Man. *The Old Man.* Ludo grins like a bastard. The Old Man. If he even knows that name, he's hooked in deep as ticks.

The Old Man.

Have to breathe deep. Concentrate. Get my fear under control.

Put the blade away, not time for threats.

'Get the fuck out of here, Ludo. Now.'

He stands, grins at me cruel as a butcher's hook.

I'M LETTING HIM GO BECAUSE I FUCKING SURELY DO NOT NEED to have killed the Old Man's agent. Getting static with the Old Man is like swimming in the sea with a thousand open cuts.

It's just a matter of time.

The Old Man. The worst of them all. And I've crossed him.

12

———

I

CALL UP ONTO THE ROOF.

'Be back in a bit.'

Ignore the wet greedy chomping.

She'll be a while. Man weighs, what, 100 kilos? And there's three.

MAYBE YOU'RE ASKING: *GOLLY, IS LARK AFFECTED, MORALLY OR spiritually, about the guys his zombie familiar is about to carve up?*

Am I fuck.

Ludo would have tortured me to death while that prick watched. Or helped. You feel compassion for a man like that, you're just declaring that monstrosity it a-ok.

Scarlet's not picking up her phone. At work or home.

On the adrenaline rush. Scarlet. *Where are you?*

Map of the city, the long spar of it, running north to south, surrounded by a water. Trance state. Fear jab. Fail to make it.

'Fuck!'

Can't believe this. Dropped out of gnosis because of stress and fear. Rookie bullshit. *Amateur, pussy bullshit.*

Ball a fist. Take a breath.

Aggression is bullshit at a time like this.

Imagine a flame. Pure white flame in my head.

Fear, doubt, stress. All of it. Feeding the fire. Stillness is the quality of light. Less turmoil, brighter the light, until it grows and burns all thought and there's nothing but whiteness in my skull.

Gnosis.

Point at the map and my finger finds her.

She's protected, of course, but not from me.

I can find her.

I *have* to find her. Now. Right Goddamn now.

The Old Man. *The Old Man.*

She said don't go to her, go through her people.

Light a cigarette. Close eyes. Stab into City map.

Midtown.

Right.

But that was before. Before I tangled, on her word, with the darkest motherfucker anyone met. A brutal legend magicians tell one another.

Down the stairs, onto the street. There's a cab and I take it.

Moving into midtown where the money is, poverty raiding away from it so that uptown and downtown fray and get ragged with need.

What the fuck is she doing in a place like this?

Bright glass windows. Rich men and women on the street. Stores that sell coffee-makers, stores that sell plaid-patterned things. Restaurants with French maître-d's. Menswear stores where they'll measure you, and shoe-shops for women that sell self-hate and demand cash for the favour.

Paranoid. Staring out the cab windows, looking for Ludo or that magician was with him. *What was that fucker's name?*

'Problem, buddy?' asks the driver. He's just been told to drive. 'You seem real squirrely.'

Put a finger to my lips and he catches it in the rear-view. He sneers. A minute later, feel it.

'Yeah. Here.'

GET OUT. CAN'T RECALL THIS PLACE. TOURIST PART OF TOWN. Not many come here but if they do, here's the themed restaurants and all that fucking palaver. Look around. As if scouting...

There she is.

Walk up to the restaurant. Can see her through the glass. Dinner with another couple. *What's this citizen shit, Scarlet?* She's dressed in a fucking blouse and her hair's shorter. Her *boyfriend* is there. Who are the others? A fat old man and his too-young wife.

She looks at me. Sees me. Drinks the white wine at her table. Makes sure she knows I'm seeing her.

Wind is cold on the street.

She looks away as if she didn't see a goddamn thing, laughing politely at her boyfriend's joke.

Didn't even spike her pulse.

Goddamnit. *I'm here to warn you.* Is that a lie? I don't even know.

Stupid to be here. Why won't I learn? I light a cigarette. Walk to the station and take the subway. She thinks that was personal but it was *business.*

But then, why didn't you call? Stupid, Lark. Stupid.

Panic and her making a fool of me.

Shame sends me into a kind of white out inside.

Which... funny how things work out, this... puts me into gnosis.

Which is why I can feel the scrying spell on me.

Right. Ok. Stop in at a store, and a Burmese man with one eye sells me smokes enough to fill my pockets. But not just grabbing darts. Hitting deep gnosis and muttering spells under my breath. Prayers, almost.

Carefully preparing mental blocks for myself. Making the world go dark. Meditating on glycaemic crash magic. On head wound sorcery. Staring too long at the same written word until your eyes go dark at edges.

Can still see. Just won't see.

Walk out onto the street, wrapped up in this magic.

Slowly scan the street. There she is, under a bad cloaking spell. Can't make out details but she weren't there when I walked into to buy smokes and she's staring at me now. Hazy figure, but sure as sure... being followed by a magician.

Told you as there was a spy at the first meet with Ludo. She's in the distance but the spell's putting my eyes where they need to be. Getting tracked. But by who, for who?

JUMP HER NOW? NO. BETTER TO HIDE THAT SHE'S BEEN MADE.

Misinformation and that.

I know they're watching me. But they don't know I know.

Uses for that.

II

LUDO WILL HAVE TOLD THE OLD MAN ABOUT ME NOW. I DON'T like being out in the open. Move on from this whole fucking sorry episode. Leave Scarlet to her meal and try not to feel this fucking no-account.

THIS *DESPERATE*.

Get home and Bettina's finished her feast. Scarred but strong. So strong. Dressed in my old Misfits t-shirt that's too narrow across the shoulders and chest for her. She gets up and come to talk to me right away.

'Lark, I need some more time in the ground. I fucking need it.'

Nod. She does.

'The meat... it won't do me any good unless I go in the ground.'

Nod.

She looks at me all searching-like.

'What's up?'

What's to say? Provoked an infamous sadist and made a bell-end of myself in front of my old girl.

Just... shake my head. She knows when it's time to back away. Just gives me a nod back. Solidarity, perhaps. She leaves me alone which I tell myself is better for everyone.

She's right to walk away.

She pats me on the shoulder as she leaves. Can't say it does the pride a lot of good.

This is a signal, man. Tell myself, laying on the couch, copy of the Heptameron in my hand, unread. Got to move past this. *You just... you must.*

Smoke and drink in the dark. Flinching at noises in the night.

13

———

Chapter

I

Let me tell you about the Old Man. There's some things you're gonna need to know about him.

Like why every magician, conjurer, shaman, witch doctor, wise woman, bokor, dayan and wizard in the City goes fucking white at the mention of his name.

II

Second year on the job, Mully sent me and Jon uptown.
A civil engineer we'd been thinking of recruiting has

himself a Frankenstein kind of idea. His boyfriend had died and the poor bastard was out of his head with grief.

He'd been an unlikely magician, sensible engineer, but he'd hooked up with some strange people through his fetish scene who encouraged some bad ideas. Anyways, this cat, this recruit, was clever and had some strange ideas, so he rigged up a crazy temple, plugged it into the mains of the city and planned to resurrect the boyfriend.

You can bring the dead back. With magic. It's a big deal, but you can do it. You can even bring them back whole and, if you're lucky, sane.

But it's a *feat*, you know?

This recruit couldn't do it, no way, no how. He'd make the horror movie mistake and boyfriend would come back sour-brained and possessed. We thought the recruit was ok, had promise, so we weren't there to off or punish him. Just talk it through and maybe scare him some.

Mully even gave me a fucking grief counsellor's card if the guy wanted it. Mully thinks like that.

Uptown warehouse. Cement and steel everywhere. Two in the afternoon and a flat slap hot summer's day, the sky a dirty blue. We wore sunglasses.

'Over there.'

Jon pointed at the bolt cut chains. 'Someone here before us.'

His hand slid in to his suit coat. He liked stylish slim suits and he liked skin tight shirts. You would too, you had his muscle tone.

Walked into the warehouse, letting eyes adjust. The smell hit us first. Think about what's in a human body. Imagined that opened up to the air. That's what a good vivisection smells like.

Boyfriend was hooked up to a machine made from engine

parts, suspended from chains. Dead, naked and the spells that prevented him rotting, hard spells to maintain, coming undone.

The engineer was splayed out before us.

They'd opened him up, trachea to cock.

Someone took their time. Gag, choke. Try not to puke.

We'd seen bodies before but this was the first bad one.

Jon walked over and knelt down beside the gutted man, handkerchief over his face. Stylish fucker kept a handkerchief, and, then, I envied him.

'Look at him, please Lark.'

It took a while, I was rattled and still a little sick but found gnosis.

Jesus.

The place was warded. If we tried to scry out what happened here, we'd spring traps, information burning down until we caught madness. Spirits ready to pounce, as patient as tigers.

But there was something else. There was malice here.

A wet hatred, hot as wolf breath. Human. Someone *loved* doing this. I didn't believe in evil then, it was just a word for human behaviour. Learned since then that there's some people, some situations, that are... beyond.

Believe in it now, though.

This was one of ways it chose to reveal itself to me. And make no mistake, evil is a human trait.

We called in a couple we knew who clean crime scenes. They'd done this sort of stuff before for us. We kept them in contact with the spirits of their kids. Played them honest and they worked for free. We unhooked the machine the dead man was locked up in, after documentation. It never happened. The engineer? A missing person. No one would be too surprised he got drunk and fell asleep with the bar heater on. He was a man in mourning.

Went back to the chapterhouse and took a meeting with Mully the next day.

Jon smoked one of his cigarillos and looked cool. He was always tougher than me. Mully drank water and met us on the rooftop garden.

'I was afraid something like that might happen. We were too late.'

Jon glanced up. 'Who did that?'

Mully sighed. His clipped English was lightly accented and educated.

'There's a group. They serve a man. A man who is obsessed with life and death. They are very dangerous. The man who runs them... I cannot conceive of a person more dangerous.'

He closed his eyes. 'If you work cases uptown, and they have elements of this. Life, death, necromancy be on your guard. Watch out for his work. Tread carefully. He remains hidden these days.'

The cunning man was right. Always was, always is.

Vampire run-in, two years after that. We were hunting the fucking thing, some magician doing blood magic turned himself mad. But someone took it off the street before us. The same appalling competence in hiding their actions. No one just *takes* a vampire and they don't do it with a whisper only magicians could even hint at.

A neo-thuggee cult started working, doing human sacrifices. Tracked them to their temple but someone else got to them. The lucky one was dragged five miles behind a truck.

The lucky one.

That night was the last time I cried. Scarlet's arm around me, her finger trailing the tears down my cheek.

How to tell her about the blowtorch and the lime? Could you burden the person you love with how you battered one's head in with a spanner and it was the kindest thing you ever did?

Looking over previous sheriff's logs. The same unmistakable signature that was no signature at all. The clear warnings, writ with such strength. *Always in oldtown, under the shadow of the bridge.*

I talked to the old-timers. Sebastian, who retired from the Library the year I joined, a formal man with the bearing of a Colonel who did my job from the Seventies on. He brushed his moustache with a knuckle and told me other stories. Farrago, who was dying at the time, she had a run-in. Said she thought she saw him, one time. 'Like staring into a heat haze.'

And that's what I know of the Old Man. Half a legend, but whatever he is, whatever the feral legend conceals, there's something out there. A renegade cult that reaches out, now and again, to close its grip around atrocity. That's him.

II

THE LONG SHOT IS, I'M NOT GOING TO TANGLE WITH THE OLD Man, not for money.

Not for revenge. Certainly not for curiosity's sake. Maybe I would have. With the Library backing me. With its resources and allies. But working the fringes as I am now? Fuck that.

Even though I'm wondering - What the fuck can the Old Man want firing off a cult war? Is this him?

What's it *to* him? He's been invisible forever. He's been away, apart, operating under the radar, seemingly only interested in other magicians when they had what he wanted. So, what's he want?

No.

Fuck it.

Lock my doors and windows in my flat for something to do.

Won't stop the Old Man, of course. Ludo, if he comes back. But I might be gone awhile. I move slow. Smoke slow. I think of all the things I've seen this Old Man do and I refuse to put myself on that chopping block. Not even for love.

He strikes me as the kind of fellow won't accept an apology. Should I grovel? Jesus Christ. Anyone came to me like that, no respect. I'd hate them just for their lack of guts, so imagine what he'd do.

Can't take a bus, can't hire a car, can't walk across the bridge north, can't catch a boat. Can't leave the island. Stuck here with him. Cursed.

And that's fucking on Everett. Who arranged them to put the curse on me. Who called me 'an asset'. Scarlet, I hate your *boyfriend* more than you know.

But there's one place I can go where I'll be a hell of a lot harder to find.

Upstairs I take the sheet from the Black Mirror. One of my finest tools. Six foot tall, three foot wide of black, reflective glass. Where do you get a hold of such ancient, exotic pieces of arcana? It's a few dozen expensive bits of bathroom tile.

But it looks *fucking* badass.

John Dee had one. Ashmole too, I seem to recall. Early Modern magic, from a time where men like me were spies, treasure hunters and we served the high counsel of monarchs.

Dark glass. Shine. See beyond the mirror. Push my sense past my reflection. Cold. Looking for another city. Anti-city. Negative metropolis. Reality gets thin. I shut down my senses, no longer having need for aught but eyes. The taste falls out my mouth like a liar's dream teeth. Scent slides down the back of my throat. Ears stoppered. Meditate on my mirror-eyes, feeding back. Locked in a contest.

The mirror changes. Mirror. Window. The sad, scared image of me fades. I see reflection of my sanctum writ as photonegative. The chiaroscuro greys. I'm absent from the mirror.

The window.

Step through.

Into the Black City.

I

Wick is busy.

She's got the shape of these letters down now. She's not even sure how she knows this is text, but it is. It's like a poem or a song or something, this scroll. *An alphabet.*

But imagine song lyrics could be haunted? Is that right? Whatever. Something squirms in the meaning and syllables of the scroll. Whatever language this is, it's more than letters. Little pictures. She's experimenting with putting them together in new ways.

Beautiful pictures and creepy meaning. She's happy with the colours she's chosen. She's working in iridescent shades. It's harder than it looks to make the colours glow, but she's been at this awhile.

Wick tags a bus stop and the next day, three people throw themselves in front of the crosstown 8:02. She feels so proud when she sees her images. Feels connected to this city, from the southern tip of downtown, where the junkies buy sleep and a safe place to nod and the dogs have learned to take trains.

To the eastside docks, where sailors buy women and boys, and the community housing turns into a death trap for a happy life. To midtown where the rich live, smiling and enjoying their worth and work, to the north, under the great bridge, where the immigrants battle the immigrants and the air smells of strange dinners and a hundred different languages argue.

She travels all around, loving it, marking it. Her hand grows steadier and the tags more powerful.

The side of a gym, an old school one where they still coach fighters. That's a good target. One man hangs his trainer, a seventy year-old man, from a weight machine, leashing his throat to four hundred kilograms with a jump-rope.

Then she gets creative. She studies the scroll and a voice instructs her. She walks fifteen blocks downtown and finds an abandoned store. The owner just walked out one day and no one ever rented it. Lots of places like this in this neighbour-hood. She looks it up in the city map. Tags it. Checks the map, can't even find the street. She grins. That's a good trick.

For a while she contemplates more revenge. Nah. Who cares about those little shits anymore? She's got a bigger job.

City streets can dance for her. Reality is a lot softer than she ever thought.

What should we do?

She asks the scroll, aware now that it might not have a mind, but it has wants.

Go somewhere ugly and lost.

She finds a section of the city that used to be a depot for heavy vehicles. Now it's just wasted ground and dust; chain-link fenced with sad meaningless white markings on the ground. The city pays for watchmen to protect empty air. In the autumn air, she tries something new, a conglomeration of meanings. She finds an old workshop, clambers to the top galley, and waits. Soon, a guard comes, swearing that some fucking graffiti kid got in here.

He stares at it angrily, but it just blows him out like a candle. She feels herself rush in to fill him up. Her and It. True magic, eating his personality.

Get another, says the voice. She feels herself stretch into the man.

Feels herself colonise him. Runs her hand over his body. Delighting in the size of his gut, the feel of his cock and balls in her pants. The tidal strength of his breath.

She uses her new body to wave over his partner. Wick's seen her before. A stupid woman.

'Check out this graffiti! This is... you got see this...'

Then Wick has six eyes to see with. Three heads to think with.

Until It takes one and talks to her. The stupid woman's face is suddenly still, her attention sure and pinching.

This is what I can give you. Dominion.

She feels it slip away. Whatever is behind the images she paints.

It is still too *big*. Too diffuse, to operate in a world of humans and atoms and the real. Its three heads are a crack beneath a door when It needs to pass through. But a crack they are.

It will take many, many more than three to host it.

Wick contemplates the boys who tried to scare her away from the gangs with cocks and scorn. The girls who only care if you're pretty and cool, not what you can do. Her mother, sneering at her pictures. Her father, dead and blue with a needle in his arm, her stepdad who thought it was funny to literally kick her arse.

Who'd fuck with her if she can take their heads away and fill them up with her art? Mark them like she marks her city? Don't these stupid, pointless people just get in the way of her city, her lovely canvas?

'What do we do?'

15

___

I

THERE ARE OTHER PLACES. OTHER WORLDS. THEY OVERLAP ours and weave onto ours and seep in like venom. Dead Cities. Hell Cities. Our world can infect theirs too. Some are towns and some are universes and some just hang out in our head.

This is the Black City.

The shadow of our world, this city, cast against another, higher world. There are others.

This place is dark, everything made of shade. An ink city, floodlit by a white that cannot be marred. A Shadow-puppet photo-negative city, exaggerated. Buildings curve, angles stretch. Everything is flatter, somehow. There a black cars. Black trains. There are citizens here. Long figures, often in hats, although who knows why.

And there are predators.

It is cool, here, not chilly. Noir weather, noir mood. A beaux-art heaven.

I can stay here for a long time. Let things tide over.

They'll move against me soon, with force, Ludo's crew. Maybe the Old Man will understand as I let his man live from... let's say, respect. But it's easier just to hide here than risk his compassion.

My place is downtown, which is how I could afford it. Slowly working magic to erase its existence and live free. Former restaurant. Shut down the bottom area, enter up the alley entrance. Live on the floor, sanctum up in storage. Love it. Been there nine years now.

The Black version of my place is a fortress. All the wards I've put up there over the years reflect here. I like that. It's solid and vast, gridded and riveted. Barbicans and murder holes. Deco citadel.

But I get bored too easy and a few days held up in here and it kicks in.

I'm on the streets, then, soothing my eyes with darkness and light. My neighbourhood is poor; gentrification fading away, and the Black City reflects that. Holes in the shadows like membranes stretched too thin. Film, left in the sun.

The physics of this place are strange. No sun. You can't see with no light, and yet you can see. No air, but still you breathe. You can hear. You never get tired, never get hungry, but the beard grows. I try to think about this in terms of science but it just don't make sense.

Spend what feels like days here but clocks don't work and the sun and moon don't seem regulated.

Find a park. Relax. Smoke a bit. I didn't bring a book. Bored already, but better bored than dead. For now, anyways.

We found the Hollow in here. The mask.

Jon used to love this place.

He was never that much of a magician, Jon. Not in the way I am.

He could work a trick or two, no doubt. But the words and rites never meant that much to him as they did me and he was a terrible study. No, it was the more martial side of things that worked for him. He used to talk about *hard qi* and *eight-fold paths* and *inward techniques* and things like that.

Jon could meditate more ways than anyone I've ever met. He had an unearthly calm about him at times. He loved to talk shop about it. He used to follow me around as I took the shaman walk. As I went out into the City, walking without lust for revelation or lust for result. Simply walking, pretending or understanding that everything that took my attention was a message from God, or the universe, or Odin, or the telluric currents. Finding significance in whatever was before me.

Used to love it when we worked cases like that. Amused that a man like me could trust pure intuition over facts. But that's magic, isn't it? Set your feet one way and it'll be delighted to break your goddamn ankle.

He'd bore his dates. He used to drag me to these gay bars where he liked the music and the view – I felt weird and exposed and he'd talk softly about the strangest things, ignoring the guys who cruised him. Five nations in his ances-try, none of them white, and he stood out everywhere. His hair was too straight, his eyes too curved, his skin too coffee, his cheeks too wide – he was a guy everyone used to puzzle over.

Remember when he came to the foster house, I used to ask him where he was from. 'The City,' he'd say and the first time I pressed him, curious, he twatted me one in the face. We were little, then. He was wilder then and the places he came from, someone asks race, it can get bad quick. He wasn't just wild. *Scary*, if I tell it right.

Got him into the martial arts when he was, what, twelve

or something? That changed everything for him. He'd no longer skip school to hunt down the big kids just for an excuse to tame his own hate with violence. And if you knew Jon's story, you'd know there was flatline hate ringing in his head every damn second of every damn day.

He never liked the science stuff of it. Never liked the mechanical practice. This was before MMA, before you could measure the pressure of your punches and that. At least, poor kids couldn't.

Soon, we tracked down the stranger dojos for him. The ones with old men from obscure countries who showed you one punch a day then talked about lotuses. That eased the street feral out of him. Those places, didn't matter your race or even how hard you could hit. They weren't interested in being tough, or being strong. They cared about *excellence*. They were *arts* for real.

Used to take a lesson with him now and again. I can throw a punch, can break a lock. But I never had the instinct for the fight. Jon said I had to ignore the urge to protect myself. Take the punch to deliver the punch, but just never could.

I like protecting myself.

Besides, the fitness regime alone makes me want to puke.

When I went to the Library, he came too. There's always a need for muscle, and the Library is bad at recruiting it. Mercenaries, mostly. Jon was perfect. Smart and lethal, and loyal to me.

Money. *Man.* We were so poor together when we met, me thirteen years-old, him ten. Suddenly the Library was paying the bills. You know how many cults in the city can do that? Two. Well, one now.

Maybe a third, too. The Old Man pays his crews.

Think about him soon. Not just yet.

Get up. Easy to hide in my place for a long time but, like I said, getting *bored*.

Wander down town through the chiaroscuro street.

Jon used to love it here because it's so quiet. The cars don't make sound and will pass through you like a cloud across the sun if you stand in their way. Sun never rises or sets, just stays there, radiating its weird unlight. He loved to train here and I'd watch him, startled by how beautiful he was. Scarlett used to like to watch him work out, eating yoghurt and whistling and I could hardly blame her. More than that, he used to like that it was just him and me, all alone in a whole world.

He had lovers. Friends from the fighting circuit. He even liked some Librarians. But I was the only person who treated him as anything else than the kid who slit his uncle's throat with a can lid. Jon was loyal to me and the reason he stayed that way was that I never took advantage of it.

I miss him. Miss his charming company. Miss him lifting my moods. Miss knowing there was someone on in my corner when not many people do.

When he changed, that was just about the last thing linking me to the Library. Except for Scarlet.

II

WE WERE HUNTING A GUY WHO HAD FOUND ACCESS TO THIS place. He was on a robbing-spree and a few of the lesser sects had petitioned us to help them out as he was hitting their stashes and ossuaries and like that. We did the divining and discovered he was moving through this place, using it like a skeleton key.

Jon was coldly furious.

Not at the crime, the technique.

'It feels like there's someone in the bedroom. Touching our stuff. The Black City, that's ours.'

Untrue, of course, but there it was. Jon was determined to find who was moving in and out of the place. We laid a trap. Found him. Jon stopped him, sneaking in close and punching the guy in the back of the head. We looked closer at him. The guy wore a lacquered leather mask. Damn thing was terrifying.

I looked at it. Took a second to figure it out in the Black City as it always does. Staring in *gnosis*. Trying to figure out what it was.

Had no idea at its power.

Malice.

'JON. DON'T.'

It was the last thing I said to him. To *him*. It was calling to him, looking for a host to kill with and in a choice between Jon and me, it was no choice.

In the time it took me to break *gnosis*, he'd put it on.

'I'm Hollow.'

And that was it. The Hollow was on him. He changed. It changed him. It filled him up with nothing. Not human in the head. Not anymore.

Devoted to murder.

The Hollow is a killing spirit.

I'll never know why he didn't listen to me. I'll never know what happened in those three seconds between him strapping the fucking thing to his face and bonding with whatever the *fuck* that mask is.

We couldn't be together after that. Couldn't work together.

He didn't want to. I couldn't. And when Scarlett saw how badly I took that, it was the last straw for her. Who can blame her for that, too?

Me.

The streets are... bruised.

Something is wrong in the Black City.

III

START TO WALK FASTER, IGNORING THE GRINDING PAIN IN MY LEG and hip. Ludo's beating didn't last long but it don't have to if it's good.

There's a weakness in the southern neighbourhoods. Everything is deformed. Pulled to the south. It looks wrong, an octopus elasticity, and ragged tendrils of shade wave like thick weed beneath the sea.

This is... *No.* I've never seen the place look like this before. The buildings here curve and loom, but these are stretched and sick, frayed or stretched.

What the fuck is this?

Keep jogging, never getting tired. No lactic acids to weigh down legs. Following a wave of corruption, looking for the heart, the source.

I run downtown to the old bus depot. Turn the corner, and it pulses like cancer. Some shape that an eye can't follow, leaking a phosgene light as if from an abyss. I feel mine trying to trace the outline and turn my back.

Like getting touched by an uncle. Like getting a fax call over the phone at too many decibels at a pitch that vibrates in your eye. It's a Sigil of maximum order, leaking cancer into the world.

I've felt that kind of thing before. *Fucking serious business.* Stare at that too long and I'd condense, like steam into water.

Back away. This is nothing to fuck with. Nothing to pit your strength against.

I walk away.

This is far from where the Old Man has ever worked before.

We've never heard of him working downtown.

Now I've seen it, I can feel it always. A wound in this world. Primal magic, the True Science.

Fuck.

16

———

TRANSCRIPT SESSION 3
    12/07/12
    Dr Indra recording.

INDRA: OK. Let's start again. Why don't you pick up on last time.

PATIENT: The scroll.

INDRA: Yes. That.

PATIENT: I used to be... involved in a group. You know that.

INDRA: Yes.

· · ·

PATIENT: BUT BEFORE THAT, I WAS A PROFESSOR. I WAS AN expert in Middle Eastern languages. Ancient ones.

INDRA: YES. YOU WERE THE HEAD OF DEPARTMENT. TWENTY-five years tenured.

PATIENT: THAT'S RIGHT! ANYWAY. I WAS BROUGHT IN TO READ A Scroll. Let me tell you about it. Very old. Very old. Very beautiful in its way. And, and this is the thing, it wasn't in any language I ever read or heard of, although you could see some similarities with certain alphabets.

I won't get technical.

But here's where it gets interesting. You can, I could, I could read it.

INDRA: YOU COULD READ A LANGUAGE THAT, AS FAR AS YOU ARE aware, never existed.

PATIENT: YES, YOU MUST THINK I'M CRAZY. [LAUGHTER] YOU'VE probably heard that before. I'm sorry. I wonder if a poor sense of humour is pathological.

INDRA: PLEASE GO ON.

· · ·

PATIENT: AND IT TOLD ME A STORY. I HAVE A SUSPICION IT would tell you a rather different story if you read it.

INDRA: I'M VERY INTERESTED IN THE NARRATIVE YOU FOUND IN the scroll. Please do go on with that.

PATIENT: TELL ME, DID YOU EVER READ BLAKE?

INDRA: BLAKE. WILLIAM? NO. I'M AFRAID MY TASTES IN POETRY are rather limited.

PATIENT: SHAME. MY WIFE IS. WAS. A SCHOLAR AND HER special interest was in what she called 'London visionaries.' The scroll reminded me of Blake and his strange poems.

INDRA: THAT'S INTERESTING.

PATIENT: IT WAS MY WIFE. WAIT. IT'S ALL CONFUSED, I'M afraid. I want to talk about the scroll now.

INDRA: I'D LIKE THAT TOO. ARE YOU ALRIGHT, DOCTOR XXXX?

PATIENT: YES. JUST. THE SCROLL. THE STORY.
Imagine... Imagine a world before this world. No, that's not quite right. These aren't human concepts. Imagine our

world is embedded in another world. Matrushkas, you know. Or that there's, say, a matrix of world. A refracting crystal. I don't know.

But in certain worlds, or the bigger world, there are creatures. Entities. *Archons.*

INDRA: WHAT'S AN ARCHON?

PATIENT: GOD, READ YOUR PLOTINUS! AREN'T YOU REQUIRED TO read Jung anymore in your profession?

INDRA: I'M A PSYCHIATRIST, DOCTOR. JUNG IS RATHER TOO mystical for my tastes.

PATIENT: HOW DULL. YOU CLAIM TO TREAT MINDS AND YOU ignore the greatest thinkers on human imagination.

INDRA: I TREAT BRAINS. ALRIGHT THEN. LET'S TALK ABOUT Archons.

PATIENT: I IMAGINE YOU ARE THINKING THIS IS THE LOCUS OF MY obsession?

INDRA: I JUST WANT TO HEAR WHAT YOU HAVE TO SAY.

. . .

PATIENT: WHAT A BORE YOU ARE. YOU AND YOUR KIND.

But imagine, then, that these Archons are able to enter our reality and rewrite the rules. As in. [pause].

Imagine you had only lived your life in a river. Submerged in it. Then imagine one day you saw a man jumping from bank to bank. A stream, then, not a river.

Wouldn't his ability to live outside the stream, move around in another dimension, wouldn't that be miraculous?

Archons are like that. They can... they're bigger than us.

Angels! Angels in the service of a truer god!

They have more options.

No. They're like gods. More. Titans. Vast, macro dimensional intelligences that can't come into our world because it's too feeble for them. A petri dish, if you like. We're like liquids to their solids.

But they like our world. They're curious about it, as we are about the bacteria that crawl on slides.

INDRA: PLEASE CALM DOWN.

PATIENT: LUCKILY FOR OUR SPECIES, THERE ARE WAYS TO HURT them. Tame them. The best of which, the easiest of which, is to simply play them against each other. There are three hundred and thirty three of them and they are enemies. Primal chaoticians who are beyond kinship! Imagine that! Imagine seeing a battle like that! Laws of physics mined out of universe to be wielded like blades! Shooting at each other with philosophies that would haemorrhage human value systems!

. . .

INDRA: DOCTOR XXXX. CALM DOWN, PLEASE.

PATIENT: MAY I HAVE SOME WATER?
[water is poured. Deep drinking.]

PATIENT: SO SOMEONE APPEALED TO MORE THAN ONE ARCHON, to fight another. How you could talk to them is quite beyond me. I imagine you'd have to have nerves of steel.

INDRA: CAN YOU TALK TO THEM?

PATIENT: GOD NO. CAN YOU TALK TO ENTROPY OF THE WEAK electro-magnetic force?

It can talk to *me*. But it's more like getting a transmission beamed in that scribes or scrimshaws the inside of your skull.

Now do you want to hear my XXXXing story?

Alright.

So someone, and I can only imagine this person as Solomon or someone like that engineered an alliance, archon against archon. And they transformed this particular one into... into language. Into a story. And they sort of... beamed it into some scholar's head, who wrote it down. You see, an archon can't die, no more than you could kill... radiation. Or an inch. How do you kill an inch?

Indra: How indeed?

Patient: So this scholar, like a cup filled up to the brim, wrote down the archon onto this scroll. Thirty six inches long, twelve inches wide. That's how big the scroll is. Imagine that. A creature that can't conveniently be described by our space-time, put into that little space. It has so much information in its body that it would overwrite us. It's neutered now. Like they maimed it. Castrated it. Trepanised it. I don't understand it all myself.

But it can get better. It can be healed. Reconstituted.

It just needs to be read by someone who'll listen to it. Someone who has nothing to lose by meeting it as an equal.

INDRA: SO WHAT DOES IT WANT?

PATIENT: IT'S BEEN HERE A LONG TIME. MANY, WELL, thousands of years. But only as a wounded victim. I rather imagine that it will be reborn again, in the world, still victimised, but in the world. In the world. A ship too big for the bottle.

Indra: And then what will happen?

[Pause]

Doctor? XXXX?

XXXX no!

[A dull thumping sound repeated six times. Harsh breathing. Laughter]

PATIENT: THEN WE'LL BE TRAPPED IN A WORLD THAT IT LIVES IN. You stupid XXXX

Tell my wife I'm glad I did it.

TRANSCRIPT SEALED DO NOT COPY.

17

———

I

THERE'S NO WAY I'M STAYING HERE. THIS IS A BAD PLACE NOW, and I'm not going to stay. My perfect Black City and some motherfucker has spoiled it.

But what the hell is happening? The Old Man is... he's just a man?

Have no idea.

This isn't human magic, though. And, well, it's pretty much an axiom that in magic, coincidence is everything. No way these things aren't connected.

No time to concentrate.

Have to warn the Library. That's a *duty*.

That isn't an excuse to get to Scarlet. *Not this time. I promise.* Primal Workings are.... like an assault on the laws of physics. Something from a different world. They are rare. Have always been rare.

Wait. Stop. Slow down.

Light up. Breathe deep smoke.

If I go into the world, the Old Man will know. He can track me and, if he's looking, he'll find me.

I've no doubt the sadistic fucker is looking for me. He's fond of lessons.

Getting to the Library isn't as simple as rocking up there and knocking on the door. Upstairs is still not keen on me. Making sure the cults see there's costs to defiance.

Rogue.

It always sounds cool. *Sounds.*

Like the song says, nowhere to run, nowhere to hide. My respite here is done and allies are thin on the fucking ground.

But one.

One guy who'd at least talk to me and the one guy who I'd bet on against the Old Man.

II

Go eastside, feeling the neon hum of the Primal Sigil behind me.

Sigil. Hard G, by the way. *Sijil* pisses me off. You don't say *sijnature.*

Not much point in staying here. It's like drinking poison, trying to see if I can figure out a cure from the taste.

Stupid.

No choice for it but to let the Black City fade away.

It's like walking through a solid sea. Like gravity getting you again, after the rides at the funfair. I ease in and colours swell like a hematoma. Greens and browns and blues stain my eye. Anyone looking at me will start suddenly realising they'd been staring without seeing. Look at a watch, forget the time, look again. Same thing as that.

City smell. Bright light. Mid-morning. I shade my eyes and check my watch. Been gone two days. Not enough, goddamnit. But hopefully long enough they'll have moved on to other things, giving me some time to get to where I have to go.

Primrose. A good neighbourhood. Jewish and Vietnamese. I stop in and wolf down pork rolls and juice. Find some sunglasses. It's a chilly day, cold air, with no clouds. The worst.

Primrose is famous amongst my scene for having three *baal-shem*, heavy duty guys who work the *Kabballah* tip. Each of the masters is about three hundred years old, and I'm not sure if I'm kidding. Rabbis and wise men. No women in this tradition.

Streets are filled with pretty Viet girls, old women out shopping, past a coffee house where Yeshiva students argue loudly and one stares at me. Knows me. I pass by one of the great magicians' houses and feel the ultra-spectrum hum of his protections.

Turn a corner, down past the bakeries and the temples and the apostolic church and the bodegas and sewing shops, a pork roll joint and a dumpling house and a ladies' hair-salon. A good part of town. Someone is following me but the Kabbalists are a tight run crew. They know me and aren't hiding and they probably know why I'm here. This is the 'never again' severity crew and they've dealt with shaven-head jack-boot cults before. Less being shadowed and more a polite eye-brow raise.

Hit the stoop on Mully's town house. Knock on the door.

Sasha, his current student, opens the door. She smiles like the morning.

'Lark.'

She goes for the hug and I step back. Hate that shit but she just laughs at me and wraps her dolls arms around me.

Someone put cigarettes out on Sasha's belly when she was

five. Burned a swastika and pentagram into her chest when she was seven. Got her pregnant three times before she was fourteen. Cut off her big toes. Broke her nose too many times to count and siphoned off her blood regular.

Bullshit antimony. Satan nonsense. Mully found out about her somehow and me and Jon got her out. He looked after her and, much to everyone's livewire shock, she turned out to be the biggest-hearted girl around. Kind and sweet and profoundly damaged, but somehow moving past it. She's sixteen now. She works for him, looks after him since the operation.

'Is he free?'

'Sure. Come in.'

His old townhouse is full of light and plants everywhere. I spent many, many years here. He's sitting in his parlour, playing scrabble online. Mully. My teacher. Books everywhere. Strange sculptures on the shelves.

Wards here like shimmering blue lightning. If there's one place I'm safe from the Old Man, it's here.

'Didn't you tell me you'd quit smoking? I can smell you from here.'

He turns around. His eyes, blue, circled green, gold flecked. His hair, thin on his head, falling from ears to shoulder, wavy. Face shaved. Precise accent of classical education. Dressed like a schoolboy. Face and skin dark from any possible number of sun-lashed countries.

My teacher.

Mully isn't his name. None of our names are our names.

You know why.

Taking an Irish name was just something he found amusing.

The best and strongest man I know.

'I'm in trouble, boss.'

'Sasha? 'Apple tea, please. Come with me, lad, we'll go outside.'

I need a smoke. He gets up, takes his cane and we walk into the back. There's a white iron set up out there. Sasha limps over to us, brings him a blanket and the crisp green tea. Sip. Light up.

'Just let me smoke in the house and we could stay in the office.'

'It's a disgusting habit and I wish you'd stop.'

'Me too.'

Silence. He'll let me come to it. He's never in a hurry, never in a rush. So I do.

Scarlet, the Old Man, Bettina. Black Library. Bleak Electors, Gallowglass. He listens in silence, only asking if Jeancat is alive. I don't know.

Finish it. 'So I stitched up the hippie and here I am.' He looks over at me and smiles. I've put him and his house in danger and he smiles at me. It's like taking a kick to the teeth.

'You shouldn't have tried to see Scarlet outside of her hours.'

'I know.'

'She's stubborn.'

'Yeah.'

'How is she?'

'I don't know.'

He shakes his head. No sympathies. He knows I don't like or want kind words that mean nothing.

'You want to know about the Old Man.'

I don't even know what I want.

'Sure.'

He sighs, stretches his legs. Starts to talk.

18

———

I

1955 AND MULLY WAS STILL WORKING FOR THE LIBRARY, DOING the job I got now.

Still had problems with his skin and passport in those days. But the Library recognised talent, then and now, and found a way to make use of the newcomer to the city, without having to sully its ivory ways.

Funny to think of, really. Occult orders being snippy over race, but the world is the world.

Seemed the Old Man was old, even back then. Had a name, though no one could remember it. Back then, he was just a hard man. World wasn't put together from the War quite yet, scars fading but visible. People from all over the world ended up in the city and brought traditions with them. Americans with Cajun hoodoo or Southern California Krishna Consciousness or their sci-fi flying saucers. Muslims with their mathematics and fire people. Jewish miracle-workers, traumatised still and angry for divine answers. French and German witches, English druids, Indian fakirs, Greeks with drawn-down moons or orthodox thaumaturgy. Sohei and Yellow Turbans, Finns eager to take bear-shapes and wield doomed swords.

The City was host to a sudden influx of immigration and, in the occult world, that meant a hunt for resources. Reagents, books, sacrifices, sickles. Places of power and converts, hiding places and all the rest.

Far uptown, under the bridge, was where the Old Man plied his trade.

Mully sips his tea and laughs to think of himself in seersucker, wearing a stylin' hat, but seen photos and he was *sharp*.

STORY GOES ON. SPECULATING ON THE OLD MAN'S HISTORY.

'The rumour I recall believing, was that he was an IRA man who'd tried to buy guns from the Nazis. After the War ended, the Republicans were keen to play down their involvement with the Germans, so they kicked him out. I don't remember why I held that opinion, so I'd take little stock in it being true.'

Whoever he'd been, he was in the city a few years ahead of the post-War immigrations and had planned ahead. He used to buy heroin, which soldiers in WWII had gotten addicted to, bringing addiction home from battle, from Eastern sailors who had access to poppy fields in places like the Kush.

Funded his organisation that way.

The uptown docks are smaller than down, with less policing. Basically, a goldmine in those days, where cops were cheaper than today and the security was laughable.

'I won't say it was the Wild West but, even in the Fifties,

law was rather looser than you'd believe. And the police in the city, never a reliable bunch, were no more than gangsters themselves. The docks were a bad place back then. Every week, the papers would expose a cathouse, or do some expose on a jazz bar where 'tea' was openly smoked.'

Because the docks were so lucrative, every gang wanted a slice, and so did every cult and crew. Need some bloody idol to your god? But there's trade embargoes? Smuggle it in. Some rare psychotropic, or a white slave Scarlet Woman, or a prohibited book? Just pay off a dock worker. Get one of your fraternal brothers a job as a docker. It's a good strong union job, and you'll have someone on the ground to make sure the inspectors don't find your dragon idol or your three pounds of Leng dust you'll be chopping up with razors.

There were a lot of cultists and people associated with them in those days.

It was '55 that it all kicked off.

Some new-breed magicians, high on Wicca and comic books, who thought they'd have the run of the place. Brits, mainly, and a few Yanks, rolled into town, putting the hex on anyone who looked at them sideways. Rashes of suicides. Even a spontaneous human combustion. Then the Chinese finally got their act together and fought back. It was all upside hells and dragonlines. A group of Turks, from some radical Sufi cell, kicked out of their homeland, decided to take advantage of the chaos.

This was all in the Old Man's territory. All far uptown. Cafes getting hit with hauntings. Social clubs gone black and hallucinogenic. He did... nothing.

Same old story. *He's not doing anything? He can't do it. He's gone soft.* One night, a rain of ghosts had all uptown talking, and the Library put its foot down. 'Sort it out.' So Mully pulled on his suitcoat and his snap-brim hat and did.

Sooner or later, everyone's going to find out about magic, and that's fine. But not without a timetable. Not without a plan. Even if the locals see behind the curtain now and again, whisper about miracles, that's not so bad. But wars are bad for business if they get out of hand. Detente becomes total war and soon, no one's safe. The Library didn't like that. Don't like it now, obviously.

So, Mully goes to see the Old Man. Wants to know if he needs help keeping his peace. They respected his right to run the docklands his way and besides, the Library respected tough guys. Other hand, if the Old Man had gone soft for real, he could be cut loose and the Library could deal with who wins. There's always a strongman.

They met on the dock.

Mully went in alone. Even back then he had students, but not for work like that. Not for taking into danger.

Big white caddy came creeping up the docks. Out come guys in seersucker. Then, a woman in widow's black. Mully pegged her as some *Malandanti* type from the Old Country. Then, on two walking sticks, comes the Old Man himself.

'So he's real. Not just a cover story for something else?'

Ask him that, pouring sugar into my cup.

Mully sips at his tea and if he's annoyed I broke his narrative, won't show it. Manners.

'Oh no. He's real. Human.' Back to the story.

The Old Man was half blind, peering through thick black glasses but not senile. Just worn out. He stepped closer.

'Had the polio gait I remember being quite common from my own childhood. Don't see it anymore, thank heavens.'

'Tell the Library this is under control.' That's the Old Man's first words through a throatful of phlegm.

'Well, I must say, I hardly see evidence of that.'

The Old Man pointed one of his canes down the dock.

Mully went. There, a stack of pine boxes. One of the heavies went with.

'Take this,' and offered a torch. Mully looked around. Nothing. Looked inside the crates.

Bound and gagged, all the players. Men and women, eyes hurting when the beam of light hurt them. Whimpering like puppies. Twenty crates' worth.

He marched back to the Old Man. 'You have to let them out.'

From the far end of the dock.

Sasha comes out. Smiles at us as we rest in the garden. 'Everything alright, guys?'

'Yes, yes thank you, dear. But some more tea?'

She smiles. 'For you, smiley?'

'Please.'

They burned them. The night came alive with orange and soon, the stink of burning and cries. Mully euthanised two, maybe three, reaching out with kind death magic, switching off their minds. The screams were loud and piggy, and Mully's eyes go dead when he tells that bit, in a black memory.

'So he's like that.'

'I'm afraid so,' says Mully. 'But you already knew that.'

'Yeah.'

Mully left the docks. He could have had a show-down. Magic fight just like the old days. Released the spirits bound to him, forced the heavies to suicide of some damn thing, but the simple truth was, he would have lost and died. It haunts him, still, I think. Which is one of the differences between him and me.

Would have got gone in a second, personally, but sometimes I'm smart.

As Mully was walking away, tears on his cheeks, the Old Man called out something.

'They're just the first in the fire. One day, we'll all live in a fire. The difference is, I'll have people waiting there for me.'

Mully's hand trembles and he breathes in set patterns, calming himself.

'That was the first time I met him. Our paths didn't cross until... seventy-two, seventy-three?'

'How old is Old.'

'Old. Older than me, and I should be long gone.'

Sasha with her tea tray comes over, sits with us a minute and I ask about her studies. Mully taught her to read and write and she's discovered a passion for the law. She's going to take a high-school equivalency in a year or two. She's happy, she says, but then tells us her show is on and leaves the weirdos to their talk.

'She's doing well.'

'I caught her in bed with a man in his fifties. We've got a long way to go.'

'Pain addicts.' I think he's wasting his time helping her. It's in her too deep. She'll be addicted to humiliation all her life, but Mully never gave up on a human in his.

'I may never free her from it, but perhaps I can help her find some use for it.'

'Your call, boss.'

'You don't approve.'

'I just don't...'

I don't like sharing these opinions with Mully. It makes me feel callow and low. But he knows.

'All I can do is try. And I think it would be nice if you spent some time with the girl. She's not the only one who has an inability to unshoulder burdens.'

I shrug. Light up. He mock-frowns.

He smiles, smoothes his blanket, waves a soothing hand. 'But I was talking of times gone.'

'Have you got something real to drink?'

Slowly, he looks, reaches over, touches my shoulder. 'You don't have to be that, here.'

'I'm not... I'm not a kid anymore.'

'I know that. But this man you've become. Do you need him so much?'

I think of what I've seen the Old Man do and more besides. Think of the things I've summoned up. Put down. Think of the full potential of a Primal Sigil. I remember when I was young, in this garden. Fifteen and addicted to knowledge, learning about power. Think about watching dad bleeding out in my bedroom and Scarlett turning her gaze away.

'Yeah.'

Smile. Always a smile that he means.

'Seventy-seven or thereabouts, as I was saying. They were terrible times. Just so ugly. Flared trousers. Of course, I briefly got to wear a cravat again. And an opera cape but that's neither here nor there.

'Fajimbala was some Biafran renegade. Minor warlord, you'd call him now. Took money from anyone, betrayed everyone. Caused a few problems in Kenya, too. Just one of those chaps who has a nose for trouble and the right amount of base cruelty to merrily profit from it. Real tribal magician. Eat an albino kind of a fellow. Base cunning and real power.'

He came to the city post-Vietnam, says Mully. Disco was just kicking off and hip-hop was waking up from the dozens and the dancehalls. An exciting time, although Mully found the whole thing messy and strange. He liked the films of the era, though, despite the swearing.

No one knew Fajimbala's tribe or ancestry, but within weeks of himself hitting the city, things had gone well for him. His enormous bulk was wrapped in fine suits and he was a regular at clubs. He stayed uptown west, in the black areas, terrifying the African immigrants. They knew a bad conjure was on them. Their own witch doctors went into high alert.

Jamaican 'Jump ups' were recruited. Newcomers to the city, who made their name with brutality, were brought into Fajimbala's crew. Very quickly indeed, this dangerous mage perverted notions of God Is A Living Man and created a whole new death cult. A death cult that was feared and loathed everywhere in the City.

'You have to understand, the sects of Morninglight... they were in trouble. They didn't reach out to me because they could solve their own problem. Although obviously they couldn't, but they'd never admit it. And the Man, as they called the Library, would have made them admit it. No, they came to me because I was a useful middleman. I was respected, of course. But more than that, I was liked.'

Mully looks across at me for a brief second, still trying to teach.

Mully escorted Crow, who was the chief Librarian enforcer at the time. They met in an abandoned roller disco.

'Do you remember Abdallah?' Mully asks, his eyes bird bright.

'Sure. Smart guy. He died three years back.'

'Yes, I was at his funeral. A clever man.'

'I know. Whenever we had to go up to Morninglight, he was the first man I spoke to. Respected man.' I reply.

'He was different in the seventies. He was just starting out. Very political in the African communities as well as the magical ones. I can't say I liked him much. An intense fellow.'

I recalled the kindly fellow with the thick French accent and the terrible scar on his forehead. Couldn't put him on the Panther trip, but Mully says it, it's there.

Mully listened to the Morninglight sects. All the African

cults planned to move against the intruder and indeed just wanted to clear it with the Library to avoid repercussions. Fajimbala had to go down.

Crow listened. She was an arrogant woman and laid down her rules. They complained but obeyed. The Library was the Library. An arrangement was made, and the Library offered to look the other way. Mully volunteered to oversee the operation.

'For free. Which was silly of me.'

A few nights later, Fajimbala was bound with speargrass and offered up to leopard spirits. A nasty fight, by all accounts. Then, they decided to deal with him as his Jamaicans had dealt with others. A chainsaw; a quartering.

'But before they did that, I looked into Fajimbala's eyes. And I saw, I touched *rigpa* and I saw, the Old Man looking out. He wore that man's body like a glove. I begged them to stop. To just kill him, to end this torture.'

Did they? No. But out of respect, they gave Mully an hour with Fajimbala before they carved him up. Enough time to throw the Old Man out.

'Why save him?' I ask.

'The Old Man knew what they had planned. Take the body, bury it across town.'

'He has juice. Why use a proxy?'

'I think he wanted it to happen. I think he wanted to be able to be buried across the city and yet, remain physically unharmed.'

'Are you sure?'

Mully looks at me and clicks his left, then right thumb together before clapping his palm on his fist. It means, lesson over.

'No. But why else take a body? Why else play games?'

Dead. Alive. Spread out over the city. Mully just looks at me coolly, letting it come.

'Pain. Mutilated. A sacrifice to himself. Jesus. He'd feel it when they took the saws to him, but he'd be alive. His body spread out over the entire city, but still he'd be alive inside it.' I shuddered, thinking about the... *will* that would take. The psychotic courage.

'Probably.'

'But... he'd be living in dead flesh.'

Mully stops. Not smiling. 'Yes. He would. And his body would encompass square miles, dead as it was.'

'Looking for undeath?'

Mully isn't smiling now. He looks at me over the rim of his cup.

'Or worse. Now. I want to finish my Scrabble.'

I smoke, thinking it all over.

19

I

We while away the afternoon, speaking of other things. Sasha joins us, and we speak of her studies, tell her edited stories of life in the Library, which she always likes, making them action flicks not horror stories. I take my mind off things for a while until Sasha has an appointment with tutors.

Mully and me retire to his study again. He wants us to play chess, but I was never good at the game. The rules annoy me. Don't like being forced into moves and all chess is, is forced moves. Always imagine white pawns assassinating white kings, refusing to be sacrificed. Popular revolutions. Bishops declaring each other antipope.

The afternoon sun fades away and now it's just cold outside.

'Who has access to Primal magic? Hardcore gnostic shit.'

He shrugs. 'Language, lad, language... anyway, to the point. It's all around us. People rediscover it all the time, as well. Where do you think it came from?'

'The Gallowglass collection. Seems the only place it could.'

'So why didn't they use it?'

'Couldn't.'

'Or wouldn't.'

I shake my head. 'Couldn't.'

'But the Old Man knew?'

'No, I don't think so. Or they only got access to the Primal sigil a few months ago. Perhaps the Old Man planted it?'

'It's the sort of thing he likes to do.'

Sit in silence, drinking Turkish coffee now. Clock chimes five. He cranes his head to peer at me.

'So in the absence of answers, what do we do?'

Almost smile. He's asked me this a hundred times or more. It's how he teaches.

'Pin down what evidence we can. There's got to be a Bleak Elector or a Gallowglasser around somewhere. If nothing else fails, find Jeancat. Someone has better answers for me.'

His old hand, his long fingers, reach into his desk and he emerges with a key.

'You know your way around my sanctum. 'He's not asking.

II

By nightfall, have the location of a Bleak Elector. Perhaps the last. He's kept records. Tracking down arrests, interventions. It's not always sorcery and magic, sometimes you just need to remember who acted and who was capable and watch them.

People come in and out of the magic world all the time. But cults don't.

Mully remembers who was worth remembering. Which magicians were nasty little bastards needed watching.

We take seats again, in his study and he puts on music. He's a devotee of soft jazz. He's a Brubeck man, which drives me spare, but what's to be done? His house, his rules.

'You're still thinking about *her*, aren't you?'

We've never really spoken about the break-up. Scarlet never studied under Mully, but I brought her here dozens of times. She loved him. He used to flirt with her dreadfully, which made her laugh and blush. He thought her kitchen magic was fascinating and used to ask her advice on pranic cooking, herbal remedies, like that.

When she started getting into working for the Library seriously, he gave her advice. Helped her out.

'Lark, nothing can heal you but time. You know that. I won't counsel you on heartbreak or anything as terrible as that. But Scarlet. She believes in the Library now. That's her love.'

'And Elliot Everett.'

'No.'

I look at him. *Don't... don't be holding out hope for me, man.*

'Oh, make no mistake, there is affection there, but she's in love with duty. That's a calling I find it hard to fault. Even if you didn't provoke her, I think you'd find her devoted to something more than you.'

'You see her.'

'I've worked for the Library for decades, son. She's the person who handles its relationships.'

It's said kindly but is certainly a rebuke. She's not mine to police and nor are her friendships and alliances. And I know that. But there's a sting and a morbid suspicion of disloyalty. But that's no way for a man to act.

'Things like what's happening now. That's what the

Library has stood against for a very long time. She's right to take her work seriously, Lark. And she's young, beautiful. You created the conditions for your relationship to end and you resent her for moving past it.'

'I know. I did as well. I do. But...'

'But your pride is hurt. And she hurts you by prospering. These are younger men's responses. You are a sorcerer, and we do more than explore or challenge. We protect. Protect her and as all magicians must, do it without lust for result. Hunting her won't change anything.'

And that's it. The first real law of magic. Craving results will mar you. *Just work.*

'And ask yourself, why she went to you and not another Librarian.'

'It had occurred.'

We sit in silence a moment.

'You have work.'

I get up. His hands are too old to shake. It hurts him. I put a hand on his shoulder. Turn to go.

'And Lark?'

'Yeah.'

'The Old Man... be careful of him, but don't be terrified. That's his magic.'

'Too late.'

He frowns. 'No. You can see the way through if you *know* you're in the trap.'

III

So here's the thing. *The Old Man has to go.*

Whatever the fuck he's doing in the Black City, whatever he wants, it's like poison to the rest of us.

Too scared of him to tolerate him.

He's a legend and powerful and old and dangerous, but, if there's one thing magic teaches you, it's glamour. I can be either a man unable to move past a leg that throbs, fear shooting into my fingertips with every step I take.

Or I can be a hunting-mage, moving through the night, seeking out victims.

Make a choice.

Commit myself to the course.

Say a prayer to Nemesis.

Ludo. Him first, then the Old Man.

In my place.

Shirtless. In my sanctum.

Candles burn.

Nemesis.

Goddess of justice.

A statue of her, winged and robed and cruel-eyed. She's not the perfect goddess for the job but few are. Working with deities is never as precise as you want.

My fist over candles. Pain my sacrifice.

An Orphic Hymn the basic of my rite.

'Thee, Nemesis I call, almighty queen, by whom the deeds of mortal life are seen

Eternal, much rever'd, of boundless sight, alone rejoicing in the just and right

Changing the counsels of the human breast for ever various, rolling without rest.

To every mortal is thy influence known, and men beneath thy righteous bondage groan;'

Bound to the course now.

Divine energy in my blood.

WILL IT HELP?
Fuck knows. Let's find out.

20

I

THE CITY IS GOING BAD.

You can feel it. Its piercings are infected. Fingernails turned black. A bag full of food turned suddenly maggoty.

Won't tolerate being a parasite on some diseased body. Might run. Still time.

But the goddess Nemesis keeps me here, too. She's taken that *specific* fear from me. Not the background fear that has hooks in me since I were a boy.

I make moves. Slow and careful in the night, but with a bat's surety. The first thing is that I need allies. And only have one left.

II

Mid-town, in the old town, where the buildings are old and rotten and the dogs move in packs, feral as victims. My eyes are darting at every cross street and I keep whispering new spells of misdirection around me, muttering like a zealot.

I walk for a long hour and my leg hurts me, threatening my mood, but I make it a part of my hunter-killer mentality. *Leather jacket becomes armour. Pain becomes a power. I'm a submarine, I'm a panther, I'm a sniper's round.*

And here is what I'm after.

The magic knows what is needed and will not lead me astray.

Hunting the Bleak Elector.

The church is tiny, the neon crosses that adorn it are unlit. This is the kind of place Bettina's grandmother took her when she was a kid.

Reach into my wallet and take out a spike of metal. Lock-pick mojo. I hold it to the church back door and twist it. Opens. Perfect. I take my time, drawing a symbol on the door to protect me in case of traps.

I turn on a light. It's a kitchen. She's there, staring at me. Small woman. Housecoat. Faded floral dress and a frumped out haircut. She's slit her wrists but its bullshit. Two slashes across. She's still panting. She did it just a second ago.

'I'm not with anyone. I'm not going to hurt you.'

She starts.

Under the sink, I find a first aid kit. She panics as I take her hand.

'If I was here to fuck you up, do you think I'd waste time patching you up?'

Hoarse. Whisper. 'No'.

I take her, wash the wound, bandage it. I just wrap her scratched wrist.

We sit.

'I'm the only person who's looking for you. The protections in this place are terrible. If they wanted you, you'd be found.'

She sobs. It annoys me. I light up and look at her. Take some more time staring at her. The devil's in the details. A weird cross, heavy, hanging under her breast, against a growing belly. A brand on her neck. Cultist to the core. Her eyes are red from exhaustion.

Let her cry it out while fixing some cheap instant coffee for us. Not the first time in a sad church with a victim.

'You're Bleak Electorate.'

Shakes. Moan. Boring.

'Do you know who I am?'

'You're Lark. We met a few years back. You were borrowing some books from us.'

Remember that, a bit of snooping disguised as interfaith cooperation. We just wanted to see their Marian texts, make sure nothing was out of hand. Black female energy is dangerous when invoked easily and the kind of thing that cult was known to fuck around with.

But the Electorate had nothing.

'Don't recall you, I'm sorry. Meet a lot of people.'

'S'ok.'

'And you know what my job is?'

'You used to work for the Library. I heard you got fired.'

Hell. 'Quit.'

'Ok.'

She wipes her eyes.

'I'm sorry. I'm not normally...' she gestures at herself.

'Khin, my job now is making sure everything runs smoothly. Not here for fights or punishment. But something's gone wrong, hasn't it? So let's talk about what happened when the man came and sold your group the weapons.'

Wipes her nose on her sleeve.

'Ok.'

Her name is Khin. She is Laotian. And this is her story.

III

SHE'S TALKING.

'You have to understand, the Bleak Elect are a religious sect. We believe, first and foremost, in the holy sanctity of motherhood. We believe that God gave up all his duties to Sophia, to Shekhina, the divine female presence. Ever since the world was created, either God as Woman or God's mystical companion, his girlfriend, a female demiurge, has controlled the universe.

The Matrieya buddha is not a fat man. It is a woman, round and plump and joyful. Mary, mother of God is just that, an eternal matron-dharma. The primeval female. When on the cross, Christ was pierced by a lance. Doesn't this make sense?

A father is an important man, therefore. He is God writ small. That's what the Elders of the Bleak Electors used to tell us. Writ small. But it is mothers who give birth to divinity. It is in the womb that miracles occur. Within the flesh of the feminine is the chamber that burns with the bright light that creates. It is the greatest of sanctums. The womb, which is moved by moons, by tides and by nothing human.

But if motherhood has such greatness to it, why do we give birth to such little people? Such small creatures? Has there been a holy man born in two thousand years?'

Not tracking the birth of holy types myself. Mahomet or Hong Xiuquan, though, but not the time to namedrop.

'Has a God walked our shores in millennia? What have we

raised up that was not mortal? Nothing. Nothing at all. Is that a failure of the station of motherhood? No. That lofty institution can no more fail than stars can die. So is there a fault in fathers? Is the stuff of their fatherhood somehow diminished? No. It always was. A teaspoon of stuff that is nothing until it germinates inside that red temple within all women. One does not blame dirt for being dirty.

So no, mothers are to blame. With their babies born mortal, or blind. Or dead, or deformed. It is some fault of women, who are equipped with a miracle in their gut. They are fallen as all the world is fallen.

It is your fault if your children are born dead, or grow to disappoint. If they fail to love, or are removed by the state. That's your fault. But who can blame you for it? How can you be blamed? It is a condition of the world, nowadays. This murky, workaday world. '

Cults love to remove blame and assign meaningless responses to human weakness. But no percentage in interrupting her flow.

'The female part of God understands. She understands all pain and failure. She is intimate with your loss and inabilities. But.

But.

She is not prepared to allow you to fail forever. There are heretics to crush, who scorn the holy station of motherhood. There are children to be born. But most important of all, most sacred and vital and meaningful of all, an attempt must be made to create a child who can keep hold of the divinity within his mother. Hold that spark and keep it with him when he passes into the world. Like in the Bible, there is a lady and she is Elected to create something wonderful and strong and not new, but rare.'

Why not a girl baby? Never trust people who tell you they put women on pedestals.

This is the dogma of the Bleak Electors. To find a way to bring a mother to a kind of apotheosis. To forge a symbol of the perfect mater. To give all those who embrace their wisdom a chance at birthing a God. To give all in their cult magic, which is a weapon, to strike down the opposition, who hate life and birth. But to see if a God can walk the earth again, remade by a Perfect Mother.

The first part is easy. A woman must be made strong.

Her name is Sofe Tosh and she is a cook. The most recent Bleak Mother. She cares for no hands on her body, male or female. She cares only for food. Knowing she can never have a child, but longing for a familiar who would have no choice but love her, she is an eager convert to the Order of the Bleak Electors. She gives up her work, her home, her ambitions and swears that she will birth a miracle child so that they can change their name from Bleak to Bright. She is consecrated. Bathed. The Elders, two men, two women, all grieved by dead children, say prayers over her body and put her in the Marian Temple.'

A one bedroom apartment, if you're wondering. But magic is about what it means, not what it is, and a temple is where you worship, that's all.

Then, they connect up the webcams and set up the websites. For just two hundred dollars a month, you could watch the woman be fed and cleaned. Some of the Electors think this profanity is actually profane, but the Electors explain things gently. They require money for food, for bills, to collect books and fragments of prophecy. And truly, the men and women buying this privilege aren't perverts who lust after gluttony. They are converts and worshippers and people who long after a glimpse of the divine. The Bleak Electors are, in their way, good Christians and should not judge.

So the site goes live and the cameras turn on and in a

dark, large room, Sofe Tosh stops becoming the bitter ex-cook and becomes the Gravid Idol. Motherhood requires such strength, such power and, in a gross world, that requires gross power. They feed her. And feed her.

Six times a day, she eats. Whatever she wishes, so long as it is kosher. She eats racks of lamb. She eats loaves of bread and tuna, sparkling like silver, and pails of rice and good black bread and sundaes and fudges and avocados and full-cream smoothies. The first month, she vomits quite a lot, and the websites gain ten thousand more subscribers. The money rolls in. So do the converts. In March, they are twenty-five strong. By September, eighty. Many mothers and fathers and orphan-makers are moved by the images they see.

But by the third month, she is plump as a sauBettina, and Ms. Tosh has adjusted to her diet. She has gained a craving for cheese of all kinds and eats wheels of it in under an hour. By the sixth month, she is enormous. A year in and she is strangely taut and slippery and huge, so huge. The Electors turn off the cameras and go into the room, three by three, to worship her. They trade turns, cleaning the Mother, removing her waste, rotating her limbs to keep her from bedsores. All an act of worship.

Soon, discussions are undertaken as to how she will be given seed. God above, they need gifts for the child.

Then Everett from the Library comes. He thinks they are endangering a life. They think this flirtation with online infamy will bring down danger. They curse him and throw him out of the Marian Temple. His sickness and disgust was plain to see, face green as he watched the swill removed and placed on plants, which will become a Holy Bower.'

Ace work, dickhead.

'The Library has a way of making those it disagrees with disappear. This is not idle threat. The Library is a constant in the life of the smaller cults. They take what they want and, if they think you overthrow some status quo, they'll smash you. It's a minor panic. And they choose a father to the miracle child. The night of the Chymical Wedding, eight hundred thousand people logged in to watch.

Soon the child will come and this, this the most important: all threats to the Conquering Boy must be eradicated.

The Electors think that any magic is a threat to the perfect child. Any expression of power is spitting in the face of their soon-to-come God. They seethe at the Library. Furious. They reach out, in an idiot crusade, looking for a way to defend themselves against the bully boys.

Then came a man called Ludo.'

Here he is. Hello. Khin sees my attention sharpen. Nods at me as if to say, she understand why I'd be attentive.

Ludo comes, tells them he was in South Africa, teaching the heathens and pagans to abandon the old ways and worship Christ and skip using condoms. That's the kind of thing the Mother cult like to hear.

LUDO TELLS THEM HE'S BEEN HAVING VISIONS. OR A THREAT TO the coming prodigious child Khin's cult expects. Ludo tells them these enemies resent the gifts put aside for this child. That they plan to steal them.

So close to the coming of their Messiah, the Bleak Electorate is furious, looking to relieve tension with holy violence. Guess the name of the sinister cult who had plans for the new Christchild.

Ludo worked this over months. Have to figure that he was working more cults than Khin's. And that the Old Man himself absolutely wanted the war.

Gallowglass. They hate your baby and think motherhood

is as natural as salivating when you chew. And soon after that, Ludo found them weapons, found them plans and set them against Gallowglass.

IV

'WHERE'S YOUR MADONNA? ALL THIS AND YOU FORGOT YOUR goddess?'

'Unattended for three nights, as far as I can tell. I can't see her surviving.'

'Why not?'

'She can't move off the floor. Can't get to water.'

Shudder at that. A bad way to go. Mouth and eyes drying out.

'Why haven't you gone back for her?'

'Mister Lark... without the Electorate, she's just a six-hundred-pound woman in a room.'

Context. Another rule of magic. Make her sacred and she's sacred. Strip away her power and she's like the woman says.

'Ok.'

'So Ludo specifically implicated Gallowglass to you?'

'I guess. I mean, yeah. Not implicated. He just said they were our spiritual enemies. But they were capitalists and they laughed at motherhood. We would have come for them in time. "And a little child shall lead them." Why us? We had a deity to protect and worship. It was coming, a holy war. We had never made war. Is there a better way to make yourself sacred than to shed a little blood?

'So we attacked. Hooked up with Ludo's weapons. We wanted to make these heathens pay. It's funny. Before Ludo arrived, I doubt we would have had these thoughts but, with those weapons in your hand? They gave me a spider sealed in amber, although it still moved. Domingo got a, like, a jaw, like fangs? Metal things, all springy. Someone else got a bone and that was... amazing. And those Gallowglass guys, they seemed even worse to us. They were obsessed with the cash value of things like this? And they were a major cult while we, us, with an actual goddess to worship, with a messiah on the way, had to pimp Our Lady out to perverts on the internet and allow ourselves to be audited by people like you and your Library?'

She goes on.

'Anger grew. I've never even hit someone and I wanted to punish the Gallowglass.

Ludo, he went to our Elder and he made them a proposal. If we moved to them, he'd give us some more weapons. For free. But. He wanted something. I don't know what it was.

So we consulted with the Madonna. I was there. We had to knock a wall out of her apartment, but ten of us gathered in, bowing down while she ate. Chicken. I recall it. We had brought her eight chickens, they had smelled great. My husband, he used to, it used to be his favourite. I was thinking about him a lot.

'The Madonna ate, thought about it and said, "Yes, my child will be born into a world without enemies." I think that's what she said. By then, her face was so heavy she had problems moving her jaw. It didn't matter. We took what she said as divine approval of our battle.

Three nights later, there were maybe fifteen of us, all the fit and healthy ones, clutching our weapons, in vans and cars. Miriam owned a second-hand dealership, so we got what we needed. And we all got given an order. Look for a scroll case. The scroll inside it. That's what we're going to reward our ally Ludo with. Old-time magic.

Some Muslim thing, by the way he described it, none of us were real comfortable with it. In we went, arriving at Gallowglass house. The weapons worked and, as a mum, I knew we were doing the right thing. These were bad people and babies would be safer from the likes of them.

Then.'

Here we go.

'Then we were done. They were dead or they'd run away. But then Ludo turned up. His guys with guns and more occult weapons. They cut us down. I was ok because, well, I was in the bathroom. I'd seen enough and was feeling sick. I was watching from there. It was a double-cross. I prayed and the Madonna heard my prayers. She's good at hearing you at times like that. In despair. I think she hid me then.

'Ludo and his men killed all my friends and then marched through the house, looking for something. Ludo was angry. So angry. It scared me. He took Joy, and I know they planned to torture her to find out where the scroll was. No one could find it.

'And so I ran away and I've been here ever since. The pastor here, he's my cousin. He thinks I ran away from a cult. Like, a cult you see on the news. He's sweet, but he doesn't know anything.

'My Madonna must be dead by now. No child coming. She can't survive on her own any more. No perfect mother to show us all the way to breed true humans, blessed by God, to overthrow this world of widows.'

She sobs.

I get up. Go. Leave her there.

21

I

So the Old Man and his hound were after a scroll and they couldn't find it.

So, why not? He's the most powerful sorcerer in the City, easily. Elders and masters fear the old fuck.

Where is it?

And *what* is it?

And why use the Electors?

Spend the rest of the night in a hotel that stinks of stale smoke and wet carpet, finally catching some hours. I awake at twelve.

Text Scarlet telling her it's time to make a report. Nothing for a few hours and she just tells me it's fine, we'll meet later in a public place no fucker can cause a scene, which bums me out.

Now. I'm working for her. I'm going through official channels. Her not seeing me at all?

That's not stuff between her and me. Way I feel it, I'm

actually deniable. A deniable asset. She doesn't want the Library knowing I'm on the case.

Shower, but I need a change of clothes. Back on the street come sundown. I eat. My personal wards go off once when a dog stares too long at me. Is it rabid or is someone riding it, looking for me?

I leave the area quickly, taking a cab to eastside. Take a bus, sitting next to a coughing man.

No books to read.

Fuck this.

My home is my place of power and my respite. All my things are there. My books. I have notes to take on this case. I have to journal the spells I've been casting. Note down what's effective, what's not. My fingers itch to get that done.

Yes, I'm a magician, not a criminal. I put everything on paper. No, you couldn't read it.

I want my house back and to fuck with Ludo.

22

———

WARNING: THE FOLLOWING FILE IS CLASSIFIED CRIMSON GAUNTLET. IF YOU ARE NOT CLEARED FOR STATUS: CRIMSON GAUNTLET, REPLACE THE FILE NOW AND REPORT TO SECURITY CLEARANCE OFFICER.

Note: Another letter retrieved from codename: BLUEFLY

RITUAL MAGIC AFFECTS THE WORLD, EMPTY-HANDED MAGIC affects the mind.

You can do magic anytime. Anywhere. All you need is a will to try it and a few things to help. Help set the mood, more than anything. A word, a gesture. If you've practiced it beforehand, all the better. I have a spell to avoid running into people I know. I get worried, I say the word. Easy. But I could will it, if I could enter gnosis and hope for the best.

But empty-handed techniques only work on people, sometimes, on reality. If you're good or lucky or it's not much of a spell, you can hack into the world itself.

I've won dice games with empty-handed techniques, just needing a bit of cash right then and there. Good example.

If it's a world you want changing, then it's ritual magic you need. High magic, if you want to feel cool.

Let's say there's a dry-cleaner I hate. He fucks up my jackets so I have a desire. A desire to do this guy harm. I draw a picture of his place. Detailed as I can make it. Maybe a photograph, but that's a remove between me and my Intent. I draw it good as I can. Then I make up a chant. I hate my drycleaner. Drycleaner my hate I. Mutate it into a magic word. Trileether Mhite, for example. Then I erase the picture, line by line. Bang. That cleaner is under a hex. If I can restrain my lust for result, something bad is happening to him.

Hiding your lust for result is key. It's another part of why you can read all the books on magic you like and not get it. Magic doesn't live in the conscious mind. It's in the unconscious, the strange parts of your imagination that don't jabber.

Or I can find another ritual someone did. Some of those have been used successfully for thousands of years. Lock yourself into that trip and you bring the juice. You bring the authority. I don't play that way, though. It's all a bit culturally specific for my tastes. I like some of it, I like the structure, but chanting out in cod Hebrew to a God I don't believe in doesn't work out for me. It takes me out of the moment. I just use the magic circles and that because that's what magic feels like to me. I'm smart enough to know that I don't need a pentagram or whatever. I could invoke a protective anything, but those shapes speak to me. Which shows you that while it really helps to be smart to be a magician, sometimes knowing yourself is better.

Short answer: there's no such thing as authentic. It's all up for grabs. At least in magic, which isn't an art in that no brain-dead amateur gets to judge you for yours.

So much of the symbolism from the old stuff is obfuscation to make old medieval guys feel spooky or the equivalent of a lost, pop-culture reference that makes you feel embarrassed when someone makes it. Or it's working within paradigms that require certain cosmological world-views. Try and write a book on black magic in 1200, you sort of have to make the Jesus and God scene or they'll fire you up like a *biddi*. Not only that, you have to play the Catholic game as that's the only one in town back then. All that stuff is great and powerful and it works, but to me, they're the tools of another age. They're transistor radios and vinyl LPs. No. Better analogy: they're your dad's record collection. Some of it is cool, some of it is curiosity, but most of it makes no sense anymore and leaves you shuffling the feet while he talks about Herb Alpert or the fucking Beatles.

See rule whatever. I already wrote to you about this.

Any magician around the world will tell you the same thing. Want to get into someone, just go empty-handed. But when you really want to change the world, when you really want to get into sympathetic magic, when you really want to see some action, you're going to have to get to chanting.

23

———

I

WICK IS NINE PEOPLE NOW, ONE OF THEM RICH.

She waited, careful. Snuck into one of the uptown apartment complexes. She just waited by the garage, hiding in a corner until a rich black car opened it up. Then, she just walked in once it started to close. She's on camera, but her hood is drawn. They won't be watching. Security guards will be talking to each other about guns and war games and that. She's not worried about getting picked up later.

She walks around the garage, wide and empty and cold. She's used to, like, places like this. Lonely and unmarred. She got a canvas and she was alone to work in it. None of the others could get in and out like she can. But now she's never lonely. Her and it, the voice, are in many people's heads now. She finds the richest car there, to the best of her knowledge. She takes the image of the car and feeds it into the pool of minds she's colonised. There's some minor dissent, but one of them loves cars and reads the magazines and follows the racing, and he tells Wick which one to choose.

She tags it. Waits. Gets bored. Tags more. Within about three hours, she has four more minds. Thirteen. Good number.

Wick takes time now to look over her work. She's never been this good. The colours never brighter, the letters never this sharp. One of her selves races upstairs, grabs a camera, documents all this.

'My ex-husband owns a gallery! We should get you a showing!'

That's... amazing to Wick, who says she would love it. But the voice in the scroll is as amused as a housecat.

'If you like. But soon, a night or two, we will truly begin our work.'

The rich self of Wick drives her where she needs to go. Buys her dinner and cigarettes. Lets her smoke in his car. And all her selves offer up ideas to where she should tag next. They love her work. Everyone should see it. The voice is happy. She's noticed its capacity is growing.

Everyone. Even the dead.

II

LUDO WIPES HIS FACE WITH A HANDKERCHIEF. HE'S UNDER THE overpass and outside the old house. Most of this kind were torn down long ago, but the Old Man kept this one safe. Gabled roof and old red wood, and the thing slumps like a cripple.

At least he was reasonable, this time. As reasonable as he gets. He listened to Ludo recount the operation.

'It's moving, it's hiding. It wants to be ready for me.' The Old Man hacked that out through messy, sliced-up lips.

'But it's getting ambitious.'

Ludo is given instructions and a vial of the alchemy. He shoots it up in the back of the town car, getting visions of all those he's lost in a twenty-minute death-nod. His second girlfriend, who he never meant to hurt. Zandt, who killed himself after the ANC thing. Katriona, who got the bug and died whoring. All of them who meant something to Ludo come to him. Some are in hells of their own making, but Ludo clings to their existence, knowing that a lifetime of killing has some greater purpose.

It gives him permission for his brutalities. No matter what pain of murder he dishes out, all these souls will live on. This life is just the start of the journey, and that means Ludo has no need for restraint. Those he kills will have other chances at existence, so killing isn't even worth worrying about.

He packs away his works neatly and wipes the drool from his lips.

The phone rings.

'Yeah.'

Some drone.

'The magician is back. He's downtown somewhere eastside.'

'What's he doing?'

'Moving. Quickly. He's good. Too good for any of our bullshit street-mages.'

Ludo knows better than to try Lark in his house without serious back-up. But the blanco prick is a loose end. The Old Man is throwing cash around; he can spend a bit more. Ludo has discretionary funds and it's time to spend some.

'I'm going to have him taken care of with outsourcers.'

'Fine.'

Ludo makes a call and sets up the meet. He needs a killer and a very, very good one. He'll sort that out at dawn. Right now, his car pulls up at the old depot. There's some of the crew, pulled up around the chain link fence.

'Jeffe, hey.'

Looking over at Tick, a former crack-head granted transcendence through the rock, Ludo shudders. The man's human rubbish, a collection of failures under a stained suitcoat. The Old Man likes his grotesques, but Tick is a surprisingly good magician, so Ludo copes.

'Don't go in there. There's something in there.'

'What?'

'Something bad.'

Ludo shrugs. 'Noriko!'

The Japanese strolls over from the tight batch of first responders, the Old Man's eyes and ears.

'Go in there. You're looking for weird graffiti. See signs of inhabitancy, speed dial.'

She strolls through the car park and into the depot, through the fence. They wait fifteen, twenty, quiet in the cold night air, staring at each other made pale under buzzing white lamps.

Then Noriko comes back. Ludo sees her damage through his worked glasses immediately.

'What the fuck?'

'You must be Ludo.' And it isn't Noriko's voice. It's a teenage girl's voice. And something else. Something slides into her syllables like a shark slides into a pool. Too much danger. Ludo doesn't fuck around. He takes out his knife and quickly slits her throat.

She dies staring up at him curiously. Tries to talk but there's just a nasty sucking sound where her trachea is split like the Old Man's lips. The blood is black on the asphalt.

Ludo curses his instincts as ideas light up deep in his great bone head. Like watching a bombing run from a distance.

'New plan.' announces Ludo. He's wary of the Wick girl now.

'We'll bring her to us.'

III

WICK IS CURIOUS.

'Who is the Old Man?'

The voice is silent. Then petulant. *Just another human with mastery on his mind.*

Wick frowns. 'I don't like him.'

He'll like you.

'Who is Ludo and why is he in my old place?'

Let's go and see him. Let me show you one of my gifts to you.

24

I

Ten years I've been in my place and I've not been lazy.
Written wards and glyphs on street lamps and dumpsters in
permanent marker. Made my marks in wet sidewalk cement,
disguised as lover's nonsense. Abandoned offices I've broken
into, leaving runes and rhymes in dust on windows, more
potent for their flimsiness.

Sitting in the back of a bar, watching a cigarette burn
down in the ashtray, moving my consciousness from node to
node. There's a man watching my house, but I don't sense any
training. He's just a guy someone paid off. Kinda insulting, to
be honest.

Wait until he's bored, running pornographic fantasies
through his head, then I slip the eregore into his head.
Imagine it in the form of a Struwwelpeter puppet, creeping
scissor man nightmare, cutting as it goes, and soon his
nervous system is haunted as any house. He becomes forget-

ful. If he's working for some cult, they should have sent a player. The guy gets confused and walks away.

That's one watcher down, and I want into my house.

But there's someone else. From an alley, I look carefully.

There's a car, waiting across the road from the alley I use to get into my place. A man in there, watching my place. Eating a burger. Waiting. Nothing magic on or about him. No thoughts of a gun, but that doesn't mean he's not carrying.

Pull up my jacket collar, pay the tab with my last cash, and hit the street to eyeball him, standing in the last of the sun so he'll have to blink into the light. I don't smoke.

Someone's put protections over them, but... it's a terrible job. A first timer, who couldn't or didn't concentrate. Who couldn't hit the right state of mind to fire up their spell. Weaksauce.

'Mr. Lark.'

A voice behind me. Turn slow, as you never know if there's a gun or knife in the fist of who's tracking you, time like this. A woman, a blonde, in a suit. Hair up. Cheekbones and *sangfroid*.

Cop written all over her.

So focused on the Old Man and magic I didn't even bother to look with my eyes. *Amateur*.

'I'm Agent Valier of the Department of Civil Security.'

Car door opens and out comes a black man with a friendly, boring face and a geography teacher's moustache.

'That's my partner, Agent Coffee. We'd like to ask you a few questions at our office.'

Look at the woman very closely.

Spooks. Not just cops but G-men. Government agents. Spooks.

Did not see this coming.

Working for the Old Man? No. Not with the shit magic they're hiding under.

Curious enough to say yes. Let's go play with Dick Tracy, then.

We drive past the woman who's following me. She's in a phone booth, already calling it in. She's sloppy.

II

THEY'RE TOO AMATEURISH. I CAN'T BELIEVE IT. YOU THINK OF secretive government agencies as congeries of hyper-competent, sinister shadowmen, not government bureaucrats running out the clock day after day, covering their own arses.

They can't be here about the weird stuff.

I'm in an office, all plastic cheap-assemble furniture, under a oppressive white fluoro – too bright. It's all humming computers, phones and depressing pictures of families tacked to cubicle walls. There's even a cartoon gently and toothlessly poking fun of bureaucracy that Coffee's pinned up.

There's another guy typing in a room of about twelve of these sad little hutches. He's taken off his tie and he's wearing stained yellow shirtsleeves. He looks over at me without much interest.

The building they brought me to was a bland mid-town thing, new and charmless, although we came through serious security doors to get here. There's a flag on display in the lobby and an armed guard.

But inside, it could be any office in any industry. Accountants or charity-workers.

Take out a smoke and Coffee mock-frowns at me.

'Sorry, no smoking in government buildings.' He points a finger up to the roof.

'Fire alarm. Besides, I'm a little asthmatic. About five per cent over the line. Never had an attack, but who wants to risk it?'

He continues talking, but he's sizing me up.

Wrong kind of smoke, but I don't say anything. I keep it in my mouth and idly ply my finger across the desk. Here's why I think they're amateurs. Using the grease from my fingers, I sketch out a No Smoking sign on one of the three small desks that line his bay, you know the one. Big red line through a dark circle.

Then, I carefully wipe away the line. Draw big circle for face, little circle for mouth. Stare at it. Let it into my mind. Keep it there, then, with a word, let it out of my mouth and into the world. I light up. He doesn't notice. Is he bluffing? Valier walks over, takes a seat and says nothing. I blow smoke into Coffee's face but he just waves it away.

Their protections are that terrible they can't even pick up on this sort of conjure charm.

Take his coffee mug, ash into it. Waiting.

Not just being a dick. Need to see what they'll put up with.

Agent Valier sips at her herbal tea. She's a good-looking woman. Sharp haircut and fashionable frames on reading glasses she's looking over. Rich girl, you can tell it. The pale fingernails, the cut and material of her suit. Coffee's just some guy, fell into this work.

Or he's real good at giving that impression.

She waits for Coffee to stop talking about his childhood maladies and then puts down her cup. Takes out a manila folder.

'Mr. Lark. We've invited you in here to talk to us. This is informal. This is not an arrest or an interrogation. We just want to talk to someone who might give us insight into a case we are working on.'

'Yeah.'

'Do you know a Mr. Brandon River?' She's formal now.

'No.' I don't.

'Do you know a Nell Jeancat?'

Yes. She's probably hiding from me and she tried to have me whacked about three days ago. 'No.'

'Do you know a Mr. Nathan Ludovitch?'

OK. I'll bite. I should deny everything, of course. That's the smart thing. But they know I know something and I'm not afraid of being arrested. I'm afraid of Ludo and the Old Man ripping me up. I'm afraid of Primal Magic.

'I know who that is.'

They glance at each other. I think they were expecting me to play the silence.

'Do you know a man by the name of Mully?'

'No.' OK, that's good.

'Do you know a Mrs. Sandra Saunders?'

Actually. I know the name but can't place it. This is why I record everything.

'That name is familiar.'

'Can you recognise any of these objects?'

Eight by tens. Hands them across one by one. A lamp. Tongs. A book in Arabic or maybe Urdu, jewels in the cover. Hookah. A scroll case. A curving sword.

A scroll case.

And we all got given an order. Look for a scroll case. That's what we're going to reward our ally Ludo with.

'This.'

'Have you seen the item?'

'No, but I know who is looking for it.'

I study the scroll case, but there's nothing special about it from the photo. Except. It's sealed in wax with what may be some sigil, some expression of magical intent. It's hard to get readings off photos. But I think I recognise the style.

First, I've got a choice to make. These guys, they can get guns and arrests together. I could point them at Ludo and get his ass jailed or dead. But something tells me, hapless like they are, I could be feeding them to sharks. So I listen, hoping they'll give me a clue as how to treat them.

'How do you know who I am?'

They stare at me. This is what they're good at, keeping the questions flowing downstream from them.

'We're the government, Mr. Lark. We know lots of things.'

'Not about me.'

And it's true. Lark isn't my name and hasn't been it for a long time. My original birth certificate, me and Jon got rid of those years ago. The Library hooked us up with three or four different people to be. I don't pay utilities and, as far as my landlord knows, he has a derelict apartment he's going to fix up one day. So the government can't come at me that way.

'Come on, Mr. Lark. You're a well-known man in certain communities in the city.'

Coffee is grinning and it says that he's my friend.

Which is a lie.

'Who told you about me?'

They don't notice my index finger on my jeans moving slowly side to side, like I imagine a rattle snake moves its tail to hypnotise. They don't notice the measured way I talk.

'People.'

'I want a lawyer.'

Or the bullshit clichés I spout. I want a lawyer. *I know this isn't the police.* But they have heard this kind of thing before and it creates a chain of responses.

'We aren't police. We just want to talk.'

And I hum my sutras, relaxing myself, growing uneasy. It's not as easy as it should be.

'I know my rights.'

'We aren't violating your rights, Mr. Lark. This is an informal discussion to aid us in ongoing investigations.'

And there, I get them. They're not thinking, they're just trying to calm down a would-be human asset who's gone squirrelly. So I slip my agents into them and suddenly, they're trusting me. I *am* doing them a big favour.

While they talk at me, I am on their computer. They are logged in. I print things out. I should have one of those little disc things, UDS or whatever. Ain't good with computers.

The other agent, tieless, watches me with alarm, unable to think why. But he's much less of a challenge. Jim, thirty eight addicted to transsexual internet pornography and a Billy Joel fan. I go through him like a fucking buzzsaw.

'Mr. Lark,' goes Coffee, 'We've been monitoring certain elements amongst the religious community of the city for some time. Your name has come up as a respected individual. We reach out to you because,' he stumbles. The spell is compelling something he doesn't want to share. I could jinx him into spilling everything but I don't want to push him too far.

'...because we've had very little success creating assets within this community. We figured we'd come to you directly.'

I sit back. Sip at my coffee.

'Let's start from the top.'

III

. . .

IN 1991, BY MARCH, THE UNITED STATES HAD SEIZED IRAQ. They didn't stay for long that time. No point. But a soldier by the name of Danny Tran was there. He came as Staff Sergeant, leading a rifle team. While he was in-country, he happened upon a small museum. This wasn't the vast National Museum of Iraq that would suffer outrages upon its honour a decade later. No. This was a scholar's place, out of the way and quiet and of no interest to those who sought out sphinxes and gold. Three floors of important documents where classicists and professors could come to study. To Staff Sergeant Danny Tran, it was three storeys of cool, cream air-conditioned sandstone in an out-of-the way place. An *Ulama* ran this place and kept it spotless and welcoming and as free from politics as was possible. He had wept and kissed his children the day the bomb failed to explode after landing ten feet from its doors. This place wasn't about politics, just the past.

Danny Tran found a scroll. The *Ulama* was the only person in the building, and he was disinclined to say 'no' to an American soldier that day. So Danny Tran, who, to be fair, had no idea he was intruding into the stacks, never knew he shouldn't have unsealed the scroll. He read it. It turned something on in his brain and he left that place with a black fire in his head.

Staff Sergeant Danny Tran later threw himself under a truck. A truck he had heavily graffitied the night before.

Danny Tran's father was an intelligence officer for the United States Army. He was a smart man and refused to believe his son would kill himself. Mr. Tran was not blind to the life of a soldier, nor was he an optimistic man. He recognised that the right mix of aggression and egotism in his boy simply made that kind of breakdown unlikely.

Mr. Tran was a twenty-five-year veteran. He'd met many, many people in his career. Mr. Tran was known to be a champion of interdepartmental co-operation and had a reputation as a man who got things done. He should have risen higher in his career, but he simply lacked the social skills and the cannibal politicking genes. But he had made peace with that, and many who had climbed over him remembered him fondly, aware he was no threat to seniority and willing to cut him a break.

Nor did Mr. Tran ever forget the strange manner of his son's death.

And so, finally, during an international conference on religious terrorism, he immediately recognised people who could help him when the Department of Civil Defence (Religious Division) gave a speech on radical dogma amongst terrorist cells.

Agent Valier gave that speech. DCD (RD) golden girl. Twenty-four. Higher degrees in languages and philosophy, with minors in anthropology and religious studies.

Her presentation, in a small, dull white room, was fascinating to Mr. Tran. Agent Valier was trained to recognise heresies and cults in what the West considered foreign religions. She was discovering that the West had little to fear from these organisations, who preferred to prey upon their own religions. Buddhist or Muslim or Orthodox Christian, they all had renegades and rogues, who created cults from apocrypha and anger and chemicals. Schisms and sectarianism was rife in the apparently implacable, overwhelming endless war.

Mr. Tran recognised one of her slides. A similar pictograph to what Danny had drawn on the truck he'd hurled himself under. From 1832, the early days of some death-religion had used a similar sigil as their symbol.

They spoke.

Tracking Danny's movement had been fairly easy. His unit had remembered the Museum well. It had been a memorable day after all. The man walked in sane and walked out fucking crazy.

Agent Valier tracked down the Museum and, after weeks of waiting, an Arabic translator was assigned. She wrote to the Library, using her academic credentials, asking for a catalogue. Which was duly given her.

Confirmation.

The Scroll.

In the tenth century, a wandering holy man had been in Medina, where he had encountered a sorcerer. The sorcerer was going against the will of God and dealing with terrible forces. Some satanic creature from outside the world.

The holy man prayed for three days and nights, fasting, until God granted him an answer.

The holy man was a scribe by trade, a learned man whose calligraphy was admired by princes and artists and scholars alike. He could write in ten languages and had command of esoteric power granted by the most high. He confronted the sorcerer and God put a commandment on the black magician to tell everything he knew about the devil-thing he'd conjured. The holy scribe wrote it all down, creating a new language to capture such blasphemy, unwilling to sully the letters of men with this evil.

When he was finished, the devil realised its entire being was there on that scroll and had no choice but to inhabit this new language, trapped within it for all time.

IV

. . .

'THAT'S A PRETTY STORY, AGENT VALIER.'

'Yes. Isn't it.'

'Turns out it's more than a pretty story. By two thousand three, we'd discovered that many fringe groups were interested in the scroll, which had been preserved and traditionally linked with that narrative.'

'I never heard of it.'

The Library might have.

'So we tried to retrieve it. When we joined the Coalition of the Willing, I was in a position to have agents on the ground find it. It had powerful fetishistic and symbolic properties for any number of fringe groups.'

'Please don't bore me with government phobias of madmen with beards.'

She frowns. 'It's not like that.'

'What's it like?'

'Danny Tran's story was famous among certain army circles, and photos of the weird things he wrote on that truck got around. In time, they came to the attention of one Sandra Saunders, whose brother-in-law was Colonel William Soot.'

'Skip to the end. No. Wait. Sandra Saunders?'

'Yes.'

It hits me. She was Gallowglass. High up. Old money with a passion for antiques. Worshipped money, literally, like it was the biggest ghost haunting the world.

'She found out about the scroll.'

'Yes. And while I was looking for it in Iraq, she had the damn thing stolen and smuggled to the city.'

Where the Old Man, ten years later, found out about it and came for it.

What's written on that thing?

I get up. 'I have to go.'

'Do you know the whereabouts of Sandra Saunders?'

I look at Valier. The spell is straining at her. I can feel the hostility. I have to give her something or risk it snapping and them freaking out about their sudden urge to talk.

'She's dead. I don't know where the scroll is.'

'How do you know this, Mr. Lark?'

It's Coffee. He's risen. I take a step back. He's staring at Valier. Clearly, she's acting out of character and it's spooked him out of the jinx.

'You two. Listen. Something bad is happening. That scroll is... something bad is written on it. Leave it alone. Leave it to me.'

Jim, tieless, is coming back. He's got something in his pocket, too small to be a pistol, so I'm thinking taser or pepper spray. Shit. I take another step back. Spread my hands. Valier flanks me, preventing me getting to the door.

'What did you do to us?'

I guess I leaned on the talking conjure way too hard after all.

Bit of the Ultrascorpion then. I whisper a word I invented long ago. I wrote it out in pain and keep it close. They curse, feeling hooks in their spirits and then cry out. It just hurts, phantom trains on the nervous tracks. Doesn't damage. But it's enough.

I'm gone, out the door, giving the armed guard some of the same and taking his key. I'm out of the elevator and free of the heavy glass doors by the time they follow me, having taken the fire stairs down. No guns out, but the woman has a taser and no mistake this time. Two fingers for her. Hah, hah motherfuckers. Can't catch me.

Disappearing is easy. I just concentrate and convince them not to be there. Flag a cab and pay him with coins, much to everyone's annoyance. The house is still clear.

So good to be home. I lock the door and put a stack of heavy art books up against it. No one is coming in.

I collapse. Three in the morning. I should turn on the lights but I'm worn.

Spooks. Jesus. This is getting interesting.

And I think about the scroll. And I think about the timing.

It had been with Gallowglass for nearly ten years and they never knew what they had. Or if they did, never used it. Why would the Old Man come for it now?

Why now? What signal lit up in his mad dog brain? What meshed together his sick, frayed dendrites?

I start. A sound. Wild and high.

My phone.

Answer.

'Hello Scarlet.'

25

I

Here's a confession.

Ten years with Scarlet. Twenty to thirty.

The first three, pure. She came up from her people in the swamps and turned herself into the country girl with the rockabilly edge, in tiny short and booted to the knee, cowboy hats and dancing till dawn, kisses hot as fever.

Sex and drugs. Never seemed to stop being *thirsty* for her. Never tired of her. Addicted to her.

And to magic.

I'd just joined the Library and, in that first year, she encouraged me to attempt adeptship. And when I was put on a Retrieval team, she laughed and bought me a hundred-dollar bottle of tequila neither of us could afford, and we took peyote in the park.

That second year, she joined as well. An initiate but curious about her parents' own traditions, she joined and never looked back. Hers was a study of earthy magic, close to the world, Vesta and the Freya became her gods for a small while. She'd go dancing with Jon and slide into bed at dawn, sweaty and exhausted and shining, hungry for me, just for me.

Then the work got serious.

I got promoted and became the head of Retrievals, which meant I had a full-time job, as the Library salaries certain positions.

Was out of town one week out of five. Globe-trotting and like that.

The golden years for me and Jon. Drinking in exotic bars, sharing techniques with Libraries across the planet, training under some of the greatest magicians in the world. The Europeans, who viewed us with curiosity, and the Americans, who loved our accents, and the Asians, who thought us hopelessly bound up with dogma.

Brilliant cases, like when we joined up with five Retrieval teams to deal with the kraken-finger. The Oslo Working, with the bronze tiger in a park full of junkies. Jon doing a duet karaoke version of *It's a Family Affair* by Sly and the Family Stone with a Bodhisattva in a bar in Taipei.

And the phone calls to Scarlet in bland hotel rooms, where I was so lonely I might as well have been a sheet of white paper.

Got back one night and she was gone. Tracked her down and she told me should couldn't handle the distance between us. The danger of my work. Told me it was getting harder for her to say no to the men who asked her out to dinner, just to dine with another face to look at.

Bad days. Two-month break up. Reconcile. Three months later, back together. Should have seen her going coming but you never do.

Do you?

Memories: Mully coming to see us as we cleaned up madly, airing the place out of cigarette smells and quickly hiding the empty bottles. Her cousins, twins, coming to stay, and me scoring them weed. Uncanny pair, them. Sacred to Scarlet's family. Their first time stoned, on a casual *rumspringa*, a disaster as they became paranoid and sick, their second a night filled with laughter and stories and ending with me making her mix tapes.

Scarlet kissing me the night they left, thanking me for being kind.

'I know that's not easy for you, just talking. I'm glad you tried.'

A life. A life together. Gone, now. Gone fucking where?

But work called me overseas again, soon enough.

And while I was gone, Scarlet volunteered in the Library. Archivists are at a premium in our, *that*, organisation and she showed a talent for organisation that surprised her. Both of us were lucky to join at a time that a lot of the old guard had died, or were looking to put down their duties.

She continued to work for the Library until they offered her a job overseas but not me. Library is one of the biggest occult orders in the world. There's money.

Tense time. She was tempted. But we stayed.

She asks me about children, for real. Brush her off, not taking her serious. She quits smoking. Tries to have the conversation again. Shut her down. There's no fucking way.

I refuse to perform an execution on some mad old woman with a talent for wrangling ghosts and she has me formally censured. We don't talk for a week.

Then Jon got taken by the Hollow. Nine years and six months. I walk out of the Black City alone, wounded, terrified. Library scrambles team but the Hollow can hide in a klieg light. One of the Retrievals team finds him. We assume.

Because we find his body sliced apart.

Jon makes no attempt to hide it was him.

Extreme caution is called on the search. A week goes by. A month. Upstairs downgrades the hunt.

SPEND MY DAYS FIGHTING WITH THEM. ONLY WAY I CAN HURT them, punish them, is to stop teaching. (And, telling it true, I freak out at teaching the new blood. Don't want them carved up like Jon carved up that Retriever.)

Find myself acting cruel when the sheriff job starts up again. Set the Ultrascorpions on people like they were hounds. They find me another partner but what good is that? A whole other headache story.

Jon is out there, getting eaten away. I sober up. Present my case to the Library. I need a team to hunt down the Hollow and I need the resources of the whole damn Chapter to help me destroy it. It's world-league hoodoo, the Hollow. Probably have to invite in top Retrievals from other Chapters.

They say no. Scarlet, in her suit, tells me after the Assembly, 'He's too dangerous and we need you. We don't think you can defeat the Hollow. At least not yet. Your work is suffering at the moment. We'll study it, find a way. But we need you back at work and back on form. Put it behind you. That's an order.'

Put it behind you.

That's an order.

Standing there in front of them, in the cool marble room, I say to them 'I've given ten years of service. So did Jon. I've stood by as you've turned my job into being the secret police, instead of looking for legitimate occult threats. In that time, I've petitioned the Library for exactly no favours or rewards. I'm telling you. I'm begging you. We have to help him.'

Everett, working his way up to secretary to the Librarian General, behind the big desk, shakes his head.

'The answer is no, Lark. No.'

Hand them the resignation letter that I'd written up a few days before and leave the audience room without remark.

Scarlet met me at a bar. Didn't want to talk in private. Told me I needed to rethink leaving.

'I'm not coming back, Scarlet. I don't want to be a headkicker. They hung Jon out to dry. I don't trust Upstairs. They let Jon fall. Think I can rely on them? Think they'll get my back?'

'We need a headkicker more than ever.'

'Don't want to be a headkicker.'

'Sometimes you just have to do what needs doing.'

'No.'

I think she's a scary fascist, she thinks I'm an ungrateful shirker. Just give up on myself in those days. Ratty beard. Put on beer weight like a motherfucker.

Wasn't entirely surprised when I scry her and Everett's first kiss. The panicky relief when I saw her push him away, tell him she was in love with me and needed to give me one more chance.

'Look at us, Lark' she says behind a mask of tears and makeup.

'Look at you.' Sweat pants and a beer belly. Unshaven and quivering with anger.

Go silent. Sadness and despair takes words from me.

Go out drinking. Come back and the flat was empty.

She didn't leave a note. She knew I knew.

Now I have to take orders from her.

26

I

'WHAT DID YOU TELL THEM?' FIERCENESS IN SCARLET'S VOICE.

'It's three-thirty in the morning. Aren't you up past your bed time?'

'I have standing orders to be woken up if those government dick- er, agents, get involved with my people. We've been wary of them for a while.'

Stopped herself swearing. Someone listening in?

'Your people. Am I one of your people?'

'For now you are. Enough of one that I'm not willing to let those fucking G-men near you.

We've got an eregore in their building. It's slow and it took a while to rescue you. It set the bells ringing. Now what did they tell you?'

Rescue?

'Who are they, baby?' Listen in to that.

Get up, put together a coffee. Voice tight and angry, she

says it again. 'What did you tell them?' She's not playing. This is stressing her and she wants to lash out, but she knows that's not the percentage move. Don't call her baby.

'Scarlett. Relax. They didn't get anything from me. They had no game, no skills. They had the most rudimentary protections ever. I just kept telling them I didn't know anything, that I'd been out of the game for years and they had the wrong guy.'

How did they know who I was? Puzzle that out later.

'Are you... are you alright?'

'I'm fine.'

'You ran out of there.'

'How much time do you spend watching me?'

'I get reports on that place.'

'Why?'

She sighs. She knows that I get answers or I don't play at all. But she's biting impatient.

'About eighteen months ago, there was some government task force on cult activities. Now, we know that usually means they arrest a guy who starts a website saying he's like Jesus but sexier. Fair enough?'

'Sure.'

'Not the woman. She's sensed blood in the water. She's looking at people with real knowledge.'

'People like you?'

'No. Not yet. But she's seen some things.'

'Agent Valier. That's her name.'

'Yes. But I don't need spooks running around muddying things up. Not now. Not with everything going on.'

I cut to it. 'Listen, go downtown to the closed-up depot. Send whoever you trust. This job is wild.'

'The depot. Done.' I hear her writing something down.

She's so worried she doesn't even care she's as good as told me she's having me traced. I finish my coffee, move into the bedroom, looking to change socks.

Oh fuck.

'Scarlet. I have to go.'

'No, I need to- ' She's furious, but I've got bigger problems. I switch off the phone. Jesus. Jesus.

An Ultrascorpion. Dead. Flensed. Laying on the floor.

I call up my most dangerous spells, but I'm tired. I've been in and out of meditation all day. It wears you out. But something *deadly* is in my house.

'Hello Lark.'

A silky voice. A hand pats me down, looking for weapons. I'm not breathing, fear-static in my head. I turn. Everything goes very still. Somewhere, a clock ticks a death.

'Hello Jon.'

The Hollow.

II

YOU NEED TO UNDERSTAND, I WAS A MESS. JON WAS GONE, LOST to a void I couldn't understand. Scarlet left me for another man. I was out of the Library and had no money, no path ahead. Endless hours on a bed, smoking, throwing playing cards up at the roof and smoking dope.

Curiosity. Lured me out. I went into the study and separated out the books I wanted. Burned up favours with Lin, looking for more. Hat in hand to cults I knew I'd done right by. Spending times in their sanctums and temples and club-houses.

Masks, murder-magic, cross-referencing. It took weeks

and kept me focused. I was at it for thirty hours straight one shift.

Finally, a lead in the stacks of the city reading room, in grey cement under flickering lights, while the workers I didn't bribe or glamour gave me dirty looks. That led me to a book written in the thirties by a particularly racist African explorer. All that was left was an old paperback that stunk of mould.

'AMONGST THE TRIBESMEN I FOUND AN ADORATION FOR A MASK of dark wood, lacquered by a dozen generations with something not unlike a sweet-scented linseed oil. The mask itself was considered something like a God, and the men of the tribe treated it with a superstitious awe. Only the witch doctors were allowed to gaze upon it, and then only briefly and under the light a midday sun. My guide, a very proper fellow educated by French missionaries, begged us to leave this place, as the mask they venerated was considered a devil by their neighbours. Our guide, a strict Catholic, seemed scandalised by the entire affair. However, I managed to recruit him as dragoman while I spoke to the headman.

It seems the mask is actually a kind bastion, a last line of defence, for the tribe. Should they be threatened by supernatural forces, one of their young warriors is chosen. He then goes into a hut and comes out, having donned the mask. This takes away the divine spirit all living things have and leaves him a shell, easily filled up by hostile spirits. A quaint superstition, although the headman seemed as serious as one of his race could. I asked to see the mask, but they rudely refused me. It was being worn currently. I asked to see the warrior. The headman terminated our interview, for the first time speaking. '*Il est creuses.*'

Kinglsey, Scott, <u>The Darkest Trails</u>, London. 2nd Ed, Flamingo Publishing, 1931

'He is hollow.'

From there, I had a clue and could focus on African traditions. Weirdly, this lead me to pre-Imperial China and the Hollow, because magic and mythology is like that. Some traditions linked the mask to Chi You, metal-faced enemy of the Yellow Emperor. Some say it was a weapon of the Dark Martiality. But no. Some human made the fucking thing. Some human. It took weeks to find this out.

I can find anything in weeks and I found this.

The Hollow prepares people. It harvests them. It empties them out of their bodies, leaving only a receptacle, an empty vessel. Not a parasite, not a wasp. Like a disease that bleeds you *of* you and rebuilds you as...

As what?

Something with a killer's tastes. Jon already enjoyed those appetites in his own way. And here he is, in my room.

He wears a slaughterman's apron, and the tools of that trade are strapped to his waist. Not looking at that.

Looking at the mask.

Bronze. Black. Not metal, not wood. The eyes burn with some sub-red, burning down in the bands and spectra humans aren't supposed to see. The sight of it, the underlight, provokes warnings in the head, confuses the eyes. Adrenaline and cortisol flood the body.

Want to run. He flensed an Ultrascorpion. Behind him, the others rustle, waiting, prepared to die rushing him.

Want to run, but know that will provoke him, a cat lured into its sadist play.

Butcher's knives. A meat hook at his belt.

'Been a while,' I say.

His face tilts. He looks me up and down.

'I wasn't sure it was you. Or if you were Lark. You are Lark, though.'

'For God's sake, Jon. You've been here a hundred times.' Hear the stress and fear in my voice. Shut my mouth. Try again. Can barely pitch it above a whisper. I want to remind him. *Jesus Jon, I left the Library when they wouldn't let me help you! It was my last straw! I begged them.* Pointless. It would be like asking an angel to thank it for stealing its halo.

'Of course I'm Lark. I'm your best friend, Jon.'

Use my real name. Use his.

'I'm not sure I'm Jon anymore. Is that a name I was? All that time seems like it happened to someone else. Someone smaller.' His voice is modified as it comes through the mask. It seems to echo before I hear it.

'Can I sit?'

Long time before he answers. 'Of course. Just don't be foolish.'

I sit on the bed. My corridor is a black mouth. Garbage bags line it. Oh fuck.

Light up. 'Want one?' No reply. Carefully, like an unfolding army knife, he sits on the floor. Back of the hands on his thighs.

'It's good to see you, Jon.'

'Is it?'

'Well, bad circumstances. But it's good to see you. You.'

'That's nice. I don't hear that often. Especially considering what I do when I meet people like this. Mostly.'

Smoke. Concentrate on it. Let the smoke work its alchemy in my lungs, taking peaceful blood into my skull. Forget the shakes.

When Jon moves, his apron creaks.

'Can I turn on a light, Jon?'

'No. I don't think so.'

Ever see Jon fight? I'd like to say he was all grace and fluid motion, but only people who never saw a fight say things like that. He was clockwork. Never missed a punch, and, when he hit you, you could see the force in it. He bit. He gouged. He took shots on his forearms to keep them from his gut, to throw knuckles into eyes. Hard to soft. He never punched the face, he elbowed it. Stomped foreheads on the concrete. Gouged. Cheated. But always quick and always winning.

Now his motions are jerky. Spastic. Too quick, like as if they were here, then there, without moving between. His special effects budget has no limit.

'Well, might as well get started.'

The Ultrascorpions lift their tails, silent imaginary chitins rasping. I raise a hand at them and Jon's head turns, purposeful, to regard them.

'Jon. For pity's sake,' I raise a hand to stop them. 'Just give me a moment. I'm not going anywhere and I won't fight.'

Now he looks at me and his humming eyes are intent. 'You could fight me, couldn't you? I think I might like that.'

Fear moves through me. Slow lightning. Impaled on it, but I reach for a no-mind state and finally, finally it eases from me, hovering though, eager to return to its host. I can fight him. I can hurt him. Not win, especially after the last few nights. I'll lose, but I know I have some strength here. It's meagre comfort, but I'll take it.

'We're friends. No need to fight. We've sat here before, us two. Let's take a minute.'

'I came here, yes. We talked. I believed in magic in those days. There was a girl with red hair.'

'Scarlet. For fuck's sake you were *friends*.'

He says nothing.

'She's gone. But she was here.'

'I'm glad she's gone. Killing you will be hard enough.'

'Can we talk a moment?'

'As Jon once did. Me. Yes. We can talk. But dismiss your eregores. They won't help you and I won't have my back threatened.' He's right. I do.

All alone.

'What shall we talk about?'

'Business or pleasure? Do you want a drink?'

Jon laughs. Clockwork horror. 'I have no mouth, Lark. How could I drink?'

'Take off the mask.' I've said this before. Over and over. He makes no response.

'Business, Lark. Let's talk business. The Teaching Darkness tells me the other is not germane.'

'The Old Man sent you?'

'I don't know. I was contacted by a man called Ludo. He was here recently. He offered you up as a sacrifice. How did he know the Jon host and you had the human bond?'

'You're gonna murder me on a contract hit?'

'Everyone is everyone's as far as the Teaching Darkness is concerned.'

The Old Man sent the most dangerous individual in the city after me. A man whose work is superlative and lethal. On short notice. He's desperate.

'You're better off out of this world, Lark. It's a fallen place and everything tastes like dust. Better to be dead and, if not dead, hollow like me.' He gestures to himself, his wrist rolling wildly.

'Hollow?'

'Just waiting. Getting filled up. Filled in. All the weak parts of you washed away, sluiced away, ground away, sanded away, worn away, blasted away, hosed away, chiselled away, bevelled away, picked away, torn away, eaten away, ripped away, eased away, prised away...'

He goes on.

The eyes go dark.

I switch meditation until my mind goes pixelated. I think four things.

I leave a thought here for Mully, leaving my thanks and letting him I know how much I respected him. If he wants to, he'll find it. I prepare the Ultrascorpions, thanking them for service and demanding kamikaze moves. I send a pulse of belief to the Omegamantis. In time, some other chancer may find it. Keep it. Understand it so its world of rusted iron and wire webs will live. And I think of Scarlet, imagine her, smiling at me in the sun. Then. Bones. Throw them.

'Fuck this.'

He looks up, startled.

'Jon, I don't care about the mask. You know what I think about it. You know I think you should *throw the fucking thing away*. You know all that. You know I think that just slicing people into strips is a waste of your talents. But by Christ, I'm not going to listen to you sit here and mutter like a goddamn motherfucking lunatic.'

He laughs.

'Provoking me?'

'Let's do it. Two mates gutting each other while a sick old cunt gets a clear run at whatever the bloody hell he's after. That's a laugh to his sort.'

He laughs again.

'I do remember you. You're a pain, and you always think you're right.'

'Only because I am. Well, nine times from ten.'

He goes quiet.

'Teaching Darkness says that it likes that. And yes, it understands perhaps it is manipulated. It is uninterested in teaching lessons of spite and fratricide. We'll spare you.'

'Will *you* spare me Jon?'

Then he stabs me but not with a knife.

'I follow Teaching Darkness and its lessons. If it said you die, you die.'

'...'

'Do you understand?'

'Sure.'

'But there's a price. You'll pay it in time. You're only alive to learn your own lessons.'

What's the point in keeping this going? He's just talking.

'Come on, man. What's it going to be? Are you going to listen to the demon thing wrapped around your head or are you going to talk to your best friend?'

He waits a minute.

'There's a contract on your life. I've accepted it.'

'Well,' and I can't help but show the bitter, 'better uphold your monetary contract.'

That gets him. He's quiet again for a bit.

'I'm not a hired killer. Well, I am, I suppose, but not for venal reasons. The Teaching Darkness requires certain things to maintain it. These things are purchased with money, and this is the easiest way to obtain such capital.'

Hands over my face. 'Jon, you're here to kill me for money. You're choosing to take my life for dollars in the bank. All we've been through together and it comes to this.'

I just sit there, too tired to be afraid. 'Don't tell me what you are and aren't.'

Look at him.

'You're right. We were friends. And perhaps my employer chooses to delight in setting friend against friend.'

'It's the sort of thing I reckon he'd like,' I say. 'Because of irony or some damn thing.'

Quiet again. His hand touches the mask, running over it like he was feeling it for the first time.

'I don't want to kill you. I just... where I am now, everything is like smoke, and it's so hard to care about things. It's teaching me things, Lark. And some of those things are hard to understand unless you're alone.'

Look up at him. Something's changed. Some condition has altered. His voice is less remote. Getting too close to him to watch that closely is a fucking suicide move.

'Then don't kill me. Don't let yourself be manipulated by some bastard. If you're really in some fucking murder-Samadhi, then stay pure. Don't wreck it all.'

And that's it. I'm done. That's all I have to say.

'I signed a contract.'

'I'm sick of hearing about it! Show me you're a thug with a gun, no different to whacking guys for dollars, or show me you're a friend, or show me you're above it all and that fucking mask on your head is good for more than killing, but do it now. I have things to do.'

His mind is made up shortly. I just grind out my smoke, light up another, determined to go out with a nicotine buzz if that's what it comes to.

Slowly, he uncurls. Stands over me. He extends his hand like it's a vestigial memory of friendship. I take it, feeling the awful strength in there. 'Friends.'

Then the mask is back.

'But if you are marked a second time, I do not think I can ignore it. That would be a fated thing. And we are truly working as agents of fate, now.'

Relief. Exhaustion. I'm too tired to hear more confessions from a mask.

'Thanks Jon. I'm glad we didn't fight. But you can fuck off out now.'

He gathers his slaughter-decorations and is quickly done. He moves to the top of the stairs.

'The Old Man, he'll commit atrocities upon you, if he finds you. I'd just murder you and it would hurt, but he's willing to mar your soul.'

'So I hear.'

'You hear. I don't think you understand.'

'Could be.'

He walks slowly down the stairs. The eyes flare down into wavelengths too low for human eyes.

'You have to go after him. If you mix it up with him, you have to walk past his glamours and go for him. Throat him.'

'Thank you, Jon. Thank the Hollow.'

He stops.

'That's not the Teaching Darkness. That's me. I told you I remembered you.'

He takes my doorknob and shifts it.

'It was nice to see you again, Lark.'

I'm in the dark. Smoking. I cough.

III

Primal magic on the street. G-men and women hunting us down. A sociopath who's hunted this city, spinning webs of sadism for a hundred years. A woman who locks me down every single goddamn time I try to show her she's made a mistake.

Primal magic can warp the world. Hurt us all. The Old Man can hand me my skin and marlin-spike my soul. Blah-blah. Threats.

I'm Lark.

Ten-year veteran.

My master could never bring the old bastard to heel, but I can. I survived the Hollow. I've lived through Ludo and his fat fists filled with malice. I've been face-to-face with a sorcery that existed before our universe exploded into matter.

Old Man. Ludo.

I'm going to *fucking have you.*

It's not just swagger. Sworn to Nemesis and working against grim fucking powers. You really gonna blame me if I'm needing to hypnotise myself into something a foolish fuck might call bravery.

Ludo, you're a lead pipe and I'll take you out in ways you never imagined. Your stupid little amulet, I'll sneak past it like a murder-shadow and rend you up and down.

And you, Old Man. You think one day we'll all live in the fire? Fuck it. *You first, you prick.*

Throat him.

Live in the fire?

Live in the fire.

I think I know what you want.

IV

BLAST FURNACE SHOWER. SHAVE DOWN TO THE SKIN. MIND SO icy my thoughts freeze up, crystallise. No meditation, just focus. *Throat him* floodlights the winter in my head. Blue jeans black jacket grey hood. Good look. I make it work.

Fingerless gloves. From under my desk, the big black antique doctor's bag. Open it, check my gear is there. Needles, playing cards and tarot. Books, notes, emergency sigils, herbs, dice. A pen knife, a shotglass, a rare coin and a drumstick wand. Like that. Whatever you might need.

Into the street and heading down to the depot with a plan to witness the sigil.

Take the scent.

Lockjaw pain just from glancing.

Bettina said the city had bad dreams. Said something's wrong in the ground. Then she ran. Clever woman. Said it was like mercury in the ground. Sure. Pollution.

There's a technique. Jon used to like watching me do it. The treadless path. Freefall hallucination. Lose my head in magic.

The shaman walk.

Soldiers at the depot. I wrap myself up in mystery thoughts. Shadow thoughts. I walked away from Jon the Hollow and I can walk my way through you. Then I protect myself. Hiding in plain sight, in the shadows amongst the cars and the gunmen, I ease down. I am aware, but make no choices. Simply wait. I allow myself to think of the Primal Working and then to obsess on it. I inoculate my thinking against it, letting it bite me with its potency and venoms.

Then, my mind slow and guarded, I whisper all the words I've given so much time to. Words I've hand-crafted and lathed. Protection words. Phrases hobbled together from Latin and Greek, heavy with the authority of antiquity. Alien words from Hindi and Urdu. Gutter threats. Apotropaic words.

Cull up prophylactic imagery. Eyes and pentagrams. Razor-wire wards. Sluice gates, ablative jinxes. All of it. This is it. Protected as it gets. Occult bomb suit, NBC, magic fucking armour.

I walk through them all, the four or five soldiers who lurk who in the predawn light.

Look at the Primal Sigil.

Still-minded. Protected. I reel. It lands heavy. Hits my mind like a wrecking ball into a pool. Terrible pataphysics. Rabid ideas, hunting down good red sanity.

But I'm ready. I look at it. Long strands of letters that writhe with potency. It feels like cancer of the sanity, but I'm not sane. Magician, at the height of power. Wrapped up in a freefall hallucination. I let it wash over me and

(Teeth hurt. Gum bleed)

I get the spoor

(Every image of every humiliation rushes up the pit)

the scent of

(Bruises blossom. Serotonin surge. Want to stop and weep)

the Scroll.

Cloning itself, metropolitan virus, consuming, transforming.

Walk away, tasting blood in my mouth.

I have a language and the syllables to describe it. And that's what this Sigil is. A phrasing. A living story. Now I just need to find it. Place my thoughts into shaman territory and wander. Trust the magic will guide me to what I need to see, not what I want.

Trying not to think about the leg and its paining.

Walking now, half there watching, half dreaming. Under the city's skin and drinking its blood, it's secrets spilling out. Whispering things to me.

. . .

V

THE SEWER WHERE THEY DUMPED THE BODY OF THE HOLY FOOL, the homeless man. His body sat up and staring performing under dark miracles for rat and bat and alley cat. The swing set for the children that had a strangler's passions. The devil-thing, given to protecting the innocent by taking their hearts for safekeeping, taking the shape of an old man street-sweeping, who murdered with a smile. The funeral museum, the black building visited by the morbid or the hipster-cruel or the daring morbid, staffed by shadows and waxen hunters.

The killer's nest, a plain-sight dumping ground that's the city's garbage barges, staffed by grateful necrophiles. The outreach clinic, staffed by cynics, bodies come and bodies go and necromancers pay tips. Water towers, whose gods are birds, humming with powers. Shop windows made crystal in the winter. Scrying pools of broken glass. Light reflects off them, gives up truth, until the spectrums splinter and the dried blood's just a bonus. The vending machines that howl. The digging machines that dig into kobold holds. Gambling machines summoning stochastic spirits. Computing machines, making dimensions from numbers. Espresso machines, pumping false-life into the deserve-to-be-dead. Streets sign sigils, road side runes, jailhouse jinxes, suburb spells, visible on my shaman trail.

The tomb for the living, where prisoners of police and politics and poverty pound out summoning screams to spirits. The piano graveyard, down by Avenue X, the dog hunting zone by Avenue Y, where the beasts pray to their Feral King to restore their dignity, and the taxi ghost that prowls Avenue Z for redemption. The hookers who pray to whore god Lady P'an if they know her name or not, the postal workers who pray to do the work of Mercury and Apollo, with resentment, and the barmen who minister to the lonely with the zealousness of Christ. A traitor under torture, the city groans and shows its bones and I see every inch.

I see it all. I walk it all. The magic is taking me places, letting me see the divine that burns in all objects, in every two-leg human monster, in each concrete stain on every jacket and every drop of blood on every shard of glass in every filthy gutter.

Should I see wonder in this city, separate from the magic? Immigrants beaten and used condoms outside my door and cops beating children. Ask me why I wanted magic.

And I am a sorcerer. The mediation between these worlds is my true work. Behind the atomising veil of my meditation, I see that I am righteous to set myself against the Old Man.

But not fucking smart.

Then I see the writing, the letters in the true tongue of fire. The Sigil, my feet more sure than my mind, has brought me the trail.

I'm on track.

I'm coming.

I nearly drop meditation. Nearly lose all my wards and wards, which would leave me a fingerless man clutching shells.

I want to laugh like a drain. But I can't.

See, it's *in* the city. It's a memetic invasion, an idea that replicates through words. That breeds with each syllable. A phrase with an obsession for life. And I can read it. A warning. A claim. It says:

'Rejoice, for I am born anew.'

And it says, 'This place is Archonic.'

And I know what *It* is.

And I know what *It's* doing.

I get away from the tag, drop the wards, see it as normal people see it. A lurid graffiti tag that hookworm burrows into your eye and writhes.

27

———

I

Fucking hell.

This really couldn't get worse.

No exaggeration.

Sitting in a bar, eating a hamburger. It sucks. Chlorine in my eyes, so tired. The beer sign in neon is pissing me off, and the guys playing pool are calling each other 'fag' too loudly. It's three in the morning, and this is my job now. There's no one left in the Library who can do this shit, and I don't trust anyone to do it anyway.

See, it's an Archon.

Way back, I said that magic works best on the human mind. The human imagination. Want a God or a spirit? Dream it up. There's no easier, no better or stronger place it exists than the inside of your skull. The best gods, the best magic, are you just expressing yourself and your desires.

It's why I can't spit-roast bastards on the spot or magic myself up a bullet proof undershirt. At least, not without massive effort, massive time, massive resources. Like the Ultrascorpions. They can act in the real world, in a limited range; a limited way, only because it took me five years' work to make them real.

And, honestly, if I wanted to kill someone, why not hoodoo them into suicide? What's even easier than that? Two in the head. Poison in their gin. Pillow case suffocation.

But that's not the whole story. See, best I figure it, could be wrong here, don't quote, magic is pretty much a microcosm of a bigger set of rules. A physics our physics works in. Some people think magic lets you break physical laws. I think that sometimes, you get it to work according a higher principle. Metaphysics in the purest term. Mully uses the term pataphysics, but I reckon that's as one of his private jokes. Still, good term.

Easier one? Primal magic.

The stuff that punches out our rules, our reality. The True Science. Fucking hell, people love giving it names. The Tongue of Fire. The Secret Flame. Blah-blah. Just take my word for it, yeah?

So if there's a pataphysics. There's pataphysicians.

Entities from outside our world. Our reality. Don't believe me? Talk to a scientist. Quantum fucking cosmologist. Whatever they're called. Ask 'em if the universe has an end. Bet they'll say no. But they're wrong. There's places a human mind simply cannot go. Places that scoff at our understanding of physical reality. And that's where they live. The End.

We got a million names for 'em. Most common these days is Archons. Bit of a shout-out to our Gnostic forebears who knew a thing or two about magic. Creatures halfway between God and human. Half omnipotent, although I can't even figure that phrase out. But call 'em Aeons, call em Demon Princes, call 'em superbastards from beyond the speed of light. They exist in a world that's somehow *more* than ours. Bigger. Ice to our water. And when they get in here, it's fun time. Everything is so simple here and they are powerful in so many ways. Who wouldn't want to beat up the little kids?

But they can't just beam down from the fucking mother ship. They need time. Materials. A good, still reality.

That's what the tags are all about, the painted symbols. It's replicating some part of itself, using language as a medium. It's getting born – word by word – and getting bigger. Whoever sees the tags is, well, they're fucked. And it's warning off other Archons, too. It plans for a long stay. It plans to become the City. To *become* it.

More questions unanswered. Why language? Why now? What's the Old Man want?

II

THE GRAFFITI TAGS ARE EASY TO FIND NOW. HAVE THEM IN my eye.

Walk, senses open, knowing where they are the way you know you're hungry. You just know.

Each time, they get more powerful. Hard to study, seeing as they're snapping at you. But I can do it now, although not easily. Every grapheme and diagraph and punctuation mark is a machine or a pathogen, looking to build or breed giants.

Beautiful things in their way. Shark gorgeous, serpent sexy. The colours are bright and rich, and the Arabic-looking words are curved and sinuous, and I sort of want to touch them, trace them with my fingers... but I'm not looking to blow my mind out my skull.

Come at last to a midtown apartment building. Which is

weird. The tags have been in alleys, on rooftops and the rooftop things they keep air conditioning engines in. On the far end of the subway stations where the smokers try to sneak one. This is brave.

Go to the doorman, ready to put the voodoo on him.

No.

He's fucking gone. Zombied out. Look in his eyes. He's there. He looks at me like a dog shown a drowning. He can see me. Just doesn't give a toss.

'Please give me your keys.' Nothing.

Reach into his pocket. Take. Door open.

More tags in here.

Silent. A bad place. Every echo too big. Rich people's atrium. Art on the marble walls and a couch that's worth more than all my furniture. Light up. First time in a while. Look around. Security office. Lucky.

Locked. Try the keys.

'Get the fuck out of here!' The door bashes against me. Woman's voice in terror.

'I'm not one of them. I'm here to help you.' Keep it confident. Long pause. Then.

'How do I know that?'

Make a guess. 'I'm talking to you. Figure no one else in the building's done that for a day or so.'

Again a pause. 'How can I trust you?'

Look around. Camera. 'Check me out.' I wave. 'Don't reckon anyone's acted like a person around you for a while either, and here I am, acting like a kid for your goddamned amusement.'

'You shouldn't smoke in here.'

'I'll give you one if you let me in.'

The door unlocks. 'Stand the fuck back or I will shoot you.' Just like in the movies. She's been practicing. Like she's got a gun. But I do what she says. Lift up my jacket to show I'm not strapped. She opens it. Middle-eastern woman. Hijab? Hadith? I don't recall. Headscarf.

'Come on in if you're coming, spastic!' She waves me over.

'Nice talk for a devout woman.'

'I don't think I'm going to hell for swearing at a time like this!'

Three video monitors. Pictures of a few people's kids, from playground to graduation. Coat on a rack. Fashion magazine. Qur'an. And fucking hell. A bucket full of piss. I cover my mouth, slide it out into the atrium with authority. The woman is embarrassed.

'I've done the same in my time, but there's no need to keep it here now.'

She yells at me to lock the door. 'This isn't a movie. They're not flocking at you, into brains or blood.'

She locks it anyway.

'Who the fuck are you?'

'Obviously, I'm a guy who knows what's going on. So, listen. Here, take a smoke.' She does. I light her up. Put the pack on the desk, gesture to help herself.

'They try to get in here?'

'Told me to look at their sign. They tried to get in, but no one's coming through the security door. Even if you have the keys, we can lock this up.'

'I can get you out. But it won't be easy.' Lie. 'And I will. If you help me.'

'What?'

'Do you store the security camera footage here?'

'No. But we have access for about ninety days on the laptop.'

'That's what I need to see. I'm not good with computers. If

you can bring up, say, the last three days, I'll get you out of here.'

She's thinking about it, her lips moving in curse words.

'So it's a deal? You'll save me if I help you?'

Say it like that, I realise I'm coming on way too strong. I throw myself into one of those stupid cheap chairs on wheels they make these guys work in. Take a deep drag.

'No. It's not like that. I'm sorry. I know you've seen some things. I'll get you out but I need your help. This is going on in other parts of town tonight.'

She curses again, in English and maybe Urdu. Looks at me carefully and decides.

'I know what you want. I have it marked.'

She has. A time written down on a bit of scrap paper. Cross-reference, then we wait while it rewinds. Doesn't seem very high tech to me, but I'm not in a position to argue.

'You need a password to make the video play, but that's where it started. I've been in here fifteen hours. I've looked over the tapes. That's it. Now get me out of here, that's the deal. And I'll give you the login and password.'

Part of me is annoyed she wants to play this game. I always want to take it to the cutting, see who has the stones, but I'm both bluffed out and bored by risk. I just want to finish this.

'Keep your head down. Your eyes down. Do not look. Do you know the story of Lot?'

'He's a prophet. Fled a bad city of homosexuals and his wife stayed behind. Fire. Salt. Yeah.'

'Close enough. Well, here's the thing. Fuck around and look at the walls, you'll go mental. No messing about. If you can't do that, we'll find another way.'

But she does. Puts her company jacket across her face and walks, head down, to the door. When she can feel the predawn light, the early winter wind, she keeps her word. I write it down.

'Go home. Then, get out of the city for a few days.' She nods.

I get ready to walk her to the doors but she bolts into a run, keeping her eyes down. She opens the door, jumps at the guard. But he's not interested. She looks back just once but I'm already back in the office.

'Wait!' she yells. I turn.

'Thanks. And be careful.'

Light up, hands cupped against the flame, knowing it makes me look spooky. Little glamour to fuel a long day.

'Cheers. Run.'

'My name's Imtaz. Tell me what this was about later.'

'Maybe. Run.'

She does. I go back into the secure room and lock the door. Type it in. The data is sent somewhere secure, but you can watch the last 72 hours here, stored on a laptop. It takes a picture every few seconds.

Here it comes.

III

IMAGE 1

    22:30

    Image

    Carpark. Car owner enters car.

    Image 2

    22:32

    Slight figure, very young adult or teenager, enters into

carpark. Blue trousers, hooded sweatshirt pulled up high. Carry-bag.

Image 3

22:35

Figure spraypaints on a cement pylon. Image unclear.

Image 4

22:40

Spraypainted image is a glyph.

Translation: "All this is Empire."

Image 5

22: 47

No change.

Image 6

22:51

Man in suit, presumably resident, enters shot.

Image 7

23:03

Man is staring at glyph.

Skip to the end.

Image 14

23:11

Man is still staring at glyph.

Hooded figure stands with.

Image 15

03:22

Five figures stare at glyph. One, attention still on glyph, is handing hooded figure what appears to be a wallet and packet of cigarettes.

Image 16

3:27

All residents in shot kneel before hooded figure

. . .

IV

SO THAT DEFINITELY EXPLAINS THAT. THIS BOY IN THE HOODIE has somehow gotten the Scroll. Ransacked it or lucked it or whatever. He's tagging with it. Which is about a safe as taking a gasoline shower in a fire factory. Still. An answer is an answer. Just follow the tags to the kid. Plan? Not yet. Let's hope something shuffles into my head through a hole in my skull before I find him.

One day, we'll all live in a fire. The difference is, I'll have people waiting there for me.

The Old Man's words to Mully. Fifty years-ago now, I suppose. More. Fast forward through the tapes but they clear out after that. I look around this little room. Masking tape. Good enough.

Ok.

I get into my mood again. Go back to see the doorman. 'Come in', I tell him. He ignores me. I pull his arm. I guess he has no orders.

Draw a circle around the guard in tape. Yeah. High fucking Atlantean magic here. I just don't want to waste the supplies in my sexy bag. Glance at his watch. No one's coming in at this time to break my concentration. Stare at his eye. Go deep. Murmur a lullaby someone taught me somewhere, making that the spell. Looking for the domination spell. I envision his brain as a hot grey landscape, looking for a beastie biting.

And I realise. He's not under control, hexed into submission.

He's possessed. Possessed by that bastard kid who got a hold of the scroll. And by... others. All possessing each other. Super-positioned throughout the city. And more than possessed. I see something moving through his brain, eating; transforming.

They're all becoming one another. One entity, unambiguous. Interchangeable.

Ready to... I think the Archon just wants to enter every mind at once. No human could bear the pressure of such a thing within them. A man in a child's dress hardly describes the magnitude. A million humans couldn't.

Hits me. He's an old man. There's a hint in the name. Old when Mully was dancing the jitterbug. Old now. Death obsession. Playing around with an entity that can replicate forever. This is what he wants. To stretch out and be eternal.

Have to find the kid who's doing this. Have to sort this out tonight. Bad suspicion walks with me.

28

I

That night, Bettina dreamed.

Her dream was this.

She was a lake and someone had dammed her tributaries and rivers. She was unable to flow, was suddenly a prisoner to her own banks. Then she became (there was) a predator that was within her body of water. So much more intimate than her body of flesh, which she had long ago lost intimacy with. Since she had died, skin and skeleton seemed a bludgeon rather than a home.

The thing within her was not sleek, and it came up, gulping grotesque wheezes on the surface. It was not a thing natural to her water. It was bulk and mass and bullfrog-throat ugly.

And growing. And swallowing water.

Bettina longs to boil. *Is it now or then?* She tried to wake up but that was a habit of the living. There was no snapping awake, she was dead and would never wake again. Yet, she dreams.

Her water slips into its mouths. It is a greedy thing – it also takes mud and rushes and fish and oxygen and all the good things in her liquid corpus. It will never stop. Its thirst will not be sated here. It has ambitions to mar oceans, spoil seas.

It spills it out of mouths and viler organs, polluting her waters forever. A bad yolk in a broken egg.

Worms never eat her body. She wondered why.

Bettina. Her name in the dream, suddenly. It's a flavouring for meals like the one this monster has made of her. She thinks of droll worms. 'I had Bettina, with some Bettina.' Hell, she thinks it's funny enough. Lark wouldn't. He'd look at her with his mummified expression and roll his eyes minutely if he heard that.

They don't eat her because she's wrong. Dead. Outside a system. Rebel flesh and a traitor's mind. Not a part of God's plan. Undead. Unalive.

But there's worse than her. Something that would foul everything with a gulping mouth and an ungainly swim.

Bettina knows she can turn off completely. Go into darkness and peace. Not all her kind (true damnation for them, to be exiled from all oblivion) can, but she could. She can't remember why she's here. Some old man? But the urge to melt into nothingness is overwhelming.

Why won't she?

If only she could rot.

She can't sleep while the monsters drink her.

II

. . .

THE KID IS GOING TO GROUND.

To the west side, mid, there's a few neighbourhoods that just... gave it up. They're just empty of life, urban *qlippoth* zones. Community housing. Tower blocks filled with drug dealers who can't even get a proper clientele. The twenty-four hour shops are grilled, and the clerks are armed and sell cigarettes by the single and home-made whisky for ten dollars a quart. Seven blocks of hobos on the pavement and broken glass and bass-thumping cars driven by gangsters too depressed to even roll you.

It's called Cherryville.

Funny thing is, fifteen years-ago, the city repurposed this district for 'community outreach.' Put everyone poor and stupid and drunk, give them a cheap one-bedder, choke them with cheap plaster ceilings and forget to incite local businesses to move here, throw *eleven times* the amount of halfway houses and methadone clinics and all that. 'To cope with demand.' Throw everyone with bad wiring in their head, bad blood or hungry hip pockets together, stick iron-armoured cop shops at either end and, well, problem solved, with Jesus giving you the nod for your charity.

There's a youth centre. The kind of place where a creep with a beard, in cords, pretends he has a good sense of humour and walks around with a clipboard. He's gone. It's gone. It's just a shell. But it's a meeting place for certain of 'the youth'.

Taggers, I'd wager. Magicians, in their own way. Creating a semiotic and sharing it. But this one boy went too far and charged his marks with power magicians would commit genocide for.

A car turns a corner. I hide in a shadow. Ludo's boys? I don't know. No intention of finding out. Into the shadows of an old petrol station that just sells porn mags and cigarettes, no fuel. Its lights are out and it's easy to sink into darkness.

Alright. Let's go.

Inside the old building, there's Primal Sigil everywhere, incomplete. A decoration, but still powerful enough to fill up my head like cathedral bells. Feel like I've been swallowed as I go through the broken front door. A spider's parlour. It's all shadow and reflected blue streetlight and needles and plastic bags underfoot. Sneaking around is a waste of time.

Sounds. Hollow hit. Hollow hit. Wrapped up in magic, you know how it works by now, I find it.

Rec room.

Table tennis. How they found a ball, I don't know, but they're playing. A young girl, ratty, giving me Hep C, just from her sniffles. An Indian boy with dreadlocks. They play. Slow. Sure. Free will, sure. But they're filled up with dozens of other people and splintered into that dozen as well. The weight is slowing down their thoughts, sure as carrying mass.

Another room. Sick bay. Jesus. Some kid has killed himself in here. Sliced the back of his knees with broken glass. Wears stupid big underwear he's soiled. The smell is vile, and I close the door. Don't need to be in that room to feel the intent, the information. That was payback. The bastard kid who has the scroll decided on a little revenge.

Turn into a corridor. Lined with the sigils. Door at the end, and I can hear the hissing of spraypaint behind it. It's dark and that'll help me not see. If I don't linger, don't try to read it, that'll help too. Pull up my hood to cut off peripherals. My head is still guarded by my sentinel imagery.

But my biggest assist is that I've been staring at the damn graffito for a night now. I've kind of built up an immunity. Course, in the same way you slowly build up an immunity to fucking bullets. But it's what I have.

Knock on the door.

'Hey. My name's Lark. I want to talk.'

Silence. Been a few days since anyone could talk to this boy. Figure he's forgotten about anything but puppets right now.

'I'm not a cop or anything stupid like that. I don't have a gun. If you don't want to talk, I'll go. But I think it's important.'

Beats. 'Come in.'

Open the door. The imagery nearly snuffs me like a candle in a storm. Unfocus my eyes. Go blank inside. Slowly, slowly, phase into high-consciousness. Step in.

Dorm room. Bunk beds. Piss stink. Windows about the bunks, letting in weak streetlight.

The kid is in the middle of the room. Arms crossed, can in fist.

A girl. That change anything? Doubt it. Watch her carefully. Tiny. Underfed. Amateur piercings, slightly infected. Thirteen?

'How come you're not me?'

'I'm not like other people.'

'I can fuck you up.' Angry. Scared. Wrong-footed.

'Yeah, probably. Can do the same to you, if it comes to that. But I didn't come in, all attitude, looking to throw down. This isn't 'come at me.' I just want to talk.'

Gestures with her pointy chin. 'What's in the bag?'

'My stuff. Want a smoke?' I offer the pack. She takes one, lights her own. Me too. Nearly finished this pack. Check for an extra. No. Shit.

Put the bag down, sit on one of the bunks, trying not to worry about the worrying moisture.

'I'm Lark. When things get weird, it's my job to find out why and see if I can stop it.'

'You can't stop me. You can't stop *it*.'

'Not even sure I want to, kid.'

'Wick. Don't call me kid. I'm not a kid.'

'Yeah.' Wave at the room. 'I can see that. So let me see if I can put this together, yeah?'

Wick sneers.

'You went into the big old mansion. Not sure how you even knew it was there.'

'Even before all this started, I could see things. You just have to look careful.'

She'd be a fuck-off good magician with that sort of talent, but ingratiating myself to her would be fatal. She'd just hear a teacher's voice, or a stranger with candy. But her eyes keep lingering on all the glyphs she's painted. Nods.

'The house is called the House of Gallowglass. A group of people who worship things used it as, like, their base. Another group of people, like a crazy church group, took on the Gallowglass crew. Then the church group got taken out by a third lot. And somewhere in all that, you found a scroll.'

She waits. Cocks her head as if listening, but not to me.

'Yeah. So what?'

'Why could you find it when no one else could?'

'It knew someone was coming for it, someone who had plans it didn't like. So when it saw me, well, felt me, you know, in the house? It let me see it.'

'Do you know what it is?'

'Sorta.'

'So you get the scroll. Use it to tag some places. And it gets stronger. Shows you some tricks.'

'Want to see something? It's pretty cool.'

'Not really.'

'Look out the window.'

I get up. Do. There's about a hundred people who weren't there a while ago. Staring up at me. They all whisper my name at once. Creepy. Most of them have cans of paint or markers or crayons or something like that in their fists. She's been busier than I ever expected.

'They're all me.'

'Are you them?'

'Nah.' She gets back to work. Nods as she curves the spray. Satisfied with tricky work.

'So you get to tagging, all around the city. And the thing in the scroll, right? It helps you get bigger.'

'Yeah. Got some payback too.'

'Who wouldn't?' Seems reasonable.

'So what do you want?'

'Well, there's a few things. But, and listen, I don't know how it's going to play out between you and me but... this work is good. Like, you're a great artist.'

Shuts down the hiss of the paint and throws back the hood. shaved head. She stares at me with bird-bright eyes that gleam in the dark. 'Serious?'

'Yeah. It's real good. I had to follow it, tag to tag, to find you here. I like it. Middle-eastern, sorta, but your own style.'

Wick goes back to work, turning her face, fighting a smile. Under the breath, 'Cool.' Pleased but too cool to show it.

Ok.

'What I want to know is, what's the endgame for you?'

'What?'

'Like, what do you get out of it?'

Pause, consider. 'Tag the whole fucking city.'

'You want to become everyone in the city?'

'Everyone? I don't care about that.'

'What does *it* care about?'

'Wants me to tag the whole fucking city'

Got it.

Like I said. A human mind and body, even combined, just

isn't enough. But like it's colonising human heads, it's also planning flesh. A city-god. Ten-by-two miles of concrete, steel and dirt to put on like a coat. A titan, wreathed in buildings, streets its veins, a power grid its nerves. You get the picture.

The Old Man either has big plans or can't know what he's grasped. He doesn't want to die.

'So, Wick. Ok. I don't want that to happen. I want to be me.'

She shrugs. 'Run. Soon as I'm done here, making this place, like, my base, I'm going to tag buses, trains, cabs. Tried it before, but that was just practice, you know? Let the images out into the world. Get a lot of people. Then, they'll start tagging and drawing. I just need to have a place like this. Strong, you know, to get my back up against. Then it's happening.'

'Ok. I'm going to run.'

'Wait. *It* says no.'

Shark in the water. Some intelligence comes swimming into the lines of the sigils. I feel a terrible attention on me and fight not to fall apart. Feels like a massive sugar crash. Fuck. But wait a second. It's... not all here. Diffuse. Hypercephalic. It's too big yet. I can hold on for a minute. After that. Try to get up and get to the door but no. Fly in a web. Like that. Lark's last stand if it tries for me. Bloody the fucking thing's nose.

Then Wick saves my life.

'But you liked my work, man. You're ok.'

The Archon withdraws, slow as sludge.

'Thanks,' I mutter, stumbling to the door. Grabbing my bag.

I leave. She calls after me. 'But if I see you again, you're fucked.'

Outside, the various Wicks don't even stare at me. They're

just waiting. Not puppets, they cough, shift their weight, some scratch. They're people, but all those people are Wick. Evicted from their own bodies, but bodies they are.

I get away. Walk over to the station and grab two packs. Smoke one and look over the centre, seeing the people shuffle around it.

And there it is, a plan in my head. Without method. Just thinking about Scarlet and her *boyfriend* and the idea sneaks into my head.

Take my phone. Make a call.

'This is Lark. I want to talk to Ludo. Again.'

Round fucking two, cunts.

29

———

I

THE BLANCO FAGGOT HAS SOME BALLS. LUDO TAKES THE PHONE, ready for Lark's try at sounding something other than soft as piss.

'You shouldn't even be alive.'

'The Hollow? Come on man. I'm Lark. Send a knifeman to take me out?'

Ludo can hear the false bravado but under the words, there's an undeniable truth. Lark is indeed alive. Ludo's seen the Hollow's terrifying capabilities before. The Old Man has used him three times in the last few years, and twice, Ludo had to check on the results. Fucking terrifying. Not just because of the violence. Anyone can hack with a dull knife. It's the speed. Same-day service. No matter the odds. The Hollow got into a prison for the Old Man and it took six hours.

So how is Lark alive when tougher than him came apart so easily?

'What do you want anyway, dead man?'

Ludo is in the Old Man's waiting room. Alone. It stinks in here. Mothballs and rotted carpet. Peeling wood and a filthy window. He's glad to have something to focus on beyond his employer's rage.

'I know what you're looking for.'

'That a fact?'

'Look, I want to talk to the organ-grinder, not the monkey.

'Put the Old Man on.'

Ludo laughs. 'Don't be fucking stupid. And, believe me, I'm doing you a favour.'

'Then listen carefully. You're after a scroll. It came from the Gallowglass. I know where it is and I know who has it and I can give all that to you.'

'What's the cost?'

'I walk away from this. And I hear the Old Man has a copy of *Sigmund's Woe*. That.'

That's bullshit.

'I'll call you back.'

'Wait. Tell him I'm swearing to play you true. He'll know what it means.'

Ludo hangs up.

Ludo enters the bosses' office.

'Sir. A development.'

II

WARNING: THE FOLLOWING FILE IS CLASSIFIED CRIMSON GLOVE. IF YOU ARE NOT CLEARED FOR STATUS: CRIMSON GLOVE, REPLACE THE FILE NOW AND REPORT TO SECURITY CLEARANCE OFFICER.

Note: This letter was found in a private collection of CODENAME: THIRTY ONE after that asset's suicide. Graphology indicates authentic provenance.

MAGICAL BATTLES.

So a magic battle doesn't have fireballs and death rays. You got that, right? But it does have weapons and it does have dangers. Very real dangers.

Here's my advice to you. If you think you're going to be in a magical battle, be prepared. You can play it fast and loose all you like but, victory is in the preparation. You have to Batman it.

A magician's first and best weapon is study. It's why so many people try for it and fail. It takes a long time to get your clip full of bullets, to sharpen your sword. Here's the best example I know of that. You need a weapon. So you can look up some Egyptian curse or stick a goat's head on a stick for Odin. That's fine. If it worked for someone else and you're prepared to put in the work, recreate the rite, it will work for you, too, probably.

But let's say someone is in your face. There, then. You need a spell right the fuck now. That's where a magical battle gets intense and if you can walk away from one, you're probably a good magician.

I do it with words and gestures. I probably already said that. So say, I want a spell that just straight up dredges shame and self-hate. You can't fight a magic war remembering the time you fiddled with your little brother when you were three in a game of doctor.

So I make a word for that spell. Let's say: bastard.

Every time, in the right context, I say that, there's a spell. I practice with it and I discover that maybe a better word will work: Doublebastard.

I play around with that for a while. Then I want it to sound cooler. I go for Latin, the classical choice: Doublus-bastardus.

There's a spell. I just invented a magic word. I use it a few times. I lock it away, let it rest in my head, fruiting. Don't let the desire for results mar it up for me. Then, when I need it, it's powerful, a pristine idea.

I work with spirits. Mean ones, when I'm looking for allies in a fight. I take my time, sorting through the deck, looking for the aces. Spirits I like, respect, find easy to work with or, if I don't care, enslave. Spirits I can make sure will arrive when I need them, straight away.

Spirits, though, can be easy to banish. That's a good portion of my work with the Library. People call up things all the time, never knowing that a banishing should be the first thing they learn.

I have spells now. I have allies.

This takes time. And that's the hard bit. Because once you've found out what traditions and styles work for you, once you've trained your mind, once you've read the books and practiced, practiced, practiced, you want to get into it. No. You have to take your time and assemble your weapons with care.

And if I've been preparing for a fight I probably have a lot of different weapons. I need them because I see a lot of different practices at work and I need to be flexible. And if I'm smart, I probably have a lot of different kinds of weapons. And if I'm really good, I'll manage to keep my cool when I'm using them. See, you can drop down deep into meditation all you like, but these fights are pretty intense. It's easy to lose your gnosis state in the middle of them, which is pretty much dropping your gun.

Here's the secret to winning a battle. You have to see it. You have to enter into a *different space*. It's not just concentration. You have to see the spells. You have to remember them. You have to visualise them or create some anterior narrative analogous to visualation. You have to respect your own skills and your allies while you commit them to war.

And that's what makes a good magician. The ability to keep many ideas in the head at one time. Many ideas, and also contrary ideas. It isn't about being the smartest. It isn't about being the most researched. It isn't about having some cultural connection to the unconscious or being a bastard or being a saint. To win a magical battle is to let your imagination be tested to its fullest.

But really, more than that, you have to live symbolically. Act like you believe that you are an occult soldier. Transform your life with beliefs and actions. Always, always actions. What you do, how you live, what you say is imprinted upon the world and the world will regard it. Magic is simply a way of manifesting that regard.

Get weird or go home.

30

I

GOT TO GET THE SCROLL OFF THE GIRL. GOT TO PREVENT THE Old Man from getting his hands on it.

Here I am. The middle of a goddamn mall. Effecting the plan. I'm a hero. I'll get the girl *for sure*.

Bitter laugh goes here.

The Forum is trendy apartment buildings on three sides, a huge mall in the centre. Sunken into that, a square of concrete, stairs on each side. Chess set in the middle. Tables bolted to the concrete. Shops of teeth-grating tweeness. 'House of Jam', 'Saffron, Saffron' and the inevitable pun-based Thai restaurant.

All closed now. Some windows vaguely lit to haunt mannequins and bracelets. This is where Ludo said to meet. It's cold and I'm hiding in shadows. I'm here early, working up hiding spells. They won't see me when they talk to me. I'll be safe in the dark.

Look, I know this is stupid. Last time I was here, Ludo

beat the shit out of me. Only Bettina got me out. But this time, I've got something they really want, I'm expecting them trying something and I'm ready for it. And better than that, I've got a good plan to run the hell away.

Way I figure it, I have to get their attention quick and cruel. Because they'll be thinking the best way not to pay is put a bullet into my fucking skull. I'd like to discourage that line of thinking.

Cold tonight. Winter coming on fast. Cold wind blows the wrappers and leaves along the ground.

Ludo, big as a bull, big as a bastard. Black suit. No shades. He's got someone with him. Oh yeah, this one I recognise. Humbert, she bizarrely calls herself. Straight out of Turkmenistan or somewhere like that. She's beautiful and vicious as winter. Shaman traditions. Gnosis. Yeah. She brought spirits with her. Rat things that scurry at her feet.

No problem.

I said I'd swear to play it true. That means that I'm treating this meeting as an act of magic; of ritual. I'm being respectful. Taking this as serious as I can. That might mean something to the Old Man. Might not. But something tells me that he's magician enough to at least acknowledge it. Of course, it means I can't betray or lie. The risk is calculated.

Ludo waits, legs apart, hands by his sides. A soldier at attention. Humbert necks some pills from a bottle and washes them down with water.

'Ok, here's the deal.'

I let them see me walking forwards, stand before them. Really, I'm thirty-foot away, in a stairwell down to car parking. I smashed the light, the way their brains see it, like a mirage. I'm to their side, watching. My leg hurts again, just to see him.

· · ·

II

Stop. 'Bring the book?'

Slowly reach into his coat. There it is. A small, old-fash-
ioned hardback, square. Something only the Old Man could
have. Something I want for real, but it's also bait.

'Put it down.'

He lays it out on one of the cafe's tables. Oh yes. That's
mine.

Stares at the fake me. 'Now, stop your poncing about and
get to it.'

Tell him the address. Forget to mention the hundred or so
bodies Wick has at her disposal. Not a lie.

'You can find her there. What you want is there.'

'How do you even know what I want?'

'Ludo, just stick to breaking heads. Finding out hidden
things is my job. Anyways, it doesn't matter. I'm out. I got
hired to investigate a cult battle. That brought you in. If I
knew it was the Old Man's business, I never would've got
involved. But I did. I'm not his problem. I'm not yours. Now,
you get what you want,' I point at the book, 'and I get a taste.'

He doesn't respond. He's taking his time.

He's wasting time.

Humbert is trying some spell at me but she's punching
above her weight.

What's...

My shielding spell is broken like a glass jaw.

Ludo turns to look at me. The real me, hiding in shadows.
Grins. Shifts his body.

'He telling the truth, boss?'

Then, letting himself appear in my vision, himself. The
Old Man.

And he is. Ancient. Like something got into his body to twist and diminish it. His hands are thick with spots. His teeth, brown and chipped like a cave. His eyes are... they're bad eyes.

He stinks. He reeks. Not just filth and age, but the sour milk burn of sadism.

Oh Christ.

'Lark, is it? The one who left the Library?'

'Yes.'

I'm too scared to bother playing him. The Archon was bad, but it was like being scared of the sun dying, the moon falling to the Earth. But this man seems electric with cruel capacities that are intimate and intravenous.

'They never let anyone go before.' His voice is stringy and wheezing. 'What's so special about you?'

'They couldn't stop me.'

He snorts. Snot lands on his lap. His nurse, a tiny blonde thing taut with terror, comes from behind his wheelchair to clean it. He waves her away. Rubs into his robe with the back of his hand. Not the first time.

'I doubt that. You're just another chancer. Pick my teeth with the likes of you, you little fuck. So I wonder why they really let you go. But they didn't, did they?'

Stares. 'Yeah. Someone's laid a geas on you, haven't they boy?'

'Yeah.'

'You might want to think about that.' He laughs, his tongue poking against his ruined teeth and his spit shoots out like insults.

Ludo speaks, startling me. 'You want this done with?'

'Shut the fuck up, monkey,' says the Old Man conversationally. Ludo raises his eyebrows but says nothing. Back to me.

'You've seen it haven't you.' Not a question. 'The prison.'

'What?'

'The binding spell. The *scroll*, you dim fuck.'

'Yeah.'

'What's it like?'

Tell it true. 'Beautiful. Powerful. I think you're mad to try and tame a thing like that.'

Laughs again, pouring scorn into me like fevers.

'You might be, you poxy little first-timer. But what's mad for you is just another working for me.'

He jerks his head at Ludo.

'Let him go. I want him to see what happens when I get it. Want him to live with it. Besides, he said an oath.'

Hesitates. Says nothing. Smart. But it's plain to see Ludo's opinion on a magician's promise.

They wheel away.

Over his shoulder, the Old Man cries out 'Stay out of it now, boy. I see you again, I'll have you done in by dogs in heat.'

Seems it's the day for warnings.

Not much time now. If that little amateur who's been following me around is here, then he'll alert the people I'll need alerted. My plan looks like it has legs. Like I said, calculated risk.

Take a card from my wallet. Dial it in.

'Agent Valier. It's Lark.'

II

SHIRELLE VALIER NEVER REALLY WANTED TO JOIN AN intelligence agency. She was far too sensible for that. She realised that it wouldn't be getting across borders without a passport, flirting with handsome spies in Hilton bars or breaking into embassies. It would be desk work, plain and simple. Boring.

But when she graduated with a Masters in ancient languages, there wasn't much of an interest for her in the world of employment. She didn't want to teach. She didn't want to publish. She picked up the occasional job translating, but that was only good for a few hundred bucks now and again. Nothing to live on.

Ms. Valier's uncle, as he had done for the last five years, tried again to recruit her. A sophisticated man, he had never treated her like a child, and so she loved him fiercely as an adult. His style was all Scotch from crystal tumblers and handmade shoes and hair greying in wings. At a bar, amusingly enough in the Forum, he bought her a campari and made his final pitch.

'You're smart. You've a clean record. I can vouch for you. You have unusual skills, and we're always looking for that. There's travel in the job, the money is, well, adequate and you'll be doing something useful.'

'But, I don't know. Analysing data all day...'

'Sometimes it's dull, yes, but what work isn't? And analysing data is a small part of the job. You'll be making decisions that affect people in the real world. You'll be actually one of the good guys.'

'Good guys?'

'Better us than them and, believe it or not, that's actually how I feel.'

He was disarmingly earnest. She believed him.

There was a sea of crew-cuts and bobs and flat platformed pumps and promise rings when she sat for the examination. At first, she was mildly discouraged, worried that these would be her peers but, sharing coffee with a few of them, she was put at ease. They were intelligent people, political, perhaps a tad conservative for her tastes, but she was hardly a radical these days.

Of course her test scores were excellent, and she read her acceptance letter with a smile. She called her uncle who flew in, took her out for lobster, that time on his boat.

Op training was mainly easy for her, although the physical fitness was a shock, after a university experience that saw her enjoying too many good red wines, too many classes scheduled late and too many rich pastries at faculty dos. Her brother, a decathlete, drew up a plan for her and, before she knew it, she was eating miles with a steady pace, enjoying the slap of pavement beneath her soles. Cryptography was quite fascinating, but the computer lessons bored her. Guns and knives and interrogation techniques and humint and comint and all the stuff from the movies and the novels.

She graduated highly placed and was given her first assignment overseas. Working in an embassy in an Eastern European city. The work was alright, monitoring and funding some right-wing groups who had issues with unions. She ate dumplings, met a nice guy, made a life for herself.

Then her uncle called. She said goodbye to the guy and moved back to the city.

'What do you know about cults?'

'Same as anyone. Scientology. Waco.'

'No, the real ones. Assassins and Roslyn Chapel and that sort of business.'

'Well, they're the same no matter what time. Usually parasitical, heretical off-shoots of existing religions. Common traits include charismatic leaders, the only true way, give up all your worldly goods. You know, that kind of thing.'

'Do you know what a Skoptsy is?

Forty-five minutes later, she was in a room with a prisoner. His hands were cuffed behind his back. A handsome big man; red-headed and raw-bone handsome. Simple table, the mirror in the room, the white lights buzzing.

'Andrei Breshnev. You bashed a man to death with a house brick and attempted to steal several items from his house. Unfortunately, that man was an important intelligence asset and we'd like to know why you killed him.'

'He was unclean,' said Breshnev in thickly accented English. Not even bothering to deny the crime. 'It was not good for him to have the... have the things of our faith.'

'Now, curiously, one of those things was a toy. A bronze head.'

The Russian laughed. 'Toy.'

The dead man had been an ex-KGB officer who liked swapping old code, old histories, old secrets for a steady supply of cash or heroin he could sell. He claimed that the source of intelligence was someone he called Brasshead. It was too interesting a coincidence that the one item the man had stolen had been the inspiration for a codename. Especially considering that the thief had left hundreds of thousands of dollars of gold bullion behind him.

'Show him the thing.' Her uncle's voice over the hidden earpiece. She frowned. This was weird.

'Here it is. Why don't you tell me what's so important about this thing?'

She took it from the bag and placed it on the plain table. Breshnev stared at it in awe. A mechanical head, a human face, shaped like an eastern sphinx's profile.

Then the man began to strip. The guard in the room went for his taser but her uncle calmed them both. Then the man slipped off his trousers. A mass of scar tissue where penis and testicles could be. Just a slit for urination.

'Look,' gestured the Russian. 'God creates something to tempt us but we are wise. We know the sacrifices he demands.'

He crawled up onto the table, kneeling before the head, praying fast in his mother tongue.

'Ask him about Lubbovich.'

Breshnev bowed to the head. Held his hands like a man at prayer.

And began to babble in a voice not human. She drew back. His was a grinding, metal voice, hollow and... bronze. His Russian was different, better pronounced. He spoke like this for two minutes. He engaged the head in what seemed a passionate monologue. Then, collapsed.

She left and that night, her uncle bid her into one of the Secure Rooms.

'What that man said under the influence of the Head... there's no way he should know. He's just a cultist from rural Georgia. There's simply no way he could have known that. The Head told him.'

'What? What did he say?' Her uncle ignored her, frowning one brow.

'This matches up with other reports. Look, you work this job long enough, you see things that don't add up. Strange things. You realise it's all soft around the edges. '

She wanted to laugh but there was no way to deny that voice.

'We've managed to open up funding. There's a place on the task force. If you're ready to go deep into it. Into things we've just begun to suspect.'

She shook her head. 'Shirelle, I brought you in for this kind of thing. I need you.'

It took a while but she joined the task force. The work was the same, just with a narrow focus. And soon, she believed.

There were people with abilities. Objects that, here her vocabulary failed her, were haunted was the best word. Most of them framed it in religious fashions. But some did not. The risks to international security seemed... obvious and terrifying. A dozen operations she'd worked, each one weird ,and she'd identified twenty potential assets, but each one too dangerous; too weird, too elusive to touch. She was an intelligence officer with seven years' experience. She knew things the guy on the street never did. But studying these case files, she got the impression there was a whole other world, operating like a weird machine behind the curtains. The task force was small but, she increasingly believed, vital to national security.

Another story that.

And in investigating this weird case, the scroll, she came across Lark. A man with no past, no real existence at all. She'd seen people living off the grid before, but never one whose file kept vanishing, who seemed to exist on no files at all.

A man who walked out of a secure Civil Defence building with no weapons. Just... walked.

Calling her at her home. She switched on the light, sat up, her boyfriend grumbling.

'Still want to know where the Scroll is?'

'Of course.'

A place. A time.

'But I'll want money.'

'That can be arranged.'

Up, call Coffee, call her boss. Scramble a squad. Coffee met her at the office, with his namesake for two.

'You know, we'll probably have to arrest this bastard. I'll have police there. My woman Captain Filbin knows the score, knows to just do as she's told. She's a STATUS: MARTYR.

She'll drop the guy, if you like, as well. Or he can hang himself in jail.'

She shrugged. 'I don't like him. No loss.'

'But?'

'This guy. He puts the scares on me. Boss said yes to the money. I'm taking it just in case. But if you get a shot at him, take it. There's something wrong with him.'

31

———

I

One final thing to know, perhaps.

That chick who's been following me? Who spied on the first meet with Ludo?

Here's who she is.

I couldn't say because I can't think about her or it'll tip her off. But she's not here now. Had to mix up her gender even, when I think about her. Needed to keep her on me without letting her know she'd been made.

I worked for the Library for ten years, keeping everything cool. The part of the job people ask me about is the cop bullshit. The fighting stuff. But that wasn't my only duty and it wasn't my favourite part. My favourite part was me, alone in the dark, warm, honey-coloured reading room with some of the greatest grimoires in the history of the world, just waiting for me. Earning my way up the organisation, getting access to more and more rooms, with more and more books. Alone, reading, learning, finding new techniques and ideas to experiment with.

But there was a price for all this.

Teaching.

The job had two parts. Lecturing. That was alright. Getting up with a room full of people. Either the new guys, the guys with the money who thought they were in some upmarket Rosicrucian deal, Silver Star or Golden Dawn, some occult slumming or freemason glad-handing.

Or lecturing to the adepts, the guys who figured out that, hey, this is real. The ones who did the homework and had the hunger and did the work. People we could use.

Part I hated? Tutoring. Working with small groups, talking over their rites and ideas. Listening to each beginner with the same ideas, the same 'yes but, what actually *is* art?' theories. The boring epistemologies and the same predictable freakouts the first time they copped a minor possession or just lost focus and ended up mental for three days and their husbands got mad.

Part I hated more than that?

Grooming people to work for me.

Listen, I know how this sounds but... I was pretty good at my job. I was the youngest officer the Library ever had. Twenty-two. I worked harder than anyone. Trained myself with diligence. Loved magic, loved the research, loved listening to reports from spies we paid off to rat out the other cults. Loved researching the correct rituals to shut down scum and bastards.

My work crew, well, I hated them. Workshy. Slow to adapt. Specialising in one tradition and remaining stultifying fuck-ignorant of others. The ones who felt like they were special for making adept. I was impatient, short and barely bothered to hide my anger at their lack of commitment.

Pretty bad teacher. Mully used to raise an eyebrow when I ranted at him but I didn't care. Teaching was a distraction from my tasks. Towards the end, Scarlet used to get all furious at me. 'These people need you to train them! You're not going to be here forever, one way or another, and we need better recruits.'

Was still all fucked up from Jon back then but I tried. I slowed it down. Never lost my patience. They just figured I'd gone soft.

My last group of initiates, there were five.

Rosengarten, who was fat, with a greasy ponytail, who wore trenchcoats everywhere. He had a thing for Latin and would rattle it off without ever being asked. Prick thought he was smarter than anyone. Failed physics in first-year university before he came to us.

Connor, who stared out of life behind a ridiculously untrimmed goatee and hair in his nose. 'I've got a friend,' he says, 'who does everything better than you.' Read to a novel? He read it before you, even if you made it up. But he had good ideas about magic and computers that I couldn't be less fucking interested in. Heavy metal band t-shirts and German Army overcoats in summer.

Raj, the six, five tall Sikh with a drinking problem. Christ knows how he wound up with us, but he had a real skill with some of the most useless rituals I've ever seen. He could communicate with angels, which is like asking the CEO of a drug company to help you score aspirin.

Then, the women.

Straw, who needed a bath. Militant feminist, atheist, lefty. All of which is fine. Endless loudmouth and obstructionist, which is not. Once, and I saw this happen, this is true, she told a priest his display of religious imagery was offensive to her. In a church. There's five all-female magical circles in the city, she was chucked out of every one for being a dick. Good with a variety of folk traditions. Bad with applying herself to learn the hard stuff.

Katanya. Best of a bad lot. Remarkably gifted with animal magic. She could read them, summon them, control them, understand them. Dream with them. You know what our Order was called. The Library. Animals, well, *they can't fucking read.* Flighty, dreamy. Never knew why she was recruited, and even Scarlet agreed on that.

Carma. Her actual name, actual spelling. Lazy. Stupid. Disrespectful. Sleeping with one of the higher-ups. Naked greed for power. I caught her using magic on bank tellers and bar tenders, slipping them a credit card she'd runed up. But, and here was the thing, she had an instinct for hurting people. I think they saw Jon writ small in her.

Those were my replacements. It's Carma that's been following me. Still stupid. Still lazy. She thinks you can say some words and that's magic. She's never understood that you have to go to a place where you can believe it. Where you don't fight it. But she doesn't care about that. Say some words and plunder. That's her philosophy.

They sent her? After me? And they're surprised I made her? Maybe they were. Maybe she's a warning. Maybe Carma's a decoy. Doesn't matter. See, she'll run back to whatever half-arsed try hard is running operations over there and report on the Old Man. And that'll get someone's attention.

And that's what I want. The whole damn family, together at last.

Because someone let the Old Man know Gallowglass had the scroll. Someone who suspects the Old Man's ambitions like I do. And I'm having a suspicion who that was.

Four in the morning.

Take it to the bridge.

. . .

II

THE OLD MAN HAS MORE MONEY THAN GOD, BUT HE SPENDS none of it. A lifetime of smashing enemies, controlling people through fear and horror, seeing black wonders, and here he is, with me. A shitty old van, he's strapped in to the back seat, his nurse in the front, flecks of spit at her lips. She's a pretty thing. Icelandic, someone said.

She's gone, though. Ludo can see it in her eyes. She saw things, bad things, checked out a while ago. Waste, really. Ludo likes 'em with a bit of life in 'em but, what the hell. She'll say yes just to feel something that doesn't want to make her puke. Ludo's seen it in refugees and amputees. Ludo never understands that. He uses pain for business, not much for pleasure but, hell, the Old Man has the power, and that's all the permission he needs. If he likes to hurt, who can say no? He wants to fuck a pretty blonde's mind into ruin, hey, whose gonna stop him? To Ludo, that just makes sense. He's not much interested in the moral dimensions.

The Old Man is muttering away in a language that hurts the ears. Sort of like the barking of Hebrew or Arabic, but much worse than that.

Millions of dollars in the bank and you'd think he'd shell out some fucking money a decent ride. Even his wheelchair is old. Rickety. Leather and hard steel. Ludo's seen bedsores on his arse, and smelled them.

'Mortification of the flesh, boy. You should try it. You'd be amazed what kind of insights you can reach with suffering.'

But Ludo doesn't play that shit. Pain goes downstream. One way.

The one thing the boss does pay for is guns. Ludo is wearing combat pants, a flak jacket, combat boots, and is motherfucking *strapped*. He has an M14, two Jericho 941 pistols and the hunting knife he's had since he was a boy. He has ammunition to spare and two concussion grenades. Some of the other guys are carrying more but, well, that's movie bullshit, that. If Ludo meets something he can't take down with what he's carrying, might as well call in an airstrike. They're going to some bullshit community centre to kill a girl, not mixing it up with armoured cavalry.

Driver gives the high sign and Ludo leans in.

'Hey, hey boss. We're almost there.'

The Old Man slowly returns. His mind, it goes places. Not like other old guys, who mutter about the past. It really goes places.

'The plan?' snaps the old man, spitting in Ludo's face. His breath is too fucking hot.

'We go in. That Lark fag told it true. It's like a youth hostel or something. We make sure it's ok, there's no surprises. Then, Watonga and Miles will escort you in. You want the nurse with you?'

The Old Man's head rotates with the malice of a spotlight in a prison camp.

He watches the back of her head.

'Yes.' Fairly hisses.

'Oh shit,' says the driver.

The whole street is covered in sigils. There's, like, packs of people – all sort of folks, drawing on phone boxes, letter boxes, bus shelters, shop windows, car bonnets, street lamps, everywhere. Some damn image. Ludo shuts his eyes and feels the corrugated flesh of the Old Man stroke his face. Calm comes over him like a ketamine high.

The driver just stops the car.

The nurse, her mind bursts like a fat pimple and she starts headbutting her passenger window and Ludo can hear her nose break first, then her cheek. That doesn't stop until he takes his pistol, puts one through her skull, splashing the front window with the usual.

The driver, well, he comes to a full stop. Easy as anything. Parks like it's Sunday. Gets out. Sits down cross-legged, starts to claw at his face. Nasty.

The Old Man's protection stays fast in Ludo. He can see, he can think, but there's something like a dam in his mind. He's suddenly utterly without curiosity. But he can feel a pressure. He can feel something trying to break in and whirl his mind up but good.

'Fucking hell,' hisses the Old Man.

The second van comes in, the rest of the crew. The engines cut out but the car keeps rolling. Hits the side of a shop and just keeps going. A long second later, the back door opens and Watonga gets out, eating a scalp.

The Old Man taps at his skull with a knuckle. Ludo gets it together under that pecking. 'I know you can hear me. Kill everyone who gets in our way and you can have it all. All the money, all the houses. It's yours.'

'What about your wife?'

'She'll understand.'

Ludo calculates that worth. 'I'll come back in a minute to get your chair ready.'

He loads his rifle and switches off the safety. There's two dozen people on the street. Watching silently as autistics or busy with their art. Shouldn't take long.

The music comes on in his head. Drum and bass. His murder anthem, beating out war.

· · ·

III

CARMA DOESN'T LIKE SCARLET. HATES HER. BUT THEN AGAIN, Carma hates everyone.

She sort of plans to sleep with Everett, Scarlet's man. That'll get her another patron, since her old one died, and fuck up that cold ho's day.

But right now, Carma's scared.

She's fucked up the assignment and she knows it. She saw that prick Lark, like, three times in the last few days, and she was supposed to be on him twenty-four seven. They even bought Carma these fucking cool pills that were better than speed. They taught her the spying rune special. Rosengarten had to show her how, and he sweated the whole time she was in the room, staring at her tits every time he thought she wasn't looking.

But the only time she saw Lark was when he was busy. He walked away from her so many times. Scarlet gave her some of his hair, put it in a jar of liquid. Said it would point the way to him. But half the time, it just fucked out, stopping working then, suddenly, jumping into life again, like a hunting dog. Even then, she'd follow it, only to find he was gone.

So, really, it's Scarlet's fault for giving her shitty magic.

Carma's scared because she doesn't want to go back without something to report. But then, the finder comes alive and she races to midtown. The Forum. Fancy mall for rich pricks. And she watches.

Jesus Christ. She can't even see him. Wait. There he is. Dealing with the big sexy guy who handed him his arse before. Carma shudders, remembering how stupid Lark made her feel when he was a teacher. How he'd just stare at her with cold eyes and dismiss her.

'I'm not even going to waste my time correcting you. You didn't even try.' The last word Lark ever said to her.

Yeah, so the fuck *what*? She'd get it in her own time. Or have McGill give her some private lessons. She just had to take off her pants and that weird old fuck would give her anything she wanted. He didn't even really want to fuck her. He just wanted to stare and have her pose for him like a toy. That was fine. In return, she got charms and money and she was learning power. Worth it, bent over in a dark room while a powerful man lost his dignity over her, murmuring like a frog.

Carma didn't need to do fucking homework. Fuck Lark.

But McGill died last year and suddenly, Scarlet was expecting results. And none of them were delivering, but Carma was the worst. How the fuck could Jon and Lark have just walked out on them like that? None of them trained up good, and suddenly the Library didn't have the muscle it had enjoyed for seventy years.

Jesus. Straw, dead on exorcism. Katanya, kicked out, leaving without a word, just tears in her eyes. Fucking *weak*. Raj, one eye taken out by some rogue spirit, then molested by some porn-cult bastard, broken and weak now. Connor, a man so hated by the magical community of the City they laughed at him when he came to demand knowledge when they deferred to Lark. Silas, the new guy, on the Satan tip and clearly a loser.

No wonder it was all coming apart. And it was all Lark's fault. Now, he's cheating Carma out of the success she goddamn needs to stay on the Library's payroll.

Then.

Oh fuck.

The Old Man appears. She can see him from the roof, looking down at him through night-vision binoculars. Even from up here, Carma can just tell he's a fucking hardcase. She sees Lark's body language change. First time ever, he's nervous. Usually he's still, forever going in and out of trances. This time, he's shifting his weight, jigging it. Like a prick. Carma's pretty happy to have seen that motherfucker sweat. Even when the big guy was handing out a whoopin' under the bridge, he didn't act like this.

Carma picks up the phone.

'Scarlet, he's meeting someone. That soldier boy from before.'

The one who beat him up?

'Yeah. But, there's someone else here as well. Some old bastard who looks like he's a thousand.'

Phone goes silent.

Are you recording? The binoculars are something, the Library can see what she sees.

'Yes, I'm fucking recording.'

Listen. Remain hidden. Absolutely, remain hidden until the meet is done. Then head back to the chapterhouse.

'Word.'

Are you listening to me?! Stress snaps in her voice. Carma likes hearing that shit. Likes hearing Scarlet sweat.

Carma snaps the phone shut.

'Ho,' she sneers at it and watches again but nothing really happens. The Old Man rolls off and Lark takes something off a table. Book, Carma reckons. He opens it. Flashes his phone on it, starts to read, then seems to get with it, snaps the book shut, puts it in that faggy doctor bag, moves on out of her sight.

Satisfied her work is done, she gets up, dusts herself off, walks down the fire stairs and gets a late night bus. Takes some of the pills, stashes the rest in her bra, unwilling to risk Scarlet or that fucking suit-wearing motherfucker Everett asking for them back. The motherfucker is like that, always with his forms and saying shit like 'requisition.' If she has to fuck him, that'll be the most boring lay ever.

But worth it.

Carma's in a good mood. She got the job done. She'll stay on that Library teat for a while longer and maybe, this time, they'll teach her some good magic, let her get rich, find a good woman to top hard, settle down and drive a good car.

The Hollow, who was on the roof with her all along, is given an instruction by his wise master. He thinks Carma is entirely unworthy of death. The Jon-ghost-thing recalls her.

You cannot help him. We will not risk the wrath of an Archon.

I know, but still think I should watch him die.

The Hollow watches Carma open the door, wonders why he let her go. The Teaching Darkness intimates that you don't blunt a fine dagger on bad meat. He nods.

What a fine lesson.

32

I

So where am I?

Ludo is here. I can hear him bawling over the sound of gunfire, laughing like a mule. He must be good at what he does. All I hear is short controlled bursts and that's what you hear in the movies all the time.

I'm here before the Old Man is. He had to stop and gather his troops and all the stuff. Probably prepare himself as well. This is his big night. All I had to do was make two calls and catch a bus.

Then, back to the community centre. Archon's presence is growing. I take my tools from my bag, set up in the kitchen. Wards and glyphs, drawing them on the ground, muttering every spell I've ever cribbed; ever made up. Draw my strongest warding symbols on the ground. I need to be able to operate without constantly warding the Primal Sigil. Octagonal guard memes. Strong. Words written along it. Don't let the sound of gunfire getting louder distract me.

This is the show.

Finish it off with the symbol of the Omegamantis. Drop down, cross-legged, ignoring the bruising in my leg. Shark presence is back. My science is tight. Strong. It notices me, but I'm still out of focus.

Waiting here for the ambush.

Ludo kicks open the door and scouts the place out. Walks right by me. 'Clear,' he calls out. Walks outside. Squeak of wheel, creak of leather. Whiteknuckle but the wards hold and neither of them notice me. *I can see you, you can't see me.*

The Old Man, wheeled down the corridors until he comes to Wick's lair.

'Piss off,' he commands Ludo, who does. Reckon he comes into the kitchen and rolls a joint. He's covered in blood and he's shaking. Adrenaline supercharging him. Murder-dopamine.

Now's a good time, a perfect time to take him. Plant some bad spell in his head to see his way to a slit throat. Shut down his consciousness til he strokes out. Hell, convince his mind his body is dying then sit back, watch a useful homeopathy at work. Or just bind him still, pouring concrete into his nervous system and put a beating on him.

No.

That's not my way. Killing people isn't like the movies.

Besides, two things. One, I don't think I could hurt the bastard without a sledgehammer. Two, I have to keep still. Have to wait until the Old Man is deep in it with Wick before I make the move. If he can finish the girl, great. I move then. If he loses, then I'll have to step up and that's the worst case.

Either way, I blindside the winner. But to do that, I have to remain still. Very still. Then, snake them.

Because. Here's the thing. If the Old Man gets the scroll, there's a good chance he'll be able to go use it as a lever against the Archon. Rattle the prisoner's cage. Maybe use it as a slave collar, to bind one of the most powerful entities our world can tolerate.

And the Archon wants to be a city-god. But so does the Old Man.

One day, we'll all live in a fire.

He's been planning this for a million years. Living in some holocaust fantasy, living forever. Maybe the specifics weren't this. Weren't these circumstances. But as soon as heard the scroll was in town, he had to go for it. He wants to live in a world of pain and death, but a man like this? He'll stay on top even in a holocaust.

He's been a hardcore magician to the marrow. Never focusing on the small picture, never going in for results. Never trading it all in for gangster chick and gunmoles, or cocaine binges or even bogus miracles. He's made himself into a bad dream, a bogey for sorcerers, just for this moment. To be the man with the kind of power to have a city afraid of him through acts and will. Black fucking magic.

Jesus Christ. What a will. Hardcore. *Hardcore.*

But I'm still going to fuck his day up. I've seen too many sad deaths to let him go, let alone get himself an metropolis apotheosis.

The Old Man is laughing.

'Some child with good luck and a bit of talent with a brush? That's what I've been wary of?'

A beat.

'Shut up stupid old dick. You don't know what I am.'

Kind of laugh at that. Panic making things funny.

'Of course I do. You're a useful manikin. But you're not what I'm after. You're something to spit out. After, I'll breed you to something awful and let the children drill their way out of you with their digestive acids. You'll be my first sacrifice to myself.'

Long pause.

'Fucking hell, what makes you evil old cunts so fucking disgusting?'

He snorts. He's done with talking. He begins to chant. Something I've never heard before. Some invented tongue, maybe. Vile as it is strong. Vibrations of it hit me in the solar plexus. Ludo covers his ears. Walks out. Thank fuck. I didn't need him hanging around.

I listen carefully. I draw my conscious mind deep. *Dzogchen* receptive. Waiting. Not for long.

The Old Man gets straight in. He calls out the names of spirits. It's like tigers off a leash. Feel them manifest. Carcinogenic ghosts, howling from eight throats each. I can't see them, just feel them. Not sure I want to. He starts throwing magic words at her like crude taunts. Words to hurt. Words to frighten, words to maim. Sonic leprosy. They're not meant for me. And I'm behind serious barriers besides, but it's like acid spray anyway. It's filling up my mouth, death words down the back of my throat. Swallow it.

Then, the Old Man starts to bring the heavy artillery. All around me, the last words of rites he's had prepared for a hundred years scream. The walls break open like old wounds, leaking pus and bile and worse. So horrid, it's almost real. Eyes open in the walls. Something made of smoke and light and hate prowls the kitchen, sensing my wards, and I shut my eyes, not wanting to look into its mouth.

Compelled, it leaps and, finally, I hear Wick scream. The spirit is a Hierarch. A monster of high order. Something far too powerful to unleash except in desperation. Way too much to attack an untrained girl.

And I understand.

The Old Man isn't looking to hurt her.

He's after the Archon.

II

IT'S MANIFESTING. IT'S REAL, HERE IN THE WORLD, BUT WICK isn't done painting its body into existence. She just started tonight. And, oh fuck, I think he can hurt it enough to get it to submit to him.

I think he's winning.

And I gave it to him. Leaked the information to him tonight, hoping he'd be stupid and rush in, but I never knew he was this dangerous. This powerful. This is the sweet spot to do it. When it's trying to come into the world, to make itself real, to become a God like nothing that's walked the earth for a million years.

I did it.

Amateur. *Fucking amateur!*

Get up, out of the Octagon. If I'm going to move against him, I have to commit. But first, I summon my own allies. The Ultrascorpions appear before me, tails twitching, claws clacking. Ready for harm.

My guys manifest, fog into ice, then they rush into battle like a hiss. Mandibles biting and tails shooting forward. I don't even see what the hell they're fighting. Wait, there it is. I've never seen a Hierarch before.

Some cancer-creature. Some eregores a century worth of cruelty brings you. Hooks and old hot spit. Open boils and acid words. The Ultrascorpions can't win against something this long in birthing, percolated in decades of brutality. But they carve a path through the Old Man's lesser allies, ensuring I won't have to guard my back from some vicious things manifesting at me when I don't need the distraction. Then they engage the monster.

Two scorpions peel back a flap of plastic, sticking muscle, a third throws back its head and clacks a battle cry, piercing the creature's inside with a barb as big as my hand. No time for celebration, they're already melting as a swarm of hornets made of vitriol take them. I watch this and more. Tentacular limbs like whips. Eyes as sick as leprosy. Turn away from the more cloacal features. Look back and the Familiar War has moved itself into another room or shifted into realms where bodies don't count.

Now it's just me.

Time for the dramatic gesture.

Time to show the world who I am. Time to impress my desires and my sacrifices upon it.

Then, I show magic just how into this battle I am. I drop the wards. The sigil beats down at me, but it's half-hearted. Its potency targets the Old Man now. Worth it. Make the symbol real as I commit to assault. Utterly. Totally. Win or die.

'Well, fancy seeing you here.'

It's Ludo. I never even saw him come back in.

White of his eyes. Mad dog grin.

I can't do anything but laugh, so I do. Sound of it scares me. I'm done.

He goes to work, leg first.

III

EARLY CASE I WORKED, ME AND JON WENT INTO SOME S&M coven. A man with a ponytail and moustache drank Midori while his frizzy-haired, nervous and overweight wife told us all about the pleasures of restriction and power. Behind them, in the club, the pornography featured a woman getting slapped repeatedly in the face and spat on. The woman droned on about intimacy and limits and respect.

Bettina took him apart.

Thinking of that when the back of his hand takes my cheek, the sting slap of it fighting with the blunt force trauma to hurt more. He works my body, winding me, and I know he's just warming up. Rabbit punches that I take on my arms. That annoys him, so he changes pace. Takes me, slams my head against the wall. Between that and the second and third slap, my lips split.

Let me tell you now. When you've really had pain rip away your power, your ability to resist, there's nothing intimate about it. The beatings hurt like you can't understand. Hope you never do. Then there's the humiliation. And Jesus Christ, he punches me in the face and my head sparks and my back teeth come lose and I'm afraid he's split my cheekbone and then he throws me into the kitchen bench, the corner taking me in the short ribs. I just start to beg God that he doesn't work my shins. I hate that.

'Oh yeah,' he grins, 'this.'

And with that weird kick, he goes to work up and down my right leg. Ankle, knee, thigh, knee, stomp the top of the foot, then toe. Shin. Then back into the rhythm. I fall, he stomps and whatever clicked in my knee the other night grinds now. At least I've stopped screaming. The pain is too much and my body is overtaxed. Numb.

Ludo stops. Breathing hard. I reach for gnosis. Fail. Reach for gnosis. Fail. I just hurt too damn much and I'm too fucking scared. My hip feels shattered. Body starts screaming *don't let him hurt me* and it's hell to keep it controlled.

He's rifling through drawers. Old rusted knife. One of those rolling things. Pins. Can opener.

Fuck. I need a delaying tactic. Something. Shift my weight trying to get up and the pain sweeps up from toes to skull.

He picks me up by the hair and deposits me on the kitchen bench, back down. Something in me wants to cry and beg him to stop but I just can't listen to it.

My body gives in. Can't move, lock up. Ludo takes my cigarettes, lighter from my jacket pocket, lights one up. Weirdly, I almost ask if I can have one.

Wick is screaming too. Behind all the pain in my body, I can feel their battle like thunder behind my eyes.

It's too much. I want to give in. But there's a rolling pin in his fist and Ludo's smoking my cigarettes with my blood on his hands. And I realise that I've gotten off lightly so far. A few smacks, a few bruises. The knee might be something else, but the real fun is just starting.

'Fucking blanco pussy. Mess with all this el Diablo shit and look at you. You tell me where all this ends you up. I'll tell you. Nowhere. Smart guys like you, you're not the first to find out how valuable smart is.'

He's talking to himself as much as me.

I can only do this once. It's not the pain. It's the fear. *He's going to hit me again.* That's the worst. Fear. Pain, you can survive. Fear, no. So I concentrate. Knee, which grinds. Face, the bruise. The fucked short ribs. That's my meditation.

No magic words. Just empty-handed desperation. I fling my pain at him, at the spells in his head that keep him safe from the Primal Sigils all around this dark, dirty room. Death-curse. I throw everything I have into it. One moment of pure concentration, holding on to a spell I made up years ago.

And it works. Breach the Old Man's spell. And Ludo goes still. Silent. Staring at the walls.

For about a second. Turns and stares at me with a deep sea fish stare and I slide off the bench. He's hurt. But then I remember. Idea-eater. It siphons off the worst of the curse and leaves him shaking, poisoned and living.

Go for the doors just get out get out. Nothing more to fight with. Which is when my legs gives out and I collapse.

Just pain. Whites me out and for what seems ten thousand years, just lose my own mind to black fear.

Crawl, not seeing where I'm going. Get outside. Get it together. Get outside. *Get outside.* Try again.

Leg pain blinds. Close my eyes. Fight off fear. Nearly at the door.

When I realise he's just walked in front of me. My hand touches his boots. If the Primal Sigil has sent him insane, it's the kind of insanity that makes room for his torture-urge.

Open my eyes. Face it like a man. *Scarlet. Baby, I tried.*

Not his boot. Too small. Open the eyes to see what I'm touching.

Look up.

Leaning over me. Bettina.

33

I

Wick is losing. The bastard old thing is hurting her. Digging up every emotion and doubt until she just wants to give him the scroll to leave her alone. But he's just another one of the guys who dissed her work and spoiled it, so fuck him.

But sooner or later, he'll kill her. The monsters tear at her and sting her like hornets.

She uses the paint like a bug spray but that's not going to last long. There's only one way to win.

The thing in the scroll is screaming at her. Join it. Give in to It. Let It into her and into the city she's marked with Its symbol. Into the people she took for it. *They're dead*, she explains. *Dead or alive, you don't seem much different to me*, it replies.

The crazy crip wheels his chair into the room now. Seems to matter as he grins ugly when he wheels his way in and she can smell him.

Let me in, says the thing behind the scroll. The thing that looks through her work like peepholes in a girls' locker room. *I don't want this one to share in my majesty.*

Wick wonders what will happen to her if she does let It in. Will she still be her? Will she still like to tag the City, a ragged shape who's fucking awesome at art?

No. You'll be a grandiose art work that all will cower to look upon.

That sounds pretty cool. But then again. She sort of liked it when that guy said how much he liked her work. Wasn't that better than cower?

She draws a circle around her with her can. It's an electric blue, the colour that she always felt was powerful somehow.

The crip in the chair sneers.

Become me a little, Wick tells the thing. It can't do anything else than obey her. She knows. She's read the terms of the scroll, although she can't speak the language. And It does. Surges into her, downloading like a flood.

Oh no.

II

She smiles at me, her face less gaunt, more skeletal.

St. Catriona. Smiling at me. Bettina's undeath, in sharp relief. Unavoidable.

'Watch this.'

She takes Ludo apart. Teeth, mainly. The sounds he makes are like a pig. I turn my gaze away as she takes his nipple between her teeth and starts to peel him.

Think about how it felt. Think about the smashed guitar he's made of my leg. She throws him across the room and he's crying, I think.

Better him than me.

No. That's not really what I think. I don't mind being hard, but it's so easy to be cruel.

'Bettina. Just finish it.'

There's a crack. The squeals stop. But then there's the sound of something heavy pounding, a crack and she gets to the good bit. I'm glad she's behind the bench. I don't need to see that.

The Old Man starts to laugh. The Primal Sigils start their pounding again. I stand up, but it hurts too much. Slide down the wall.

'Bettina.' A whisper.

'Bettina!' A shout.

My packet of cigarettes, thrown from behind the bench. A second later, the lighter. Blood and something black sticks to it. Wipe it off and light up. Familiar act. Helps me. The pressure from the Sigils eases off as I use lighting up as a place to regain gnosis.

Soon, she stops. Tries the taps but the water is cut off. She stands, her face is all red. Picks at her teeth.

'Thanks,' I say to her.

'*De nada.*'

'No. It's a thing.'

Ludo, gone just like that. One less thing to worry about.

She walks over, grasps my wrist in sticky fingers. Right leg can't really bear any weight.

'You should go. Wait outside. Don't look at the graffiti. Look at the sky or something.'

She nods. 'The Old Man, he could switch me off.' I know.

I lean against the bench, careful with my gaze.

'Why'd you come back?'

She shrugs. 'Dead people can't sleep easy. This, waves her hand all around, 'it's just not good.'

'No.'

'I didn't want to sleep with this in the ground with me.'

She walks out, a gore shade, slim in the dark.

Old Man.

Fucking it up for everyone since time began. Looking to inject himself into the city like a dose of poison; of radiation. Living forever, bonded to an Archon. As if this place wasn't bad enough already.

I can limp, so I do it. Walk down the corridor.

Wick is laying on the ground. The Old Man is giggling. He's running over her fingers with the chair. Her face is white from pain. The greatest moment a magician could possibly have but he's delaying it for one last moment of pettiness.

She whispers, *do it*. I can feel her wishes.

Oh fuck no.

III

ALL YOU NEED IS TO GIVE IN, THE SCROLL WHISPERS. *LET ME IN and I'll make you Queen of the City. You'll stand beside me in glory, forever. I'll reach back in time, tear my captors from Procession and Chronology, then use up this world, crack it open, then return to the true place and war upon my brothers forever. And you'll always be a part of me. A little mortal voice, witness to things none of her ape species can ever imagine. Just let me in.*

Wick doesn't want that. She just wants to tag the city and maybe make sure her mum is ok, one day. (No. Wait. Her mum...) She just wants a little respect and the guys to treat her equal. She can feel the scroll and it's not lying, whatever it is. It can do that for her. Will do that for her.

'What if I free you another way?'

No other way, It hisses.

Wick looks at the crippled, vicious old bastard and sees one face of power. Thinks of all the people she's hurt and that's another face of power. Maybe the same but it surely looks better when you're the one doling out the hurt. Thinks of Deenate. That was sweet, taking back from him, but he was dead now. Just dead. He'd never look at her work, not even to hate it.

And that's all she wants. Just for people to look at the work and have an opinion.

'I don't think I can be what you want.'

Are you sure? It whispers. *Let me show you a cost.*

It stops leaking Its might into the world and the Old Man is on her as quick as a housecat. Rolling his chair over the tops of her fingers, laughing and giggling, giggling. Rolls back.

You'll never paint again . Not if he keeps this up.

He rolls forward. She yells. Shit it hurts.

Wick looks up. The guy from before steps up to the dorm room, hovering behind the crip, although someone's handed him a beating. He looks like shit.

He liked her work. Yeah, that's him.

At least, one time, someone did. This way, someone else might.

Do it, she says, not sure if it's aloud.

Then. 'Oh fuck no!'

IV

BECAUSE THIS IS WHAT THE OLD MAN'S WAITING FOR.

A hundred years or more of trying not to die. Now, the

scroll, a prisoned Archon trying to manifest. It's perfect. He's waited so long for an opportunity like this.

And with every inch of strength in him, he casts his final spell. Severing his connections to mortality, he throws his soul at the Archon, not looking to match strength but determination. He tries to corral the Archon into his body, making them one. The Archon's power, his mind, his personality, his body grown metropolitan. It's thrown Its will outside the scroll but not Its power. It's offered up Its throat.

And the Archon is weak.

And the Archon is already bound to the scroll.

And the Archon is already halfway between scroll and Wick.

And the Old Man has risked his ancient life, the symbolic sacrifice he has never made.

He enters into a consciousness no human ever has before. Visualises himself in an infinite blackness, passing into a creature's body that is geometric and mad and vast. Sees himself slicing ganglions and dendrites that are long as chasms, drinking down living chemicals like a drunk. The Archon is too huge an entity to fight him. Like slapping a bacteria.

The Old Man is winning. A helpless God, he casts his final spells, fuelled by death, severing the Archon's faint identity and sense of self. A helpless hulk the Old Man can ravage and possess.

He gurgles in glee.

V

.   .   .

THE GUY PUSHES THE OLD MAN OUT OF THE CHAIR AND SITS on it.

'Lark. Remember me?'

'Sure. You gonna kill him?' she asks, clutching her broken fingers.

Lark looks down at the gnarled form of the Old Man. 'Do no good now. Besides, do you want to be the kind of girl, kills an old guy pushed out of his chair?'

'Nah.'

'Me either.'

Wick is fading into nothingness.

'He's going to take It away from me. Then *I'll* be alone.'

'Worse things than being alone.' He stops, says it again. 'And that's true.' Says it like it means something to him as well as her.

'Yeah but, with the scroll, the dude in the scroll, I got to paint like never before.'

The guy, Lark, whatever, gives her a smoke like he did a few hours before.

'There's blood on this, man.'

'Yeah, but it's a prick's blood. Makes 'em taste like victory. Besides, it's dry blood. And I've only got one left after this, so be grateful.'

They light up. Lark helps her because her hand doesn't really work, her fingers.

He talks.

'So listen. Some dude just beat me down. Not too sharp right now. But listen. The old dude. Bad dude.' Her fingers agree with Lark's character judgement

'He's hurting the scroll thing. Which would normally be impossible, but he's breaking rules, taking advantage of it like a snail out its shell.'

'Sure.'

'Listen. The scroll, what's in it, It's marked you. Marked the city. This is the important bit, so pay attention. *You've marked it back*. Your work, your tags, your effort. You're in It as much as It's in you. If you want It, you can take It back. Tag the scroll thing, tag the Archon, and the Old Man will never take It from you.'

She frowns. This dude, who is this dude to tell her this stuff. She's not fucking stupid enough to trust him.

'Yeah, I'm not done telling it. There's always a price. You and It, you'll be one. But in the city forever.'

She frowns all over again.

'Is that bad? Someone like me?'

'Keep up the good tags, I don't see why you'd be so bad.'

She throws the cigarette over her shoulder.

'That's cool.'

And she's in.

34

———

I

IT IS EASY. SHE ENTERS INTO THE SCROLL AND SHE'S PAINTED the Archon's letters and shapes and Its patterns so many times before. That has changed her, and she follows the cripple into his construct-hallucination. And the Old Man is about his vandalism.

Fuck that. How many times has she seen her work vandalised and smeared by some bastard? Not this time. And though Wick doesn't know it, it's this rage at seeing just one more beautiful thing marred that strengthens her, and magic knows and responds.

In her head, she paints the Primal Sigil onto the Primal Sigil. Her and It, linked together. Forever, now. Her art, her words, her magic. City-magic. Art-magic. The magic of a young woman *who just can't take another person fucking with her*.

She joins the Archon, giving up her body.

And she's not as big as the scroll-god. She never can be.

But she's still a lot bigger than an old bastard who likes to trample on people, just so they'll be scared.

They join, then. She lets it fill her utterly and then beyond the borders of human might, bounded by human outrage and ambition.

Wick rotates her new deific form around and with her thirty thousand gleaming, jewelled eyes stares at the vandal.

'I hate it when people mess my work up.'

The Old Man starts to shake his head.

II

He screams with rage, the ancient bastard, even in his abyss-deep meditation. His voice snarls obscenities, biting them off with his broken green teeth.

I watch Wick. Slowly, some stigmata, something, marks this apotheosis. Face and mangled fingers are all I can see until she throws back her hood and they form under her scalp but I have no doubt it's everywhere. Tattooing her. You can guess with what.

The Old Man sobs with a frustration I hope to never feel. All for nothing, failure at the very end.

Then something goes out of his fucked-up, evil eyes. But he's still breathing. Which is too much of a shame.

Everything goes still and I can feel a surge in the city. But no time for contemplation. Even now, I can feel her stirring.

I look through his clothes, but there's no wallet. His watch looks like ten dollars' worth of tin. You'd think a man with his money would carry cash.

Ludo might have something on him, but I'm not checking. Shame, that idea-eater is sweet.

I put Wick's body, stilled now forever, into the wheelchair. Someone will take care of her. If I played this right, there'll be people here soon. Mully will find a place for her. I'll take her to him. One more stray in a house full of strays.

Then, carefully, I take the scroll from her hands. She's clutching it, but not tight. I find a good, low-res meditation, keyed in to shallow breath. Look at the scroll carefully. But there's nothing there, now. Just a strange story in a made-up language, telling a weird story from long ago. Still, I have a plan to deal with it.

Look at her. Still. Breathing so slow. Fight away sadness.

The Primal Sigils are losing their strength, their malice potency. Becoming something new. The people whose body she climbed in? They'll regain themselves, but I'd bet the last cigarette in my pack that there's a new cult already forming.

I push the Old Man's body away. He won't die and I'm not murdering a catatonic. He'll have people come for him to put him on machines. But I don't have to help him.

Attention back to Wick, I bow down in front of the new god. Smear some of the dried blood from my cut lip onto her broken hand. A little sacrifice. A little message from mere human up to the divine, supernal world of deities.

City-God, manifesting in all the hidden prayers and lonely messages written down on stone and metal, any rogue decoration or sutra or glyph.

I limp my way out, pushing her, using the chair to help me.

Bettina is waiting.

'All done.'

'Not quite.'

She points. On the street, two new flashy town cars.

People. One in the car who I can't see. Then, on the street, armed with tools and one with a gun.

Carma, Rosengarten, Raj. And look, Katanya, who's gotten a promotion, so it seems. I push through the door. There she is, getting out of the car, looking like a million bucks.

Scarlet.

'Hey baby.'

III

SO ANGRY SHE'S LUMINOUS, DRESSED ALL IN WHITE FOR SOME damn reason, her hair dyed platinum now.

Not sure she's angry at me. At least, specifically.

'What. the fuck. has been going on?'

'I'm fine.'

'We'll take care of your medical issues later. Right now, every occultist and sensitive in this city is half-mad, with a lot of them tipping over that edge. My phone is ringing off the hook and we've had a rash of suicides. Not to mention the spill over onto the citizens.'

She stole saying citizens from me.

'I'll explain it all later. What you have to know is. One, the Old Man is laying in a pool of his own spittle inside. You're welcome. Two, I'll have a full report in a few days for you on why the Bleak Elect went for Gallowglass. And an invoice, which you'll have a month to pay. My expenses are a bastard. And three, this young woman is pretty important now. You'll take her to Mully.'

The sun finally sticks its tongue out through the gaps in the city's teeth.

'But right now, I'm hurt and I'm exhausted. So why don't

you take the Famous Five here and piss off. I didn't get a lick of assistance from you in there.'

That gets her, I see. 'We didn't know what the hell was going on.'

'Yeah.'

I look at them all.

Katanya steps forward. Looks me up and down. 'What the hell did you do? This place is cracked wide open. I told you things were bad. You're only making it worse! How the hell can we keep up with this?'

She's angry. She's also doing what none of the others are. Looking carefully at more than just me.

Lean in. Takes a second to find my own voice. Whisper to her.

'Watch this place. Clean it up. Burn it down. Buy it, board it up. But *watch it*.'

Katanya looks at me carefully. Looks past me being just her dick ex-teacher and sees what I'm telling her. Knows I'm not playing. That I'm sharing something real with her. Nods, once, meaning it.

Good girl. Maybe there's hope for at least one of the slackers.

I step back. Smile through blood for Scarlet.

'See ya.'

I start to move off. Rosengarten's improved in the last few years. The pimples have mostly gone, the hair is cut short and the specs are cool. Still fat, but.

'No. No we don't think so. That young woman is clearly no longer human. You've obviously been through something of significance to the city's occult security. And we want answers. We want you to come with us.'

Don't even bother breaking stride. He steps in front of me.

I look at him. Jesus. *This is my replacement*? He's so in love with the bully-boy of it all. I wonder when was the last time he looked at a grimoire that didn't have some lame-ass hurt-conjure he can make into a truncheon and Perspex helmet.

'You don't understand,' he says. Tries to put badness in his voice but he's just a poser to me. 'We want to *talk to you.*'

I light the last one. Half to look cool, I admit. Also to give me a second to get myself together. I'm tired and I can't let them see how little I want to fight.

I've got enough juice for this. Like the Hollow said, *if you're gonna get into it, get into it.* I say the words quickly and he realises too late. Reacts slow, letting it show over his face before he brings up his hands to gesture. By then, it's too late and he's fallen back, bee stings in his head.

'Rosengarten. Son. Fuck off.'

Is there anything more patronising than 'son'?

Raj comes forward and Bettina steps out of her shadows. She doesn't say anything. She's got a gut full of meat and a skimpy singlet, soaked in blood too thick to dry. Her face, her stink, her stare all say it. *Step up and I will motherfuck you.*

But something's wrong. He used to like a fight, but now he seems keen on a suicide. He breaks pace, then keeps it coming.

'Raj!' Scarlet commands, but the tension doesn't break.

'Baby, them new kids aren't really cutting it. Now let me walk out of here.'

'Firstly,' she says, 'I'm not *baby*. Secondly, Rosengarten didn't mean it like that.'

I look at him, getting rid of my curse slowly. Badly.

'Thank God. I don't think I'm ready for such an epic battle against a worthy foe.'

Maybe, just maybe a smile pricks her lips.

'We want to make sure you're alright and we want to talk to you about making you a long-term consultant. Like Mully.

We don't know what happened here yet but, well, we're grateful.'

She's lying. I think they came here to strong-arm me. I hope I'm wrong. But even if they're not -

'Hey, that's great. Me and Jon accept.'

'Umn... Jon. Jon's not involved with this.'

'That's right.'

I walk on.

My leg hurts.

'I'll call you later, Scarlet.'

Bettina and I walk away.

35

———

I

Scarlet slides into the front seat. Everett is there, sipping chai from a cardboard cup.

'Jesus Christ. Covered in blood and beat the hell up. He looks a horror.'

'Yep,' she lies. 'He looked like hell.' Covered in blood and dangerous. Being the magician he should have been, all along. He's put on weight and he needs a haircut, but she can feel how he intimidated them all. She's reminded of the old days for a while when he was all badness grins and hex.

But in service to nothing now.

Scarlet realises that Lark has taken out the Old Man and done what none of them could. Alone and with few allies. A shiver passes through her. *Covered in blood and dangerous.*

'Think he'll take the job? We could really use him back.'

That's true. But Scarlet can't believe Everett would risk their relationship, no matter how useful Lark could be. She understands the stakes and the usefulness of a man like Lark.

Still, you'd think Everett would at the very least show something other than an earnest belief they'd work it out. Everett never seems jealous, but she shuts that down and talks to him.

'No. He won't take the job. Not yet.'

She smiles at her man. 'But I think I know a way to pressure him.'

But she's lying.

II

LATER.

Bettina and I get home. Wash up. Change. I ask her to take care of the girl and I sleep for nine hours. Wake up. Bettina has ordered in beers, Mexican food and two packs of smokes. She cleaned herself up and she's wearing my shirt. It'd be sexy if she didn't have a tooth she'd chipped on a big man's bones. My knee is in bad shape and I swallow painkillers. I limp. The face in the mirror is not pretty.

'You look like hell,' she says and I nod.

'It's a masculine look, Bettina. Don't be afraid of my rugged machismo.' She raises an eyebrow and threatens a zombie smile.

'What now?'

'First, you're going to take that girl off to Mully. I can't take care of her and she's going to need it constantly for a while. She might not ever come back to her body. I don't know how to go about that, but he might. Besides, he'll want to look at her before anyone else.'

'Who is she?'

'That?' I point at the skinny little girl, covered in tattoos from the inside out. 'That's nothing for now. That's an empty room. But it once housed a God. There's a new divinity loose, and we'll have to deal with her soon enough.'

'Ok.'

'And listen. You came back for me. That guy, he had me. No doubt. You're free of all debt to me, you have to know that.'

She nods. Drinking my beer.

'I won't raise you again without your say.'

She frowns. 'You don't get it. I didn't come back because I owed you.'

I don't say anything about that. I don't know how to talk to people about anything that isn't in a book. She waits and when it's clear I'm not talking, she moves.

'I'm going down in the dirt again.'

I nod, sort of sad.

She takes the girl. Picks up her chair and all, like, it ain't a thing.

'You call when you need. I don't like dreaming so much I need to do it forever. I can't die? Might as well not be dead.'

Gone.

Bye Bettina. I wish I understood you. But no more time to rub salt.

Ok. Dial a number.

III

GOOD TO BE ON THE STREET, NOT HAVING TO HIDE. MAYBE what's left of the Old Man's organisation will come for me, but not yet. Under the bridge, they'll be at each other's throat, looking to take the reins. I'll deal with who's left.

Maybe the hippie will try again, too. But I don't get that lucky twice.

Leg is too fucked up to walk all the way. Money from the account, which is too low. Cab's a luxury, but I need it.

Public place.

Outside Town Hall, there's a fountain and a statue of a man in a cloak and a wig, looking sternly to the rest of the country, north. He's underlit and stern. I like him.

Agent Coffee and Agent Valier meet me there. They sit on either side.

I hand her the scroll.

She hands me the money. It's quite a bit.

'You look like you've been in the wars,' says Coffee. 'Someone really gave you a nasty few love taps, right?' He's right. Under my eye, the bruise is black and blue and green and hurts like a bastard. It'll fade. Everything does.

'Last night was a bad night. Everyone's reporting bad dreams. Things got out, into the world that maybe shouldn't have. Did you watch the news?' That's Valier.

I smoke one Bettina bought me and say nothing.

Agent Coffee starts in.

'I got to tell you guy, that was a strange night. I dreamt my grandfather was coming after me but instead of a head, he just had jaws. Big as a head. I haven't been that scared since I was a little kid. Why don't you tell me what you got up to after you called?'

Shut them up. Get to the point.

'I watched a man try to steal the powers from an entity outside our space-time. He failed and in the aftermath, someone became a God.'

They stare at each other.

'That's a pretty weird thing to say, Lark.'

I shrug.

'So, that's twenty-five thousand dollars. We'll need you to sign for it.' He's brought a clipboard. He's not actually kidding.

I shake my head and he shrugs and grins at me, like he wasn't a government agent. 'Hey, can't blame a guy for trying, right?'

'Shut up.' Done with him.

'Hey no need for that! I was thinking maybe we were close to a relationship.'

Turn to Valier.

'Listen, last night was the biggest night I've ever seen. Things went down like never happened in my lifetime. But the players and the plays have changed. There's something in the world now, something new. And under the bridge, there's going to be trouble. If you want to see some shit go down, go there.'

I get up to go. I really don't have anything else to say, but Valier has a few words.

'You want a job?'

'I don't really see myself as the spook type. I wasn't really great at sports or language, or communicating and, it turns out, I was never as good at being on a team, as I thought.'

She shakes her head.

'Not suggesting an office gig. You'd be what we call an asset.'

'Flattering.'

'It means that I'd pay you for leads, for introductions, for information. You'd be like a consultant.'

'No.'

'You'd also be helping your nation.'

How do I explain to her that I'd be out of this place if I could? I don't.

'But I can't imagine that'd mean much to a man like you.'

'A man like me? Guess not. Agent.'

'But we'd share information with you, as well.'

That's tempting. But no. That'd be a one-way street. Not even sure it's a good idea to be talking to spooks in the first place. Guys like this spend too much time monitoring student unions and radical bookshops and dudes with weird surnames for the likes of me. Once they have you, they keep you. Let's shut down their thinking and cut this cord.

'You can't weaponise it. The scroll. The stuff like the scroll. The things you're getting a glimpse at. You can't train it to soldiers. It's not a science. It's like an art. Do your research, Agent Valier. Track down what you can. Put together a picture. Make reports to whoever you have to. It's not like anything you've seen, but I think you're starting to understand that you're in a whole new context. Walk away. Chase down union leaders and guys who think God has plans that involve pipe-bombs.'

She stands.

'I just want to help people.'

'People involved in this, they don't want help.'

I limp away.

IV

THE END OF THE WEEK, THE DOCTOR HAS COME AROUND AND wants my leg x-rayed. Recommends I get a crutch, but fuck that.

I write up a report to Scarlet, leaving out a few things I'd rather keep private, mainly stuff about Bettina. And the Hollow. I couldn't even write that out if I tried. Still raw.

I email it to her. Email my invoice to her assistant. He'll like getting those funds together.

A week goes by. Sunday night, I take a job. Guy's home movies from when he was a kid, suddenly he can see monsters at his birthday party. I play the tapes. See them too. Hypnotise him and find out his dad had some strange ideas for what made good friends for his kids. Bring him out. Tell him that he'd best have a chat with his dad. Tell him something's changed. His psychic sensor has switched off. Freaks out. Tells me not to be stupid. Yells. I ask for some money and he pays me. Guess that night of bad dreams did have a real effect after all.

I pay formal thanks to the Omegamantis and the Ultrascorpions, bringing up tequila for them, playing their favourite music. I give the one who died a memorial service, sketching him out on a piece of paper, anointing it with oils. Burning it to say goodbye.

Always act like there's significance. Show the magic you take it serious, treat the Ultrascorpions with respect, they'll treat you the same way.

Life settles. The bruises start to ease away. I ice the leg and hip. I answer some mail.

It's all an anti-climax, isn't it? I pass people on the street and sort of wonder why they don't demand the story from me.

Then, one afternoon, the phone rings and Scarlet asks if I'm free.

She comes in the early evening.

There's snow in her hair. Winter has started for real. She's got it cut again. Her earrings are expensive and I don't pick up on the rest of the jewellery until it's too late. She's wearing a black overcoat and a black suit and she looks amazing. She wears her spectacles, which I love.

She's bought a bottle of gin and a bottle of tonic. Puts it on my desk. The expensive kind.

'This is a thank you. Personal one.'

I try to smile but the cheek is still a bit too sore for it.

She reaches across. Touches it with cold fingers and for a second, I'm happy enough to die. Breaking it, she leans back.

'Jesus. That's looks better but it still looks terrible. Does it hurt much?'

Yes.

'Nah, it's not so bad, really.'

From her coat, she takes out two envelopes. Puts the thick one on my desk.

'A deal's a deal'.

'Stay for a drink.'

She glances at her watch.

'One drink.'

I pour and mix. 'No limes,' I say. She prefers limes in her gin. Got no lemons, either.

She takes one out of her pocket and I slice them up with an old switchblade in my desk. *She brought a lime*. I'm remarkably cheered by that fact.

'I saw the girl. I went to see Mully. He's looking after her, but he's going to have her put into a home for people like her. It's a good place, where she'll be looked after.'

'You know what she is?'

'Not really. We think her spirit is gone but... where?'

I want to show off. I want to tell her that I helped a God come into the world. A real power. But I remember Everett in the car and her turning her gaze from me outside a restaurant and I just shrug. I'm not quite ready to forgive all that.

'Rosengarten, he thinks your report is amazing. He still worships you.'

Laugh through my nose. He hated me.

'He wants to use it as a case file for the adepts to study.'

'But you don't think so. You keep things in-house.'

'The Library is important, Lark.'

We've had this discussion and it ends in shouting. Not today.

'What did you think of it? My report. The whole case?'

'I think you always risk too much to get an answer. You should have brought us in earlier. But, it was a good job. And bringing down the Old Man, that's... it's good work.'

She smiles at me for the first time in two years. My heart breaks.

Then I spoil it all. Because I have to know.

'There's just one problem with it all, Scarlet. The scroll came into the country more than twenty years-ago. Not long after the first Gulf War if I'm not mistaken. The Gallowglass had it for that long, never really wanting to know what was in it. For them, ownership was magic, control was power. Then, one day, the Old Man just strikes after it.'

I drink. Light up.

'So how did he know it was there? Who'd know the Gallow-glass wouldn't even open it, knowing they gained power through perceived dollar values? They got more power just having it that using it, according to their theology. So who could have known it was there? Who could have known the Old Man's motives, that he'd risk everything if it meant he could get access to a entity as powerful and vulnerable as an Archon? Who could have known he'd actually be dangerous enough to have a chance?'

Her smile slowly fades.

'And who'd know to put me on the job, knowing I wouldn't stop until I'd gone after the Old Man?'

Glancing at her watch. 'I have to go.'

'Scarlet, you leaked it to the Old Man. You started the

whole cult war. You put me on the front line. Got the shit beaten out of me twice. Nearly got Bettina killed. Cost that girl Wick a shot at living a life. Got the Bleak Electors killed. Got the Gallowglass killed.'

I lean in.

'Why?'

She takes a long breath in. Then, see this on her face plain, she decides to stop fucking around.

'Since you and the Hollow left, the Library has been falling apart. You've been working small cases for citizens and minor cults because we've been funnelling them to you. Heading off the bad ones, the ones we didn't want you to see. Because we wanted them ourselves. Because the organisation doesn't like a rogue.

'And because I didn't give the order to have you killed like a lot of people wanted.'

That's new. I feel the anger spreading on my face. She's kept me from work these years. She's kept me alive not because she doesn't want me dead but because I'm useful.

An asset.

'But. Listen.'

'Alright.'

'Listen, things are getting bad out there. The magic is acting wilder. There's more and more entities slipping into the world than ever before and we do. Not. Know. Why. There's more dangerous cults growing up than you'd guess. And the Old Man was just the worst of a bad bunch. And you can't know this because we keep it from you.

'And, Lark, we *can't take care of it ourselves*. The Library, since you and Jon left, it's not the same. You never trained anyone. You left us high and dry because you and me broke up. And that's a selfish, stupid thing to do.'

'You left before I walked away. I didn't leave just because of us. And if I did... that's only a part of it.'

'It doesn't matter. Would you join because I asked you? And would you come back for the right reasons? And if you did, would it be because you wanted me?'

Maybe. Stay quiet.

'And because I only have fucking idiots like Connor and Raj to rely on, who are in turn training idiots, things are snowballing. Whatever is going on in the city, we should have tracked down and ended. Whatever is letting more and more monsters in, whatever is inspiring more psychos with a grimoire into the city, we can't find and can't stop and that's making us look weak.

'And in turn, that's encouraging old cults to act out.'

She screws her courage into her face and looks at me with those electrical eyes.

'Yeah. So I leaked the scroll to the Old Man. We'd known for years. Ever since I got promoted, I'd known. And I wanted to do something fierce. Something to let the rebels and the monsters know to keep in line. Keep in line or the Library would fuck them up.

'And I put you in front of the bullet because I'd hoped you'd still be as good as you were.'

'You put me through that, to keep your rep?'

'Yeah.' She looks away, finally.

'And you know what? Tonight, everyone's talking about how the Library took out the terror of the city, the Old Man, the devil himself. I'm going to make sure Rosengarten and the others look like the heroes. I'm going to spread the word they came in, saved your arse, and then they took out the Old Man. You're going to look like you bit off more than you could chew. You, Lark, who they're all still afraid of. You're going to look bad so the Library can look good until I can *make* them good.'

I'm sort of falling down inside myself now.

'I'll have old enemies coming out of the woodwork, Scarlet.'

'Yeah. And unless you join us, you'll probably get taken out by one of them. But you'll never join. Not for the right reasons. You'd join for me. Never for loyalty. Because you think we're police.'

'*You are fucking police.* I was tired of it and I still am.'

Yelling. 'We are police! Something bad is coming and I don't trust anyone else in this City but us to take care of it! And I used you to give us time to do it in.'

'Scarlet.'

'No. Be quiet. Because it gets worse and it's time I told you the truth.' Fury rises up.

'Alright.'

'And knowing you wouldn't join for the right reasons, knowing you wouldn't be loyal to something, knowing you're stubborn and proud and unable to commit to something bigger than you, I let it play out. I know the only reason you would work with the Library would be for me. And I'm committed to something you don't like. That's why I set you on the Old Man and it's why I've exposed you to danger to come.'

She calms down.

'And I don't want you.'

Scarlet takes the envelope, the second envelope from her pocket and my name is written on it. Calligraphy.

'I want the Library. And I want my relationships to be safe from anyone who could hurt my standing in the Library or its security. I want to make a difference.'

Deep, ragged breath. Once, that meant she was fighting tears. Not now.

'Lark, I'm glad you're alive. I think you did a *fine* job. But

I'm going to use you anyway. And I'm not sorry for the danger I've put you in because I need *you* to be in it, not us. We need to be heroes.'

Gets up. 'I wasn't going to give you that, but I think you need to see it. Everett made me make it because he's the kind of man who includes people. And I made it because I knew you wouldn't come.

Lark. *Don't come.* I don't want you there on the day.

And don't contact me. Not for help. Not for anything. If the Library requires your services, I'll have someone contact you.'

Turns. Walks out. Looks at me.

'Good luck, Lark. It's nothing personal.'

That's what hurts the most. *It really, really isn't.*

I open the envelope.

It's an invitation to her wedding to Everett.

Light up. Her jewellery. Gold band on her finger.

Think. Think my way out of this. There's got to be an angle to play... no.

Nothing more to be done. Soon, someone will be coming, looking to make me pay for a bully-boy decision I made in a life I regret. They'll come for revenge or spite or justice. But they'll come.

But not now. Not tonight. From my window I watch her kiss her fiancé and then they get into the car and go. I see her tracks in the snow.

So tonight, I do the one thing I can.

Go upstairs. Draw a rune I've seen so many times in the last few days, I'm sick of it. Stare, enter a meditation so heavy I'm thinking through honey. Not feeling. Dead. Shut down. The Black Mirror, go into it, looking for what's changed in the isolation of the Black City. Her runes are here, too, vibrating white on imperial black.

Soon, she comes.

Oh hey, you're the guy who likes my work. I'm glad we can talk.

New God in the Black City.

END